Gail Lockwood and her Imaginary Agony Aunt

Lynne Hackles

Cahill Davis
Publishing

Cahill Davis Publishing Limited

First published in Great Britain in 2023 by Cahill Davis Publishing Limited.

First published in paperback in Great Britain in 2023 by Cahill Davis Publishing Limited.

Printed and bound in Great Britain by Clays Ltd, Elcograf S.p.A

ISBN 978-1-915307-02-6 (eBook)

ISBN 978-1-915307-01-9 (Paperback)

Cahill Davis Publishing Limited

www.cahilldavispublishing.co.uk

For my husband, Colin, also known as the LSO. (Long Suffering One.) It's not easy for anyone married to, or living with a writer.

1

Tuesday, 4 January 2000

Gail Lockwood saw the giant boot swing out of the sky. She felt its scuffed toecap come into contact with the seat of her jeans, giving her an expert kick that sent her sailing through the air.

'What a way to start the new millennium,' she moaned, recognising the scrapheap looming beneath her. Gently, she floated down towards it until she was sitting on the top.

Legs dangling and tears threatening, she remembered her first visit.

'Ah, but I was younger then,' she mumbled into her lap. 'Forty-five and not bloody fifty.' Now, she was too old and too tired to start again. 'And I can't be bloody bothered,' she muttered. 'The scrapheap will have to do.'

Five years ago, when Roger had left her for their daughter's best friend, she'd thought life couldn't get any worse. A classic tale of a midlife crisis. Man leaves devoted wife for younger model.

She'd spent the next two years staring at the pavement, believing that everyone was talking about her.

Poor cow. Fancy being deserted for a schoolgirl. Well, she shouldn't have let herself go. She was all grey roots and wrinkles and he was all dark hair and a twinkle in his eye. Had a look of Elvis about him. You can understand why he looked elsewhere.

Gail yawned. It was tiring just thinking about her long haul back to self-respect, but she'd managed it with the help of good friends, hair colourant, a load of clothes from various catalogues, self-improvement books from the library and an imaginary agony aunt. She looked upwards and, to the right of the fluorescent tube, visualised an elderly lady dressed in pink, smiling down at her. Her agony aunt was the sort who often gave advice without waiting for questions. And she wasn't always helpful.

'*Help? No can do,*' said the vision in pink. '*It's my day off.*'

'Can I help you?' A lad blinked at her through round glasses.

'Me?' Gail mentally dragged herself from the top of the heap, an imaginary bonfire where she'd been sitting like some henna-haired Guy Fawkes. She wriggled on the job centre's uncomfortable plastic seat.

'Yes.' The little lad, who had appeared behind the desk, brushed back his dark fringe.

'I need a job,' said Gail, 'but'—she lowered her voice—'I can't work the computer thingy.'

The schoolboy, a replica of Harry Potter, made his way around the desk. Gail was surprised to see he was wearing long trousers. 'It's very simple,' he said, leading her towards the thingy. 'Just press here and all the details come up. Let me demonstrate.' His fingers flashed across the screen—faster than Liberace's had ever done over a piano—his pudgy little hands covering the bits she needed to see, such as *exactly* where it was you had to press. Between his bitten nails, she saw words and what looked like maps flashing.

'What sort of work are you seeking?' he asked.

'Anything, as long as I can pay the bills, the mortgage...' She decided to press her own button, the mute one, and finish the sentence in silence, and in her own head. *And the catalogue clothes and the new suite—the buy now, pay next year one that's sitting in my living room.*

'Office work?'

Gail blushed. Or it could have been a hot flush. There wasn't a lot to distinguish between the two. 'No. I've been doing shop work but it's closing down. I haven't had the sack or anything like that. It's just...' She was rambling, and Harry was getting bored.

'Any qualifications?'

'Umm...' Gail played for time. She had a certificate somewhere for swimming and Brownie badges for ironing and clothes-folding. 'No,' she confessed, and was relieved to see his hands go into overdrive. There was probably a load of stuff on that computer for people like her.

As Gail waited for the opportunity of a lifetime to flash up, she examined her fingernails and tried hard not to float away into her dream world. Her nails were long and well-shaped but the dark chocolate polish was chipped in several places and she hadn't had time to renew it. Letting herself go again. Never mind. She'd probably have chance between leaving this job and starting the next. Enough time to get her roots done and give herself a manicure but not enough time for her mother to monopolise every waking hour. And she'd be gainfully employed before her daughter.

'This one might suit,' said Harry. 'Housekeeper.'

'Housekeeper?' repeated Gail.

'Yes, you know, cooking, cleaning, that sort of thing.'

Gail knew all right. She'd been doing that sort of thing for over thirty years. She sighed dramatically and loudly and, staring at a point above the lad's dark head, travelled through the years of cleaning, shopping and cooking. A motorway of sticky marks, on one side of which was an ocean of Fairy Liquid and on the other a Mount Everest of shopping surrounded by snowy peaks of Persil. If all the clothes she'd ever washed were pegged out on one long line, there'd be enough to circumnavigate the world.

And if all the pastry she'd produced in her life was rolled out in one piece, she'd have a pie crust big enough to cover Birmingham.

'Shall I print out the details?'

Gail jumped back to reality.

He didn't wait for an answer. Within seconds, a sheet of paper appeared, as if by magic, from a handy slot. 'Housekeeper to a young professional couple with an unspecified number of children,' read Harry.

Gail was immediately suspicious. Unspecified? This professional couple couldn't keep count of their flipping offspring?

'No experience necessary,' added the Master of The Computer Thingy.

Gail smiled ruefully at the idea of keeping house for a family when you had no experience. Experience was what was needed most, and she had buckets of it. But did she want any more?

'Would you like me to phone and arrange an interview?'

Gail, busily counting the unspecified children now tumbling out of the open doors and curtained windows, was about to ask who he wanted permission to phone when she remembered the Cherie Blair type who wanted a slave, because that's what it boiled down to.

'No,' she snapped, in an unusually forceful tone. There had to be something better than that. There just had to. Surely he could magic something up? 'Got anything else?' she asked brightly.

Harry shook his head and took off his glasses. 'I'm afraid not,' he said. 'Perhaps you should consider re-training. It's never too late.'

It was all right for him, barely out of school and yet to have his first shave and shag. Gail was at the other end of the scale, facing old age and a bus pass. 'No, I don't think so,' she said, 'but thanks anyway.' Running her fingers through her short, spiky auburn hair, she gave her sweetest smile and stood up to go, but Master Potter hadn't finished with her.

'I'll give you some forms to fill in. Benefits, retraining, etcetera.' He smiled as he conjured up a heap of coloured leaflets.

Gail felt an overwhelming urge to wipe the smirk off his face. He followed her to the door, holding it open for her, as if she were too ancient and frail to do it for herself.

His milk-teeth gleamed. 'Have a nice day,' he said.

Gail was glad to escape. She stood on the top step outside the job centre, breathing in the fresh air. The sun was out, the sky was blue... Wasn't that a song? It was a nice day for January. A lovely day. Sod Harry Potter. And sod the scrapheap. Her spirits soared in the cold sunshine. Staring up at a cloud, she began writing an imaginary to-do list right across its middle with an imaginary pink glittery pen. The pen that belonged to her agony aunt.

Get a job.

Sort out family relationships.

Pay off the suite.

Do roots and nails.

The cloud was beginning to change shape, the words on it elongating into curly scribble.

Get a man and get laid, Gail hastily scrawled in the wispy bit at the bottom. And not necessarily in that order. OK. She might be fifty but that wasn't old, and Gail didn't feel fifty anyway. So, she couldn't read without glasses and she could do with losing a few pounds and her roots demanded regular attention, but inside she was still nineteen. There was still hope.

There ain't no cloud... That was the song she'd been thinking about. Gail took a step away from the job centre door and posted the pretty-coloured leaflets in a handy waste bin. Things were bound to pick up. She'd get a job soon, and it would be a decent one.

No cloud to bugger up the view...

A horn blasted as she stepped off the pavement in front of a bloody big cloud in the shape of a tatty yellow Jaguar.

And it's raining... A thunderclap sounded in Gail's heart. Closely followed by a cloudburst. Now it wasn't raining. It was pissing down.

Mother. The last person on the planet she wanted to see.

'What were you doing in *there*?' Her mother struggled out of the driver's side of the battered car, a huge flower-trimmed straw bonnet falling to the ground in the process. Plainly one of her ladylike days.

Pearl Proctor retrieved the hat, plonked it back on her head, covering the long silvery wisps of hair and, with white-gloved hands, smoothed down the circular skirt of her blue gingham 1950s button-through dress with Peter Pan collar.

Gail sagged as the rear door opened and her daughter, Tamsin, shot out like a streak of lightning.

'Yes, that's what I'd like to know,' said Tamsin. 'What were you doing in *there*?'

There. Like it was a brothel or something and she'd come out for a breather between punters. Now that was an idea. A new venture for Chenwick. The town had everything but a red-light district. Sex? What was she thinking about? Gail couldn't remember the last time.

'There?' she repeated, playing for time and getting ten seconds reprieve as the passenger door of the Jag swung open and a man in a dark blue boiler suit stepped out. Gail's eyes swivelled in his direction. He was a bit of all right, probably in his late fifties but still slim and he had hair. She wouldn't mind betting he still had his own teeth too.

'That's Guy,' said her mother. 'My mechanic.'

Guy. Bit of a posh name for a mechanic.

'This is my daughter,' said Pearl. 'The one I was telling you about.'

Guy's smile was wiped off before it had chance to get started. Shit. Gail could just imagine what her mother had been telling him.

'And to add to everything, she's just come out of *there*.'

Once again, all eyes turned to that den of iniquity, the job centre.

Tamsin squealed in horror. 'You haven't gone and got the sack, have you?' A tiny blonde bundle of fury stared her mother down, standing feet apart, hands on hips. With her thumbs stuck inside her belt, the tips of her fingers, which, admittedly, were long, nearly reached the hem of her red skirt.

Not for the first time, Gail felt mother and daughter ganging up on her. The three generations of the family forming the layers of a sandwich. Pearl and Tamsin the bread, while she was the meat in the middle, and a giant hand was squeezing the whole thing together.

The bread slices were standing wide-eyed, waiting for an answer.

'No, I haven't got the sack,' said Gail, stretching to her full five-foot-two. 'I'm being made redundant, and I came here to find out what my options were.'

Model, brain surgeon, nuclear physicist...

'Redundant?' Tamsin and Pearl chorused.

'You mean BJ's is closing down?' This from Pearl.

'Yes, haven't you heard?' That was better. Gail could sense the tables turning. 'Haven't you seen the signs all over the shop windows?'

'No.' Once again, they spoke in unison, making Gail grimace.

'No, of course you wouldn't have seen them.' Her voice rose a couple of octaves. 'Because you only shop in the new out-of-town development. You are two of the reasons we're closing. Well, you'll be sorry, Mother, when they take your damned licence off you and all the local shops have closed and you have to wait hours for a bus in the freezing cold and your arthritic knees are playing you up.' Gail was warming to her subject and couldn't shut up. The mechanic was scowling and had put a large protective hand beneath Pearl's elbow.

'There'll be nothing left in the town centre but estate agencies and...' She was about to say charity shops but stopped herself in time. The High Street being left with Oxfam, Red Cross, Tenovus, Cancer Research and the like would be an absolute paradise to her mother, who never bought clothes from any-where else. And if they'd sold groceries, she wouldn't have bothered with the new superstore on the new development.

'Gwanny,' came a loud wail from inside the car.

Guy, who had been carefully studying Gail, turned to go back to the Jag.

'Hello, Jack.' Gail waved at the three-year-old struggling to escape from his child seat. Ooh, the sit-uation was all too much. Mother, daughter, sobbing grandson and bit-of-all-right mechanic.

'I've got to go,' she finished lamely. 'Dilys is on her own.' As soon as her best friend's name tripped from her lips, Gail knew she'd made a mistake. Dilys Lloyd was anathema to her mother.

'Poor Dilys,' spat Pearl. 'I don't know why you, of all people, give a fig what happens to Silly Dilly Lloyd. If it weren't for her awful daughter, you'd still be married to Roger.'

'Oh God, Mother. Not this again.'

Pearl knew when to change the subject. She held up her white-gloved hands, fingers spread, in an attitude of 'I give up'. Which she never would and never had. 'How's that man who lives in your house?'

'Will's fine,' puffed Gail. How come her mother could never remember her lodger's name, or was it that she couldn't bring herself to say it?

'I preferred Roger,' said Pearl, oblivious to Gail's reddening face and worsening temper. 'And you know what I always say...' She always said lots of things about lots of subjects. 'You married Roger in church, and what God hath put together, let no man put asunder.'

She gave another huge sigh and hoped it wasn't true what they said about each one taking a minute off your life. At this rate, she wouldn't be around to see fifty-one.

'I've had enough, and now I really must get back to work.' God, it sounded pompous even to her own ears. 'It won't be long before I join the ranks of the unemployed.'

She pivoted on her stiletto heels and marched off. Her jeans were sticking uncomfortably into her crotch, but there was no way she was going to tug at them with the dreary duo and the macho-mechanic watching her every move.

'Oh, good, you'll have plenty of time for babysitting Jack.'

'And taking me shopping.'

Her daughter's and mother's voices respectively floated behind her.

'Like hell I will,' mumbled Gail, breaking into a run.

The weak sun chose that moment to tuck itself behind a cloud. It was as if someone had switched off the light. Ominous.

Is this the end? Gail asked herself. *Drawing the dole and becoming a full-time unpaid carer-cum-babysitter-cum-gwanny?*

2

Both windows of BJ's were filled with enormous Day-Glo pink posters. So many that it was impossible to see what was inside. Gail had pointed this out to the man himself.

'Every person in Chenwick already knows what's inside,' Bradley Jones had said, smiling. 'Everything. If you want it, we've got it.' That was what he'd always boasted, and he was probably right, for only the Almighty had a clue what lurked in the darkest recesses of the labyrinthine stockrooms upstairs.

'What does BJ stand for?' Tamsin had once asked, not associating her mother's employer with his own initials.

'Bloody Junk,' Gail had answered. Now, as she hurried towards the door, stepping over plastic boxes of plastic flowers, shorthand notebooks and AA batteries, pushing past a clothes rail of flasher macs, Crimplene frocks and crocheted bikinis, she wondered how they would ever manage to empty the place.

The normal poster that adorned the door—'We Never Close'—had been replaced with a bigger one announcing, 'Closing Down, Everything Must Go.' At Gail's touch, it detached itself from its overused Blu Tac moorings and fluttered from the door to land on top of a creaking pile of assorted wicker baskets. The writing on it, in thick black felt-tip, was Bradley

Jones's best. Why pay out for printing when you could do the job yourself and at a fraction of the price? Cheap and cheerful was Bradley's philosophy.

Bradley grinned at Gail as she dashed in. 'Good morning, madam, and what can we do you for?' It was what he said to everyone who entered his little world. He'd said it for six days a week—the 'We Never Close' was a slight exaggeration—for fifteen years and wasn't about to alter the script at this late stage.

Gail gave another huge sigh. Another minute down the drain.

'You won't be hearing that for much longer.'

'No, I won't,' said Gail, the reality of it hitting her like a brick wall. 'I shall miss it, and I'll miss you.'

It was the truth. Where else would she ever see an aubergine three-piece suit with flared trousers and wide lapels? What other man still had his hair permed regularly in an effort to replicate Kevin Keegan in his heyday? Would she ever again be lucky enough to work for a man who serenaded his staff on quiet afternoons? Would she ever again be lucky enough to work?

Bradley stepped towards her and put one hand on her shoulder and the other under her chin to close her mouth. 'Catching flies?' he asked.

Gail made an attempt to smile and felt a lump come to her throat. *Don't go weepy. Not now.*

Bradley fiddled nervously with his black kipper tie, the knot of which was as big as a jam doughnut. 'Any luck at the job centre?' he asked.

A sniff and a shake of the head was all she could manage. *Bloody hormones*, she thought and dashed to the staffroom to collect her nylon overall.

Dilys was in there, filling the kettle. 'Well timed.' She smiled. Gail had often envied those perfect white teeth. 'Any luck at the job centre?'

Gail swapped her denim jacket for the pink tabard Bradley considered suitable uniform. 'Want the bad news or the effing awful news?'

Dilys tossed a teabag into a chipped brown pot. 'Surprise me.' The thing was, Dilys already looked surprised. She was wearing a permanently startled expression due to the fact she'd overslept and had to put on her slap in a rush. Her eyebrows had been plucked to extinction since puberty, and one of her first tasks before breakfast each morning was to draw in a fresh pair in Rimmel's best blue-black to match her hair. Unfortunately, the hurried ones were a little too high and a little too arched, and together with her large and dark brown eyes, they made her resemble a rabbit caught in a boy racer's headlights.

'The bad news is I'm too old for today's job market.'

'Oh bugger. I'm a fortnight older than you, so it'll be straight to the knacker's yard. What's the awful news?'

'I can spend the rest of my days traipsing around behind my mother, searching for cat crunchies with tuppence off and the rest of my nights babysitting Jack while Tamsin goes clubbing.'

Dilys poured tea as weak as gnat's pee into a large black mug with 'Boss' written on it. 'There's no answer to that,' she said.

Gail sincerely hoped she wasn't right.

'Take that out to him, will you?' The mug changed hands.

'Weak and willing, same as I like my women,' they chorused. Bradley's words, like his famous Day-Glo posters, were always predictable.

Dilys added a second teabag to the pot and waited for it to get some colour before pouring it into two mugs. 'Builder's tea for us,' she said, following Gail into the shop, which was overflowing with stock but devoid of customers. The sale wasn't going well,

probably due to the fact that Bradley hadn't advertised because of the cost and the posters in the window hadn't been clocked by any passers-by because
they were all crammed into the new supermarkets,
new clothes stores, new DIY stores and new furniture stores on the outskirts of town, prior to chewing
their way through burgers at the new burger bar or
sinking a schooner of sweet sherry or a pint of lager
at the new theme pub.

Bradley was kneeling on the floor, making more
posters, all adorned with garlands of exclamation
marks. Final Week!!! Massive Savings!!! Bargains!!!
Bargains!!! Bargains!!! As Gail approached, she heard
him singing quietly to himself. He sounded cheerful
enough. It was all right for some. Early retirement,
a few rounds of golf and slobbing out in front of the
telly. No, that wasn't fair. Bradley would never have
given up the shop if the new out-of-town development hadn't been built. He'd have gone on until they'd
all reached pensionable age together.

'Here you are, Boss.' She put his mug on the end of
the counter.

Bradley looked up and gave one of his boyish grins.
He'd hardly changed in the fifteen years Gail had
worked for him. Hair, shape, smile, fashions, all the
same. 'Weak and willing...' he began.

One hundred per cent predictable, thought Gail, and
then remembered he wasn't. Oh, no! He'd knocked
her and Dilys for six when he'd made his earth-shat-
tering announcement. 'This town is finished. I'm selling up. It's early retirement for me.' Little did she
know he was about to make a second.

He stood up, slightly wobbly. 'Oops. Been sniffing
the felt-tip again.' Lifting his mug, he stared over the
rim into Gail's eyes and yelled, 'Dilys.'

The astonished rabbit appeared from behind Gail,
clutching an ancient *Star Wars* mug. 'Yes, Boss?'

'I've an announcement to make,' he said. 'Are you two ready for this?'

Gail and Dilys were stunned into silence.

'Shut the bloody shop. I'm taking you girls out to lunch.'

No one moved.

'To celebrate my new life,' Bradley explained. '*I'm off to sunny Spain...*' His singing voice made the ceiling shake.

Gail and Dilys stared, still in silence.

'To live,' continued Bradley. 'Either of you want to come with me?' he said, still looking at Gail.

3

'Cod, chips and mushy peas.' Dilys giggled. 'Fair play. Bradley certainly knows how to show a girl a good time.'

'Well, it was a jumbo cod. And he didn't *have* to take us out. He closed the shop to do it.' Gail skipped deftly over a puddle. It was their night to go to the slimming club. They were walking there, as a little exercise was called for.

'Cheap and cheerful to the end,' quipped Dilys, wearing an air of serenity due to her newly applied eyebrows.

'He ordered bread and butter *and* we got apple pie and custard for afters.' Gail felt herself salivate at the thought. OK, so Fred's Fries wasn't the trendiest place around, but Fred had been Best Chippie of the Year three times in a row and the Formica tables were always spotless, the salt cellars always full, the butter spread thickly, the fruit pie portions generous and the custard never lumpy. She dabbed at the corner of her watering mouth with a tissue. 'All that fat. Wasn't it wonderful?'

'Fantastic,' agreed Dilys. 'Pity it had to be today though. All those thousands of greasy calories.'

'Yeah, but I didn't have any dinner when I got home from work.' It wasn't strictly true. She'd had the corner off the shepherd's pie she'd cooked for Will. And the crispy bits scraped from around the edges of the oven-to-table casserole.

'We could always give this a miss and skive off to the pub for a drink,' suggested Dilys hopefully. She'd undone the button on her skirt after that mountain of golden chips, and the waistband was still gaping open at the back. The pizza she'd eaten for dinner hadn't helped, but Dilys had made several major discoveries about dieting and one of them was that once you tasted fatty food you wanted more. In her book, cod in crispy batter only gave you the urge for deep pan pizza several hours later. She burped as the picture on the box floated before her eyes. Family-size pizza with cheese, tomato, olives, baked beans and ham topping. Disgusting. It had looked it too. Like something the cat had chucked up but, get over the appearance and, the taste was out of this world. So much so that she'd eaten the lot. One woman living alone on family-sized pies and pizzas. No wonder she was nearly two stone overweight.

'No skiving,' said Gail, gripping her friend's arm and steering her in through the door of the church hall. 'We're in this together.'

First stop was the loo. Empty the bladder. Liquid weighed loads. Standing at cracked washbasins, they rinsed their hands, applied fresh lipstick and stared at their reflections in the mottled mirror.

Dilys smoothed down her blue-black bob before removing her dangly gold earrings. 'Every little helps.' She laughed as she dropped them into her organiser bag.

While Dilys had been smoothing, Gail had been spiking, fluffing up her hair and sucking in her cheeks in an effort to make her face less chubby. 'Ready?'

'As I'll ever be,' groaned Dilys.

As one, they stretched to their full height. Busts out, chins up, breathing in deeply, hands to their stomachs to check the effect, they marched briskly into the hall. Arm in arm. A couple of synchronised slimmers.

Flabfighters was in full flight. Cynthia—in a black Lycra minidress, black tights and black suede ankle boots—stood centre stage, an aggressive stick of liquorice in charge of a weighing machine. Her captives lined up awaiting the climb to the stage for their weigh-in. Dilys and Gail took off their coats and hung them over the backs of two chairs in the second row before joining the end of the dithering queue.

'You look nice. That new?' Dilys admired the skirt and matching top dotted with tiny unrecognisable flowers in assorted colours that Gail was wearing.

'No. I've had it for ages.' Gail lowered her voice. 'It's got an elasticated waist, so it's comfy.'

Cynthia thought elasticated waists should be banned by the Government. How could you judge your circumference unless you wore properly measured waistbands with button fastenings? An elasticated size twelve could easily stretch to a fourteen or even sixteen. She had a point, regardless of the fact that a fully stretched size twelve made a lot of women very happy.

The queue shuffled slowly forward, the changing leader giving an occasional grunt or groan, or little yelp of delight. Depending.

Finally, Dilys and Gail were joint leaders.

Cynthia glowered at Gail. 'I saw you today,' she said. 'You and her.' She switched her evil eye onto Dilys. 'You were filling your faces in a *fish and chip shop.*'

Gail raised her eyes to the ceiling while Dilys, in a pretence of shame, stared at the floor.

'Well?' screeched Cynth, obviously wanting an answer. 'What were you doing in *there*?'

Gail shifted from hot flush to cold shiver as a sense of déjà vu descended on her. At this rate, there wasn't going to be a building in the whole of bleeding Chenwick she'd be able to put her nose inside. First the job centre, now the chippie. Next time she saw Fred, she'd demand he put up net curtains at his windows or provide discreet cubicles for his clientele to scoff in.

'You should be ashamed of yourselves,' finished Cynthia.

Ashamed—Gail couldn't manage it, but Dilys could do a good impression of it. Liquorice Lady could rant for half an hour, but it wouldn't change the fact that the high-cal lunch had been bloody lovely.

'Ouch,' was all Gail managed as Cynthia pushed her towards the weighing scales and her very own moment of truth.

Gail landed on the scales with one shoe on and one off. Lopsidedly, she awaited the verdict. Taken out and hung by the neck until dead.

'Same as last week,' hissed Cynth. 'Not an ounce lost.'

'Nor gained.' Gail's voice was so quiet no one heard it. She stepped gratefully down and bent to collect her shoe. With it tucked under her arm, she staggered Herman Munster style across the stage and down the steps to join the congregation of sinners.

'I'm only half a pound heav...' Dilys stopped in mid-flow, her bum hovering above the sagging rattan seat. 'Hell. Check that out.'

Making a late entrance so as to be certain of the final place in the queue was Alexandra Camberlege. Widow of the parish and left very nicely, thank you.

'My money's on her for Slimmer of the Week,' said the fat lady Gail and Dilys had christened Mrs Galleon. 'You mark my words,' she puffed as she battled her way into a soft and fluffy elephant-skin-sized, blue-grey Angora cardigan. She pulled the garment around her huge bosom, nodding sagely. A hush settled over the hall, like low cloud over a mountain top. Even Cynthia's successes had given up their little mews of pleasure.

Alexandra Camberlege was enjoying every moment. This was at least her second finest hour. Worthy of an Oscar. As had been the graveside scene at the funeral of her poor dear departed who'd been a pain in the arse during his life but had turned into a pot of gold after his death.

She wriggled her feet out of her red Gucci sandals prior to her big scene. This was it. Deep breath. Relax and onto the instrument of torture, only she and every Flabfighter in the vicinity knew that it wasn't going to be torture for her. It was about to become Triumph. With a capital T.

'Sixteen pounds.' Cynthia almost choked. She wasn't the only one. Gail stared at the apparition on the stage in envy. How the hell had she managed it?

A reverential silence filled the church hall while Cynth checked her scales.

Alexandra, still sandal-less and wearing a long-sleeved silk dress adorned with red poppies and olive-green leaves, and in a size twelve, or maybe a ten, stepped onto the scales again.

'Yes, definitely sixteen pounds lighter,' said a traumatised Cynth. Never before had she witnessed such a success.

The room erupted. They clapped, they cheered, they whistled. All genuinely pleased for Alexandra.

Gail settled for clapping and cheering. She couldn't whistle. She'd often tried but always failed. She wanted to be able to put a finger or two in her mouth ... Oh no! Surely Alexandra hadn't been doing that? Making herself sick? Gail pushed the thought aside. She couldn't imagine the perfectly groomed woman performing such an inelegant act.

Cynthia took Alexandra's arm gently, respectfully, and turned her to face the front. Joyfully, the two slimmest women in the building took centre stage.

'We haven't seen Alexandra for four weeks,' Cynth announced. The noise stopped. 'And in that time, she's managed to lose a whole sixteen pounds.'

More clapping.

'Now, Lexi, my love.' Getting very pally and throwing in an endearment.

'I'm sure we're all dying to know how you did it. So, what's your secret?'

Silence. From the audience and from Slimmer of the Week.

'Don't keep us in suspense,' entreated Cynth.

Thirty pairs of pleading eyes stared up at Alexandra. She licked her dry lips, removing a layer of Crimson Crush lipstick, and carefully studied the Crushed Crimson polish on her toenails. With her head bowed, they wouldn't be able to see that she was blushing as red as the toenails that matched the lipstick that matched the poppies on her expensive dress. Oh, and the sandals. From beneath her thickly mascaraed lashes, she peeped at the woman in the second row on the left. Gail. Gail, who was wearing a voluminous floral thing and was sitting on the edge of her seat, waiting. No doubt desperate to know The Big Secret.

'I gave up chocolate,' is what Alexandra said.

And took up sex, is what she didn't say.

With a married man, is what she didn't even think. Especially when the man's overweight wife was staring enviously up at her from the second row on the left. And he was hopefully due to land on her doorstep before his neurotic wife waddled her way home.

Over the regulation church hall's thick green china cups of tea, the conversation was all about Alexandra Camberlege.

'Lexi now, is it?' said Dilys. 'Bosom buddies now, eh?'

Gail looked across at the two women who were chatting together. Cynthia was standing as close as she could possibly get to her greatest success story, looking like a black beetle trying to climb into a flower bed.

'It's that bloomin' haircut, that's what it is,' said the very wise Mrs Galleon. 'Last time I saw her, she had long hair. Look at it now.'

They all looked. Alexandra's hair couldn't be any shorter. It was like a brown-black silky cap on her head.

'Shorter than my old man's, and they gave him a right good trim before they nailed him in his box,' continued a red-faced and perspiring Mrs Galleon.

Oh, if only it were that easy. Get a haircut, lose a stone. You'd want locks as thick and long as Lady Godiva's. Thicker. Longer.

'Bollocks,' said Dil, rather too loudly.

'Exactly my sentiments,' said Gail. 'Bollocks. But were you referring to the "get rid of your hair, get rid of your weight" theory, or is this down to good old-fashioned honest jealousy?'

'Do I look green with envy?'

'Yes.'

'OK. But life's not fair, is it? Some people have everything.' She gestured in Mrs Camberlege's direction. 'Money, looks, figure, the lot.'

That was what Gail loved about Dilys. They were both on the same wavelength.

'Have you ever seen her shopping in BJ's? Course you haven't. She's got no money worries, she lives in the best part of town and she's probably getting a bloody good shagging. Uses up a lot of calories, that does.'

'She'd have had to have been at it like a rabbit,' said Mrs Galleon.

Dilys grinned. 'Like I said, some people have all the luck.'

Gail spluttered over her weak tea. Dilys was as green as a go-go traffic light and the tea was as gross as the thought of Mrs Galleon in one of the crocheted bikinis at BJ's. Gail spluttered again as her last thought turned into a full-colour seaside picture postcard.

Cynthia chose that moment to clap her hands in a demand for silence, so it was her fault that Gail's cup crashed to the floor, splashing lukewarm tea over her feet. Pulling a crumpled and previously used tissue from the depths of her bag, she bent to mop up as Cynth made her final speech of the evening.

It was the usual stuff about taking one day at a time, sticking with it and achieving results, and it ended with a further round of applause for Slimmer of the Week.

As the glamorous Lexi waved goodbye, she threw a look of pity towards the poor unfortunate in the floral disaster. Gail didn't notice. She was too busy dabbing at her ankles with her old tissue.

Mrs Galleon watched Alexandra Camberlege sashay down the centre aisle and out of the door. 'Lexi, be buggered,' she said. 'Laxi more like.'

Gail and Dilys stared at her.

'You don't think...?' Dilys's eyebrows managed to contrive a shocked look without being touched up.

'It's either laxatives or throwing up, you mark my words,' prophesied the wise woman.

'It certainly is not.' Cynth had overheard and was immediately in support of her heroine. 'Anyone who sticks to my diet will get the same results.'

'Or it's a man,' continued the Galleon.

'Yes. There are two sure-fire ways to lose weight,' said Cynth, in a rare moment of honesty. 'Get a broken heart by catching your loved one at it or fall in love yourself.'

The four women held a moment's silence, all thinking the same thing—Mr Camberlege was dead and therefore he was innocent of adultery.

'Love it is, then,' said Gail. And nobody argued.

4

Will Bassett sat and shivered in his ancient green Morris Minor, parked on the terrace of Hill House. These January nights were too cold to be hanging around. He peered at his watch in the dim light. Twenty-past-eight. Lexi should be home soon.

Sitting in the dark, he fiddled with his long hair. It flowed down over his shoulders. When he was working in the advertising department of the Chenwick Echo, he wore it in a ponytail. That way, from the front, new customers couldn't see that it was long. He began plaiting it, for something to do to pass the time. Three strands, over, under. He'd grown his hair long when he started college at eighteen and twenty years on knew it was outdated but liked it long, so two fingers to fashion. As he wove a tidy rope, he thought of the comfortable home he shared with Gail. The cluttered kitchen and bright jewel colours of the living room. Compared to Lexi's cream designer kitchen and parchment drawing room, they were as different as the surface of the planet Mars and the moon.

Lexi and Gail couldn't be more different. Gail was down-to-earth, sensible, reliable and a great friend. You knew where you were with her. Pity he didn't fancy her. He imagined the sex would be satisfying and uncomplicated. Sex with your landlady. The stuff young boys dreamed of. Well, at least he had in his student days. He felt bad about pretending she was his wife but some sort of self-preservation was called for. Sex with Lexi, the madwoman, was fine. More than fine. It was exciting and dangerous. Too dangerous for deep involvement, so he'd had to invent a wife, hadn't he? And he'd struck gold with that. Lexi had become even more passionate once she believed he was married.

He thought of the ritual awaiting him. It was all of his dreams come true. Like living in science fiction land. And Lexi loved it too, though he knew her pleasure came from having a man who would comply to all her weird rules and regulations, and he guessed not many would. Yes, sex with a woman suffering from a compulsive behaviour disorder had its upside.

He jumped out of his car as a red Mazda MX-5 stopped in front of the triple garage doors. The science fiction dream was about to begin.

He opened the door of the Mazda. Her legs swung out. Alexandra Camberlege stood up, hair shining in the security lights. Her hair had been the first thing Will had noticed about the woman when he'd walked into her life. It had been long, blonde and glossy. Exactly as her old man had wanted it. Once he'd become the dear departed, she'd pleased herself and had it all chopped off. It was short, severe and almost black. It gave her an elfin look. Not of this world.

From the moment of the new style, the boundaries of his existence had begun to blur and, instead of losing himself in one of the thousands of books or videos in his sci-fi collection, he had only to go as far as Hill House to find himself transported to another dimension. One in which he was the key player and Lexi his co-star. His futuristic princess. His beautiful alien lover.

She moved closer to him, keys in her hand, and smiled. Pushing the sharp end of her door key into his chest, leaning into him, drawing one foot upwards and sliding it against his calf, she purred, 'Are you ready to play?'

Will couldn't speak. He couldn't even manage a nod. Though one part of him did.

'You're going to stick to the rules, aren't you?' She had him by the lapel of his shirt, dragging him towards the house. The key turned, unlocking the door.

As he stood on the doormat behind her, Will groaned. He was close but not touching. Touching at this stage was not allowed.

They stepped inside. The door closed softly. Lexi slipped off her shoes and took a step further into the hall. Will remained where he was, his feet glued to the mat, his eyes glued to Lexi. He licked his lips and swallowed as her arms reached back to unzip her dress. She shrugged it off her shoulders, wriggling so that the scarlet and olive material slid over her body and fell to the deep pile vanilla carpet. She bent to pick it up. There was a carved, dark wood chest to Will's left. Lexi lifted the lid and dropped the dress inside. Her arms reached behind her back again to unclip her white lace bra. She added it to the chest. Finally, she stepped out of the matching thong.

There was a lot less of her now than when he'd first seen her in the buff, Will noted, recalling how she'd requested a visit from him in his capacity as advertising manager. She wanted advice, she'd said, on how best to dispose of her late husband's business and wanted to know if there would be any local interest, or should she contact a larger newspaper?

Will, all ears and sympathy, had listened and advised and been sufficiently compensated when, after the Darjeeling, she had initiated him into the mysteries of sex with someone suffering from a cleanliness phobia. After that first time, he'd invented the wife. Pronto.

Lexi allowed him to ogle for a few seconds before taking a white towelling robe from the coat hooks above the chest to cover herself.

'Pollution,' she said slowly. 'So much dirt, so many germs.'

'Yes,' gasped Will. It was his turn to strip, and he did it at warp speed, hurling his fake cashmere sweater and stone-coloured chinos into a duplicate chest on his right. Lexi's would all go to be washed, but he'd retrieve his later for going home in.

For pollution, Will read radiation. Now his contaminated clothing was safely sealed away, he was ready for the second stage. Zapping. Also wrapped in a white robe, he followed his princess/captor/goddess, according to that night's script and he hadn't yet decided, up the stairs and into the shower room. Lexi, in total control, switched on the water, checked the temperature, and once satisfied it was hot enough, handed a new cake of soap to Will. Carefully, so their hands did not touch. Then she left him to get on with his ablutions while she scrubbed up in a separate bathroom.

Happily, with his mind free to boldly go into the realms of sci-fi sensuality,

he stood beneath the shower of scalding water, soaped himself, then reached for the shampoo.

His body dried, but with long hair dripping over his back, he awaited her summons.

There were two doors into the shower room. He'd entered the one from the top of the stairs. He would leave through the other. It was his airlock, and it led to the White Chamber. What Gail would call the spare bedroom but as unlike a spare room as Gail could ever imagine.

Lexi called.

Will left the anti-pollution chamber and went on to the next phase. A white bath towel was draped over a chair. Will sat down.

His alien slave, the female lead in that night's chosen story, materialised behind him, ray gun in hand. The trigger clicked at the back of his head, and a stream of hot air washed over him.

Lexi lifted his wet locks and began the drawn-out process of bombarding them with her BaByliss. Will slumped in his seat. This was the only time in his life he ever envied Phil Mitchell, baldie of Albert Square. It wasn't as if Lexi was the chatty hairdresser type. Conversation was another no-go area. Asking where she'd been or if she'd had a good day would mean instant beam-back to the tradesmen's entrance. He closed his eyes, praying for patience. He also made sure his hands didn't stray. On one occasion, he'd scratched his ear and she'd made him start the cleansing process all over again. What some men had to put up with to get a leg over.

Lexi put down the hairdryer, lifted his hair and breathed into the nape of his neck. 'You're ready,' she purred. The naked alien temptress licked her lips.

Will, his legs trembling, rose.

The hall clock struck eleven as Will let himself into number forty-two Rosehill Avenue. He was knackered after all that sex. A glass of water and he'd be under the duvet for eight hours. He tiptoed through to the kitchen. The light was on.

'You look like the cat who got the cream,' said Gail.

Will shrugged in what he hoped was a I-can't-help-it-if-women-fall-all-over-me manner.

Gail, in a maroon candlewick dressing gown, was perched on the high kitchen stool, sipping hot chocolate made with full cream milk into which she was dipping a giant-sized Flake. An empty Twix wrapper lay on the worktop.

'Feeling down?' asked Will, picking up the wrappers and dropping them into the pedal bin.

Gail's sigh could have inflated a balloon.

'I'll take that as a yes, shall I?'

'Oh, Will. I've had a crap day.' Then she remembered the fish and chips. 'Apart from lunch,' she added.

Will stepped forward and put an arm around her shoulders.

'You smell nice,' said Gail, sniffing.

Will could have informed her that it was Lexi's expensive soap, but all he said was, 'Thanks'. He took her cup and led her through to the living room. Putting the drinking chocolate on the coffee table, he guided Gail to a buy now, pay later armchair and switched on the gas fire. 'Wanna talk?'

Gail had been talking to her imaginary agony aunt, who had told her to pull herself together, to be positive. The future was looking rosy. She could do whatever she wanted to do. Gail had blinked hard and made her vanish. Now, this was the last thing she needed. Someone being nice to her. She promptly burst into tears.

Will passed her a tissue, a fresh one, and waited while she described all the horrors she'd encountered between breakfast and bedtime, not sparing him when it came to the clash with Pearl Horrendous Proctor, and only occasionally stopping to blow her nose or sip her drink.

Will listened but, at the same time, his mind kept wandering back to Hill House and his alien life form lover. Who was it who said that a man couldn't concentrate on two things at once? He could. No, it was a man couldn't do two things at once. Never mind. He was listening to Gail's condensed edition of Terrible

Tuesday, which didn't appear to be in any chronological order, while seeing Lexi purging the white chamber and its connecting shower room as if it were a crime scene. Removing all traces of DNA so that even the top forensic experts at New Scotland Yard would never be able to prove he'd had a shag there. She'd be stuffing the guilty sheets and pillowslips into the washing machine, soaking her satiated body in a deep bath, dusting, hoovering, wiping every wipeable surface with Dettol-impregnated disposable cloths. Cleaning, cleaning, cleaning. No wonder she'd lost all that weight.

'No help there,' sniffed Gail. 'And this little boy had to show me how to use the computer.'

'Cleaning. There's cleaning,' said Will, shaking Lexi and her J-cloths out of his head. 'And bar work and telesales. There's always columns of ads asking for them.'

'And no wonder. I couldn't phone people up while they're eating their dinner or watching *Neighbours* and ask them if they want double glazing.'

'Bar work?'

'They're all wine bars these days. Trendy places want youngsters, regardless of the fact that all they do is flirt and chat and ignore the customers.' Gail heard her own voice whine.

'Cleaning, then?' Will leaned forward, trying to look enthusiastic. 'You're a great little scrubber, Gail.' Trying to inject a bit of humour. It worked. She took a swipe at him.

'You could pick and choose. Hop from one to another.'

'I suppose so, if the worst comes to the worst.' It was honest work. And a few different jobs would mean she had a change of scenery. 'But I was hoping for something a bit more challenging, upmarket, not so boring. Oh, I don't know.' She sank deeper into the armchair.

'There's enough cleaning jobs advertised to keep an army in full-time employment.'

'I've had enough of cleaning, but...' She could almost feel the light bulb burning brightly above her head, the nearest she'd ever get to a halo. 'Maybe,' she whispered, 'maybe I could start my own cleaning business.'

'Problem solved.' Will grabbed her hands and dragged her out of her chair. He lifted her off her feet and made a brave attempt at swinging her around. 'Forget doing the scrubbing yourself. Employ other women to go out and do it.'

The light bulb popped, and darkness returned. What the hell was she thinking about, starting up a business? You needed brains for that. She stopped Will in mid-swing. 'It's a daft idea.'

'Why? What's daft about it?'

'Do I look like a boss?' She stared at him from mascara-streaked eyes.

'Do I look like an advertising manager?' Will dragged the elastic band from his ponytail and shook his head.

Gail straightened her dressing gown, pulled the belt tighter and frowned. 'Do you really think I could?'

'You can do anything,' said Will without hesitation.

'Me? A boss?' Being an entirely new concept, it was taking a while to sink in. 'It's a scary thought.'

'You'll be a company director.'

'That should please Mother, but it's still scary.'

'You'll have me to help you.' He planted a big wet kiss in the middle of her forehead.

5

Wednesday, 5 January

'Who cleans your house for you?'

Bradley waggled his eyebrows. 'You offering?'

'It's a serious question, Bradley.'

'Nobody. It's a tip. Had to sack the last two cleaners. They either didn't turn up, or if they did, they must have sat and read the paper 'cause it didn't look any tidier after they'd been.'

'What if you could get somebody good and reliable?'

'Too late now. I'm off to sunny Spain.' He stepped closer to Gail, who had her elbows on the counter, chin resting in her cupped hands. She had to lean to do it, which made her bottom stick out. Before he reached her, she straightened up and looked him in the eyes.

'But what if?'

'I'd jump at the chance,' he said. 'But what's all this about?'

And as Dilys was up in the stockroom, she told him.

'If you can pull it off, you'll be sitting on a little goldmine. I can't be the only one in town who's desperate for Mrs Mop.' Bradley was all encouragement. So much so that Gail began to wonder if she shouldn't jump in at the deep end and tell Will to place his ad asap and sod another encounter with Master Potter at the job centre. But could she do it? Would she get any customers? Would she make enough money to survive?

Oh, for a peek into a crystal ball. What would her life be like by Easter? She considered calling one of the phone lines manned by clairvoyants.

'Don't.' *Her agony aunt's head popped up behind Bradley's. 'They use very tiny print at the bottom of their adverts and charge calls at a fortune a minute and there's a minimum fee. They'll keep you hanging on for as long as they possibly can. You don't think it's going to be a case of, "Hiya, I'm Gail Lockwood, and I wondered if you could see me running my own business, making some decent money, murdering my mother, seeing my daughter settled before I snuff it and, last but not least, am I ever gonna get laid again?"'*

Gail blinked, and her agony aunt disappeared. 'Got the paper, Bradley? I'd like to check out my horoscope.' Cheaper than phoning.

BJ perched gold-rimmed half-moon glasses on his nose, fished beneath the counter and surfaced with the Chenwick Echo's new venture, a glossy monthly magazine, mostly filled with advertisements. He riffled through the pages. 'Here you are,' he said. 'Stars for the month, and this woman's supposed to be good. Your sign's Virgo, isn't it?'

Gail peered over his shoulder but, spec'less, could see only the names of the star signs.

'Family,' read Bradley. 'Develop patience with loved ones. Close family members may prove awkward. Money. Your bank balance is about to improve but take care to spend wisely. And, most importantly, love. Don't let the man of your dreams slip through your fingers.'

'You're right. She is good.' That family stuff was spot on. And money too. Her redundancy pay would be in the bank soon. But love? What was all that about? The only men in her life were her boss and her lodger, and neither of them had ever featured in any dreams of love she'd had. There again, had she ever had any? Not really. Not since the early days of marriage before Roger's first affair. Men couldn't be trusted, but what if...? What if the man of her dreams did exist? She stared heavenwards, which inside the shop meant up at the sagging ceiling and the top shelf on the back wall where her agony aunt was perched like a large pink parrot.

'The man of my dreams,' she murmured as George Clooney appeared between her agony aunt and a navy blue sleeping bag with red trim, which was starting to unfurl and make its way towards the shop floor. It went unnoticed by Gail, as did Bradley when he produced his widest, brightest smile as a customer walked in through the door. Instinctively, he slipped into his usual routine.

'Men's underpants? Can you see them? Of course you can.' He leaned closer towards the simpering woman. 'Whatever turns you on. Tell you what, my love'— Bradley lowered his voice—'you can feel them if you like.'

Bradley's cheery tone made George Clooney and the agony aunt melt away. Gail yawned. She'd heard her boss's spiel before, but her yawn wasn't anything to do with his ancient chat-up lines this time, it was because she was exhausted. Since hitting fifty, eight hours sleep a night was essential. Twelve would be better, and last night, she'd had barely two. The idea of running her own cleaning agency had rattled around in her head, continually changing from exciting to terrifying, plausible to impossible. It was true, what Will had said about everyone looking for cleaners, so there was plenty of work around, but were there armies of women out there who wanted to clean? And, if there were, why were there columns of small ads in the paper every week, put there by people searching for them?

She opened her mouth, about to voice all her muddled thoughts to Dilys, who was staggering towards her with a boxful of BJ—bloody junk—then thought better of it. What was the point in saying anything to Dil if the whole idea fell flat on its face? On the other hand, she'd want her friend's help to get the idea off the ground in the first place. Oh, balls. Think of something else before you get a headache.

'Tea?' she suggested.

'Lovely,' said Dilys, pulling out a magnifying mirror and pushing at a sooty eyebrow with a fingernail. 'Shall I make it?'

Gail screeched, 'Noooo'. She hadn't meant to, but she'd just seen her mother pushing at the door, trying to get in. 'I'll do it.' Her last three words floated back to Dilys as the door to the staff kitchen closed.

As one door closed, another opened, and Pearl Proctor shambled in. Obviously expecting rain, she was wearing oversized black wellington boots and a yellow plastic pac-a-mac with a rustling clear plastic rain hood decorated with sprigs of white flowers.

Dilys groaned and took a pace towards her, but Pearl turned her face away and marched towards BJ. The woman studying the button-flied long johns heard the rustle of PVC before she felt it in the form of an elbow in her ribs. Hastily, she sidestepped, and Pearl immediately filled the space, her weatherproof gear crackling as she leaned across the counter and demanded, 'Where's our Gail? What have you done with her?'

Bradley knew better than to attempt answering. Apologising to his customer for the intrusion, he lifted an arm and clicked his fingers. Dilys lifted a sensibly arched eyebrow and disappeared into the kitchen.

'You're wanted. Sounds urgent.'

'It always does,' answered Gail, leaning against the worktop, waiting for the kettle to boil. 'Tell her I'll be out in a minute.'

The eyebrows arched into the fringe as Dilys made the sign of the cross and began trembling. 'I c-c-can't,' she whimpered. 'Sorry, but I'm right out of garlic and silver bullets.'

'You owe me one,' Gail said, laughing. 'Here, swap places.' She slapped a couple of teabags into Dilys's hand and, straightening her shoulders and tilting up her chin, walked briskly back into the shop.

'Where's your coat?' The words hit her before she'd had chance to make a proper entrance.

'Excuse me?'

'Get your coat. It's threatening rain.' Pearl did a good imitation of a royal wave, relaxed hand circling around with index finger pointing upwards. Behind her, Bradley—whose customer had departed massaging her ribs—clicked a catch, and a tiny tartan stump morphed into a giant mushroom of an umbrella. Gail swallowed a giggle as her boss's hand slowly emerged, palm upwards, checking for water dripping from the lumpy ceiling above. He began to whistle softly. Gail's swallowed giggle clung to her tonsils, threatening to choke her as she recognised the tune. "Raindrops keep fallin' on my head". If she choked to death, would he be responsible for murder?

'*Gail.*' The voice was like a breadknife slicing through butter-icing. 'Don't stand there looking gormless, girl.'

The pleading look Gail gave Bradley was of no use whatsoever. Her obliging boss asked, 'Well, what are you waiting for?' If losing a member of staff meant getting old Pearl off the premises, well, so be it.

As she collected her mac from the kitchen, Gail listened to her mother's high-pitched wail as she told Bradley how her car had failed its MOT and that nice mechanic had phoned to say he'd fixed it and it was ready for collection. 'And I saw our Gail's car parked outside and thought she could give me a lift,' she finished.

'Damn, damn, damn,' moaned Gail. If only she hadn't stayed awake all night, then she wouldn't have gone to sleep after the alarm had gone off and she wouldn't have had to drive to work. She'd have walked as usual. As it was, she'd been late arriving, and she didn't want Bradley to think she was taking advantage because the shop was about to close down. Her little Clio had been more or less abandoned further down the road, away from the double yellow lines the council had painted outside the shops in a last effort to stop people from coming into town. No yellow lines near the new retail park.

As she walked slowly from the kitchen into the shop, it was too much of an effort to lift her shoulders. Her problems weighed her down. They reminded her of Little Christian in an illustration from an old book of "The Little Pilgrim's Progress", where he struggled along the straight and narrow path, bearing the weight of a Humpty-Dumpty-like burden around his shoulders. That picture had been in black and white. The one she saw began in full colour. Her problems had rolled themselves into plasticine balls—red for mortgage, green for suite, yellow for credit card, blue for catalogue, purple for family—but then they'd squeezed together, and her technicoloured burden had become one shitty-coloured lump moulded onto the top of her spine. And from this hump had sprung two arms complete with hands whose fingers intertwined and clung around her neck, melding together in a superglue grip. Suddenly, life seemed futile, and the chin she normally kept tilted upwards in an effort to ward off ageing creases around her throat succumbed to gravity and, like the rest of her, drooped. And it was only ten o'clock.

'Where is she?' Gail whispered.

Dilys nodded to a far corner, where Pearl, rain hood slipped over her eyes like a visor, rummaged in a wire basket filled with hats. Every few seconds, she gave a little cry and flung a hat onto the counter where BJ was standing, collecting them up and clocking up the prices on the till. A sou'wester, a stripy knitted bobble hat, a green baseball cap and a man's trilby so far. Bradley put a warning finger to his lips. Gail leaned against the wall, her sigh completely deflating her. Pearl dug deeper. She was leaning so far over she was in danger of falling into the depths of the basket.

'Aaah.' She re-emerged brandishing a black shiny plastic thing with a brim.

'Aaah.' Bradley did a good imitation. 'I see you have discovered the jewel in that particular crown.'

Pearl looked towards her daughter. 'What's he on about?'

Bradley twirled the hat in his hands. 'Designed by Mary Quant,' he said, 'and straight from Carnaby Street.'

It was Gail and Dilys's turn to exchange looks.

'Carnaby Street, my arse,' whispered Dilys.

'Mary Quant, mine.'

Pearl shuffled further into the corner and sank to her knees. The electrifying crackles her pac-a-mac made covered up the giggles from the two assistants. Within seconds, she was back on her feet, a pair of boxing gloves swinging from her wrist and a single dusty cricket pad clutched in her hand. 'For our Jack.' Her voice was muffled due to the rain hood slipping further. It had gone from hood to visor and was now a surgeon's mask. Another few inches and it would become a pretty garrotte. *Wishful thinking*, thought Gail as she watched Dilys bravely make her way behind the counter to help BJ prise open one of his cheap carrier bags.

Arms now loaded with colourful clothes pegs, striped tea towels, a pair of thermal hiking socks and a set of six grey beakers, Pearl struggled to the counter.

Dilys, triumphant, passed the open carrier to her boss.

'*Stop*,' commanded Pearl in her sergeant major voice. 'I don't want *that* woman touching any of my things.'

It was Bradley's shoulders turn to sag. A second ago, he'd been thinking the old dear wasn't so bad after all, but that had been when she'd been collecting up his ancient stock as if she were grabbing for essentials from a sinking ship. Now, a change of mind appeared imminent. He'd only just remembered how much Pearl hated Dilys. Not that Dilys had ever done her any harm, apart from giving birth to a daughter who grew up, fell in love and legged it to the antipodes with Pearl's beloved son-in-law. And if the son-in-law had been so perfect, why were Gail and Dilys bosom buddies?

'Roger was a big lad and made his own decisions,' said Dilys.

'Don't you speak to me like that.' Pearl tugged at her rain hood but succeeded only in pulling the knot on the white string ties tighter. She let it dangle on her chest, a Turner Prize necklace.

'I was only stating facts.' Dilys's voice remained calm. Inside, she was coming up to the boil.

'The fact is...' Pearl squirmed inside her plastic coating, making herself as tall as was possible. 'Yes, the fact is...'

Gail's breath stopped midway to her lungs. She recognised that tone of voice.

'You are the mother of the whore of Chenwick.'

There would have been a shocked silence if it hadn't been for the pac-a-mac. Then it was Dilys's turn to stretch upwards. Her glare caused those eyebrows to merge together above her nose, forming an almost perfect V. She thrust out her bust, flashed a perfect smile and came out with her bombshell. 'I'll give darling Roger your love, shall I? He's getting married, and I'm off to play my part as mother of the bride.'

Gail's breath remained wedged. She gasped and felt the wall slipping behind her. Was it the truth? Was Dil off to Australia? She didn't give a stuff about Roger remarrying, but Dil going... And she hadn't said a word.

Pearl's mouth dropped open. For once, no words came out.

Sensing the old witch's defeat, Dilys threw in an added bonus. 'So, there you are, then, see. Fancy coming with me? It'd give your poor Gail a break.'

Bradley stared at the three women. Poor Gail. Bleeding Pearl. Big Gob Dilys. He was out of his depth, so he did what he always did when there was a problem. He gave one of his biggest smiles and asked cheerily, 'What's happened to our tea break this morning?' His head jerked in the direction of the kitchen door. Dilys didn't need further persuasion. Linford Christie would have been pushed to reach the kitchen first.

'Did you know about this?' Pearl demanded of her daughter.

Bradley's grin became so wide that his jaw was in danger of breaking. Gail took the hint and forced her mouth into a weak copy of her boss's. 'Course I did.'

Bradley thumped at the till. 'Fifteen quid and I'll throw the cricket pad in for free.' While Pearl searched her pockets for her purse, he began throwing her purchases into the carrier bag, which he then placed inside another bag, to be on the safe side. He didn't want the flimsy carrier splitting on his doorstep and for the old dear to charge back in. *Please, Gail, get her out of here,* he pleaded silently.

Telepathy worked. 'Come on, Mother. Let's get this car of yours.' The pac-a-mac felt warm and sticky as Gail hung on to the sleeve and steered her *loving parent* out into Chenwick High Street. Not a word passed between them as they made their way past the row of shops, turned right at Woolworths and got into the Clio outside the deserted library.

Not a word passed between them as Gail switched on the ignition and pulled away. The reflection of her face in the interior mirror was whiter than the flower sprigs of her mother's rain hood. The bags under her eyes gave the only colour to her skin. A sludgy blue. Her red hair above the ghostly pallor screamed dyed and the spiky bits looked stupid, as if she'd stuck her finger in an electric socket. Had a shock. Yes, she had. It wasn't her mother's behaviour that had shocked her—that had merely confirmed that Pearl Proctor was a difficult woman. Very difficult. Dilys going to Australia and not telling her had been the shock.

In the passenger seat, the difficult woman had given up on her rain hood and was playing lucky dips in BJ's carrier. She dragged down the sun visor and checked out her new headgear in its tiny mirror. Now, should she wear the baseball cap peak facing forward or like one of those skateboarders, peak to the rear? Completely untroubled by the events of the last five minutes, she screwed the cap around and around on her head, trying to make up her mind.

To Gail, it looked as if her mother was screwing off the top of her head. If only she could. Then perhaps someone could drop a brain inside.

Gail stopped the car on the forecourt of the neat little garage. Wooden half-barrels, a tiny leylandii in each, stood at regular intervals around the edge of the plot. The two petrol pumps gleamed in the weak sunshine. Behind them was the main building. One door led into a small office where customers went to settle bills and pay for their fuel, the other double doors yawned open, and in the dark depths of the workshop sat the yellow Jag. There were no other cars inside and no queues for petrol. Was Chenwick Motors another casualty of the new park?

'You wait there while I make sure my Jag-uarr is ready.' Another order.

'Yes, Mum.'

Crackling like damp logs on an open fire, Pearl poured herself out of the Clio and clomped across in her wellies to the workshop.

'Yes, Mum. No, Mum. Three bags full, Mum.'

'Why didn't you say no?' Her agony aunt was sitting in the passenger seat. 'No, I can't take you to the garage. I'm busy working.' That's not difficult, is it? Why do you always trot along and do what your mother tells you?' Her agony aunt ran her fingers through her pink curls. 'If she said, "Come on, our Gail. We're going to jump in the canal," you'd say, "Yes, Mum. Of course, Mum." You're a bloody wimp. When did you turn into a yes-woman? Is that what advancing years did to you? Will you agree to anything for an easy life?'

'Easy life?' Gail snorted. 'What's easy about my life at this moment in time? Nothing. Soon to be out of work and no hope of a job, according to Harry at the job centre. No qualifications. Well, we didn't have to have them in my day. We all left school at fifteen and got on with life. I've got nothing but the dole to look forward *to unless I run my own business. Now, what did I come up with in the night? An idea for the company name. What was it? Oh, yes. Will said he'd help me set it all up, so I put our names together, and what did I get? Gail-Will. Gail will mop your floors. Gail will clean your windows, polish your antiques, scrub your bogs. Gail will because Gail will have to. The bills have got to be paid somehow.'*

She tried saying it more loudly. 'Gail-Will.' No. It sounded daft. How about the other way around? 'Will-Gail. Bloody hell. Sounds like a question. Will Gail what? Survive? Go bankrupt? Wallow in misery for the rest of her days?'

She twisted in the seat, turning her back on the agony aunt, and peered out of the side window. How much longer was Mother going to be? She really ought to get rid of that old Jag. It seemed to be forever in the garage these days.

'Oh, Dilys.' It was a long drawn-out moan. 'How can I start the business without you? Don't desert me now.'

It was then that she noticed her agony aunt had deserted her. Gail felt a sag coming on and turned to the mirror to check out how much misery showed in her face. The corners of her mouth turned downwards. With her index fingers, she pushed them up and, holding them in place, considered plastic surgery. She tried speaking without letting go. 'Will someone tell me how I can run my own business when I can't even think of a name for it?'

The tap on the window made her jump, and a fingernail stuck into her cheek, leaving a tiny horseshoe mark.

'Yeah?' She tried to frantically pull herself together and get back to the present. It wasn't easy with that face peering through her side window. How long had he been there? Long enough for him to be grinning. Definitely his own teeth.

Mother's mechanic tapped again. 'I've put the kettle on,' he shouted. 'Fancy a coffee?'

The Wicked Witch of the West materialised behind him, pushed him to one side and flung open the driver's door. 'She's only dreaming. Always been like it. Lives in cloud cuckoo land. She'll be off somewhere with a Beatle or that American actor off the telly.' The peak of her baseball cap was looming dangerously close. 'Come on, our Gail. We're going to have a cup of coffee with the nice man.'

'Yes, Mum.' Oh, God, she'd done it again. It was an effort to get out of the car and follow the mechanic and Mother into the office without kicking herself. Yes, Mum. No, Mum. An effort was called for. Gail came to a halt inside the door. 'I really should be getting back to work,' she said.

'Rubbish,' scoffed Pearl. 'Sit down there and have your drink. What'll that Bradley Jones do if you stay here all day? Sack you?'

Her mother had a point. Gail sat and immediately felt as if she was letting Bradley down. Skiving. What she craved was a giant bar of Dairy Milk.

'Choccy biscuit?' asked Guy, the mechanic, holding a tin beneath her nose.

The tin was overflowing with a selection of Kit Kats, Wagon Wheels and Penguins. Gail licked her lips, dived in and perked up.

'She didn't want to come,' said Pearl, nodding at Gail as if she were a five-year-old. 'She'd have seen me walk. Her own mother.' There was a pause while she waited for denial from one and sympathy from the other.

'That's not true.' Gail gave the denial, spitting chocolatey crumbs at the same time.

'You could have asked me,' said Guy, running a hand through thick grey hair. 'I'd have fetched you from the house.'

No, you'd sooner ask me. Gail reached for another biscuit. *Drag me out of work. This is probably only a trial run. A practice for the weeks ahead when I'm at home all day with nothing to do.*

'Never mind,' said Pearl. 'Pretty soon, Gail will have nothing to do. She'll be glad of her poor mother's company then.'

Like hell I will. Gail pushed three quarters of a Penguin into her mouth. It was back to the job centre first thing Monday, and if they had nothing, it would have to be the other option. *Gail-Will, here I come.* Decision made, she sipped at her drink, feeling better. 'Nice coffee.' She smiled at Guy.

'Want a refill?'

He held the coffee pot out. Gail nodded. Guy took two paces across the office until he loomed above her. Gail stood up and held out her mug. Mmm. What was it about mechanics? There was something about greasy, black-stained blue boilersuits, dirty hands and the smell... a mixture of oil and aftershave. Roger had been a mechanic. Roger, who used to chase her around the bedroom, threatening to leave black handprints all over her... oh, those were the good old days, when lust ruled. Gail shivered.

Guy steadied her hand with his as he filled her mug. Back in the Sixties, boys used to do that when they were lighting your fag for you. 'Got a light?' you'd ask some fanciable male. He'd produce his lighter, and hey presto. Physical contact.

Physical contact with a stranger was an unusual sensation for Gail. A man's hand, warm and dry against her own. *Don't go there,* she told herself. She was shaking enough as it was. But why? Was it because Guy was standing so close, or her mother had driven her to the edge of murder, or her best friend was going to wing her way to the opposite end of the earth?

6

Lexi, in a scarlet raincoat and matching boots, strolled past the library and shuddered. How could people go in there and borrow books that other people had read and handled? Surely some would smell of cigarette smoke? Some folk would read and smoke at the same time. And what else would they do while they were reading? Maybe eat? Chocolate or ice cream on a hot day. It would melt and get on their fingers and then onto the pages and the cover. She shivered and suppressed a retch. Besides eating and drinking, they'd get up to all sorts of unsavoury behaviour. It didn't bear thinking about. She speeded up, turned the corner and slowed down again as she approached BJ's. She'd no intention of going inside. Why would anyone like her want to go in a place like that? No, all she wanted was a peep through the window, and if she was lucky, she'd get a glimpse of Will's frumpy wife in her natural habitat, scuffing around in a hideous overall, no doubt.

Since last night's Flabfighters meeting, Lexi's curiosity had been killing her. All she knew about Gail was that she was married to Will, needed to lose half a stone and had appalling dress sense. She wanted to know more. Discussion about the little woman at home was not anything Will indulged in. Not that there'd been many discussions during their relationship. No, it was ninety-nine per cent physical, and the one per cent remaining was chat, but that was when they'd first met, business talk mostly and a few quick question and answer sessions.

'Had any interest in the business?' Will had asked after her advertisement appeared in one of the national dailies. Or 'Tomorrow night all right?'

There was nothing much she wanted to ask Will. She knew he worked for the Chenwick Echo because that's how she'd met him. She knew he was thirty-eight years old because he'd said so. What she didn't know was anything about Mrs Gail Bassett, apart from her name and Will letting it drop that she was a member of Flabfighters. That had been a coincidence. It meant she'd been able to actually get a good look at the woman, the poor downtrodden wifey who was being cheated on and didn't have the sense to know she was the third point on Lexi's love triangle. Perhaps she turned a blind eye and considered herself lucky to share Will, considering the age gap.

Will was not forthcoming about his wife. 'Leave her out of this,' he'd warned. 'No point in hurting anyone, especially seeing as we're probably never going to live together.'

Lexi noted his hopeful 'probably'. He could go on hoping. The last thing she wanted was a man about the house. Dirty, smelly things. She wandered nonchalantly towards the poster-infested windows. She didn't like the thought of sharing. Will was serving a useful purpose. He was very good in bed, and Lexi wanted him in her bed until she tired of him. The thought of him going back to Rosehill Avenue and climbing into bed beside a shop assistant whose idea of fashion was being wrapped in flowery curtains was as nasty as... no, it was actually nastier than having to turn the pages of a well-borrowed library book after an obese cigarette-smoking, beer-swigging, nose-picking, wind-breaking old pervert had finished with it. She wasn't jealous, she simply liked to keep what was hers private. Sharing wasn't in her vocabulary.

The windows were useless. All shocking-pink posters and no room to view the contents or the staff. Lexi made her way to the door. It was the same. Posters proclaimed the place was closing down. That was good news. A nice little dress shop selling some good quality designer clothing would be far more acceptable.

Lexi sniffed and was about to march away when the door swung open and a man with permed hair of all things, yes, definitely not natural, spoke to her.

'Come in, madam. Nice to see you. To see you...' The words froze on Bradley's silver tongue. He'd been expecting to see Gail, not Mrs Camberlege. The look she gave him was enough to freeze blood. No wonder Reggie had snuffed it. Poor old sod.

Lexi started at his toes. Black patent shoes. Her eyes travelled the length of his black suit with narrow white pinstripes, over his black and white striped shirt, orange tie and up to his glacial smile. By the time their eyes met, she'd composed herself. 'Thank you,' she said sweetly and stepped inside.

Two things registered in that first second. There was absolutely nothing on these premises she would ever consider purchasing, not even to top up the contents of her dustbin, and the woman behind the counter was the strange little woman from Flabfighters, the one with the ever-changing eyebrows.

Making sure that her clothing didn't come into contact with any of BJ's stock, Lexi made her way cautiously between baskets, rails and shelving, trying not to inhale.

Bradley Jones watched in amusement. It had been sheer devilry on his part, opening the door like that and practically forcing the woman inside. Her pinched expression told him she considered herself slumming it. Ha. She might look down on his store, but she wouldn't sniff at his bank balance. Not that he'd ever let a snobby bitch like her near anything of his. He made a swift check on his flies. Safely zipped up. The way her eyes had lingered, you'd have thought that, unbeknown to him, the old todger had crawled out for a bit of fresh air.

Dilys, smoothing her hair and overall, stepped from her side of the counter and walked silently up behind Slimmer of the Week.

'Hiya,' she chirped. 'Just wanted to say congratulations for last night.'

Lexi, glancing over her shoulder, gave Dilys a quick once-over beginning with the nine pounds ninety-nine trainers, carrying on to the baggy-kneed jogging bottoms, pink tabard over black sweatshirt and ever upwards, past the Rimmel eyebrows, finishing with the Harmony-sprayed blue-black hair.

'Good morning. You're one of Cynthia's Flabfighters, aren't you?'

'Yes, that's what I was saying. I saw you there last night. Slimmer of the Week.'

Lexi turned on a halogen smile. Full power. 'You were there with your friend, weren't you?'

Dilys nodded. 'Gail. She works here too. Popped out for a minute. She should be back soon.'

'Really?' Back soon. It was worth lingering, then.

'Can I help you at all? Are you looking for anything in particular?' Dilys was going for Assistant of the Week. Slimmer being out of the question.

Looking for anything in here? What a preposterous idea. As if. But Lexi did want to wait a while and see if the biggest mistake in Will's life turned up, so, as there wasn't a single thing BJ's could supply her with, she asked for something it couldn't.

'Chocolate?'

Dilys's mobile brows rippled into action, rising and falling. 'Chocolate?' she repeated.

'Only joking,' said Lexi. Was the woman stupid? 'I gave it up. Remember?'

'Oh, yes.' Dilys remembered. Lexi had told them giving up chocolate was her secret to losing weight. Mrs Galleon had hinted at laxatives. Chucking up had crossed her own mind, and they'd all finally decided the real secret was bonking. *I wonder who the bloke is*, pondered Dilys. She was tempted to ask the name of Lexi's buck rabbit and if she could have him now that Lexi had achieved her target weight, when the door swung open again, and Gail strode in.

Bradley had promised Dilys she could have five minutes in the kitchen with Gail on her return. There was some explaining to do about Australia, but Bradley seemed to have forgotten his promise. Possibly Lexi's Chanel was dulling his senses.

Gail's stride stuttered at the sight of Lexi. *She's slumming it.* It was an echo of her boss's thoughts from two minutes ago.

'Hello, Gail.' She sounded friendly. Must want something.

'Hello, Lexi.' She was buggered if she was going to call her Mrs Camberlege, and why should she? Slimmer of the Week had started off on first name terms.

'I didn't know you worked here.' Lexi's jaw was beginning to ache from all the smiling and being nice. It didn't come naturally.

Why the hell should you know? were the words Gail bit back. 'Oh, yes,' were the ones she let out. 'We've both been here for fifteen years now.' Her spiked hair bobbed in Dil's direction.

'How nice,' purred Lexi.

'But we're not here for much longer, as you can see.' Gail held up the 'Final Days!!! Massive Reductions!!!' poster that had fallen into her hands as she'd swept through the door.

'So, you're about to become a lady of leisure, as they say. You're lucky to have your husband to support you.'

'Husband?' What was she on about? Or what was she on?

'Will.' Lexi's smile was becoming a permanent fixture.

'Will?'

Lexi nodded. Poor Will. His wife was obviously suffering from some sort of dementia. She transferred her smile to Bradley, thinking how kind of him it was to employ such a befuddled wretch.

'Will's not my husband,' said Gail. 'You've made a mistake.'

'A mistake?' What was going on? Lexi looked questioningly at Gail. Surely she hadn't forgotten whose bed she'd climbed out of that morning. Come to think of it, she didn't look well. Tired and drawn and very pale.

'Yes, a mistake,' said Gail. 'I may live in the same house as Will but we're not husband and wife. He's my lodger.'

Lexi's smile slipped into her red boots. It took a moment for her to drag on the mask of an actress. 'Oops. Silly me. I saw you in the avenue together and jumped to conclusions. Terribly sorry.' Now for a quick exit, but as she turned, she came face to face with the pinstriped suit.

'For you,' said Bradley, producing a huge bunch of plastic daffodils and drooping tulips, all interlaced with fine cobwebs, from behind his back.

Lexi, maintaining the act until the final curtain, accepted the grubby bouquet with as much grace as she could muster. 'Thank you.' Her voice wouldn't have carried as far as the front row. Her exit was the speediest ever made.

'Cup of tea time,' sang Bradley as he shepherded his staff towards the kitchen. 'I'll have mine...'

'Weak and willing, same as you like your women.' Gail put an arm around her pal's shoulder as they sang the words together.

'That's right. You two have a little talk. I'll hold the fort.' Bradley brushed his suit jacket and sneezed. Those flowers were dustier than he'd thought.

Apologies from Dilys began before Gail had time to turn on the tap and fill the kettle.

'I'm sooo sorry, Gail. Me and my big mouth. I was going to tell you about it later, but when your mother started, I blurted it all out.'

'I know,' soothed Gail. The whore of Chenwick indeed. Years ago, four decades—no, more like four and a half—Pearl had threatened to wash her daughter's mouth out with soapy water. Gail couldn't remember the offensive word she had spouted to call down on herself such a threat, but it couldn't possibly have been as vicious as what her mother had uttered today. 'I'm sorry too.'

'I'm sorry for you,' said Dilys. She left unsaid, *for having a mother like that.*

'We're all sorry,' said Gail, flicking the switch on the kettle and reaching into the doorless wall cupboard for clean mugs. 'Now, what's all this about you going to Australia?'

'I'm not. Well, I don't think I am.' Dilys sat on a wonky chair and rested her elbows on the Formica-topped table. 'What I mean is, I haven't made up my mind yet. The invitation arrived as I was on my way out to work. An autumn wedding.'

Gail felt several pounds drop away. It was her heart lightening. Autumn. Loads of time before then to get the agency up and running.

'My Anne and your Roger,' finished Dilys.

'Not my Roger.' After their fifth year together, he'd become Angie's Roger, and then Sandra's Roger, and then, well, then he'd Rogered anything with a heart-beat.

'No, of course not. They're getting married. She wants me out there for the wedding but...' Dilys paused.

'But what?'

'I turned the envelope inside out, but I couldn't find a bloody plane ticket.'

Their laughter made Bradley stick his head around the door. 'Everything OK?'

'Yeah.'

'That's all right, then.' He disappeared straightening his Jaffa orange tie.

'Free tickets to Sydney. That'd be a first for my ex. Free anything. But you said you were going.'

'In the heat of the moment, I lied. Your mother could make anyone say anything.'

'You should go. After all, it is your only child getting married.'

Dilys's head drooped. 'The child who ran off with your husband.'

'And did me a big favour.' Gail hadn't thought it was a favour at the time. 'It's your chance to put things right between you and Anne.'

'It'd be wonderful, and I did consider using my redundancy money to pay for the flight.'

'You should,' said Gail firmly.

'Yeah, and what would I come home to? No, I'm going to have to stay here and look for work, same as you. There's bound to be something for a pair of hard workers like us, and Bradley will give us glowing references. We'll be snapped up. You'll see.'

The kettle clicked off. Gail turned to empty it into the teapot. She bit her lip. *Keep quiet*, she told herself. *You know the score.*

'*You certainly do.*' *Her agony aunt was leaning against the sink. 'The future's nothing but thick mist filling a gargantuan void for the pair of you. Let Dil enjoy what she can before coming face to face with little Harry and the brutal truth.*'

Gail didn't want to hear any more. She carried the drinks into the shop on a battered tray Bradley had borrowed from The Red Lion fifteen years ago. She passed him his weak brew. 'Sexy,' screamed the word emblazoned on his mug. Dil's was covered in stars and planets between which glided the Starship Enterprise. Gail's was pale blue and in white italics bore the legend, 'What a beautiful day'. Huh. 'What a load of old bollocks' would have been more appropriate. Her wristwatch from the catalogue—free with orders over fifty pounds—twinkled fake gold on her wrist. Five to twelve? It couldn't be. It had been at least a fortnight since she'd forced herself out of bed. She put down her mug and, slipping the watch from her wrist, gave it a good shake.

'It's five to twelve,' said Bradley.

'And don't shake it like that. It's not your mother,' said Dilys.

'Talking of strange women,' said Bradley, 'how do you two know Mrs Camberlege?'

'We all go to the same slimming club,' said Gail.

'And she was Slimmer of the Week last night.' Dilys was still impressed. How could anyone lose the equivalent of eight bags of sugar in four weeks?

'I take it you don't drop in for coffee or go for girlie shopping trips together?' He didn't have to wait for an answer. Their amused expressions told him what he wanted to know. 'She's a rich bitch. I used to play golf with her husband, Reggie, in the days before she drove him to that fatal heart attack.'

Dilys's eyes widened. 'He didn't, did he?'

'Didn't what?'

'Die on the job?'

'Not as far as I know, but I do know she led him a life. Always wanting something or other. Flash car, posh clothes. What she spent on her hair in a month would pay your mortgage. But she has something wrong with her, and I can't remember what it is.' He had his staff's full attention. 'Something with initials.'

'Like PMT?' Dilys loved word games. 'Or RSI or IBS?'

'What are they?' Bradley asked.

Leaving out PMT, surely her boss knew what that was, Dilys went straight into, 'Repetitive strain injury. Irritable bowel syndrome.'

Bradley shuddered. 'No, definitely not. I'd have remembered that one.'

'It wasn't bulimia, was it?' Gail was thinking of that spectacular weight loss again.

'Isn't that making yourself chuck up?' Bradley had only ever chucked up when he'd had far too much to drink.

His girls nodded.

'Are there any initials for it?'

His girls shook their heads.

'Was it an eating disorder?' asked Dilys.

'No. Weirder than that. Compulsive something.' Bradley scratched his head.

'It wouldn't be compulsive eating, or she wouldn't have lost weight like she did.' Dilys was obsessed with the woman's weight loss. Obsessed and jealous.

'Obsessive-compulsive disorder. OCD.' Bradley gave a huge grin. The old grey cells were still there and fighting fit.

'Obsessive-compulsive disorder? What's that when it's at home?' asked Gail.

'Dunno. Can't remember what Reggie said now.' Perhaps those cells weren't as fit as he'd thought.

An hour and half a dozen customers later, the door crashed open to reveal Will in his sober grey suit, every inch the businessman until he turned to close the door and revealed the long ponytail hanging down his back.

'Hiya, Will,' said Dilys.

'What are you doing here?' said Gail. Her lodger had never frequented BJ's before.

'That's a nice, friendly welcome for a good-looking bloke who wants to buy you lunch.'

Gail was even more puzzled. A visit plus an offer of lunch. What was going on? Lunch sounded good, especially as it had been a fortnight since breakfast and days since choccy bics at the garage. 'Bradley, is it OK if I go now?'

'Yep,' was all he said. It was unlike him not to make a comment. He stood, eyes downcast, fiddling with the tie with the Satsuma knot. Obviously upset. As Gail put on her mac, she thought about how the shop had been his entire life for so long and this selling up and moving abroad was a big venture.

The first thing she saw when she stepped outside was Bradley's bouquet. Instead of cascading from a vase, it was sticking out of the top of a rusty bin hanging from a lamp post. 'Oh dear,' said Gail, retrieving it and giving it a shake. 'I can't leave it there.'

'I could,' said Will.

'You don't understand. It might upset Bradley. He gave it to...' she'd been about to say Lexi when a warning light flashed. The middle of the High Street might not be a sensible place to ask him if he knew the Slimmer of the Week. She had a feeling there was more to her imagined marriage to her lodger than Lexi had let on. 'A customer,' she came up with, and then because it was a lie, she had to embellish it to make it sound more believable. 'A little old lady who came in and spent quite a bit of money on odds and ends.' Now it was beginning to sound like her mother.

Will wasn't paying too much attention. He only had an hour and there was so much to discuss. Throwing an arm around his landlady's shoulders in an all-pals-together type of gesture, he steered her across the High Street and up the worn steps of The Red Lion. They entered the double swing doors like a comic bride and groom, him in his smart suit, her in a long cream mac, bridal bouquet clutched tightly to her chest.

The place was heaving but, after a wave from Will, a little blonde waitress in old-fashioned uniform of black dress and white apron, completely at odds with her facial piercings—three in the ear, two in the eyebrow and one in the nose—hurried over and led them to a corner of the dining room. She gave them menus and removed the 'Reserved' sign from the table. Gail handed over her mac, wishing she'd worn something a little smarter than a baggy yellow sweatshirt, which Pearl had said made her look like a sick canary, and an old pair of frayed jeans. Not even fashionably frayed—the knee was ripped due to being caught on a nail in one of BJ's cluttered stockrooms. The 'Reserved' sign meant that Will had booked in advance. The least he could have done was warn her so she could have made a dash for home and got changed into something more respectable. As it was, people were probably thinking a generous but foolish executive was giving his cleaning lady a treat. Cleaning lady. A light in her head switched on. That was what this was all about, but surely it could have waited until they'd both got home from work?

Will sat, his back to the other diners. Gail fidgeted on the long bench seat, the flowers on her lap.

'What the hell am I going to do with these?' she asked her agony aunt, who was sitting, legs crossed on the bar, one hand resting on the ice bucket.

'If you were a real bride, you could've stood up and thrown them over your shoulder,' came the unhelpful reply.

Gail wondered what would happen if she did throw them. She pictured the faded yellow daffs and stiff tulips falling onto tables, knocking over wine bottles, hitting men on their balding heads, showering dust into bowls of soup. Carefully, she moved them onto the seat beside her, pushing them along the red plush, as far as she could reach. Once lunch was over, they could stop there, or a swift whack could send them into hiding beneath the long white tablecloth.

Will was hidden behind his menu. Gail opened hers and blinked. She held it further away, but her arms weren't long enough. She could make out some fancy writing in italics, but the words were blurred and she didn't have her glasses with her.

'Will,' she hissed. 'Can you read it to me? I've forgotten to bring my specs.'

'Main courses only, or do you want a starter?'

'Main courses, please.'

He'd reached the vegetarian options and was relishing the descriptions—'creamed parsnip, leek and carrot in a herby sauce, served in a case of chef's cheese pastry'—when the blonde with the pinny and piercings returned.

'Are you ready to order?' She smiled at Will, then swapped dimples and teeth for serious straight lips and eyes narrowed in sympathy as she turned to Gail.

Little cow. She thinks I can't read. Gail conjured up a smile of her own. 'I've forgotten my reading glasses,' she said. 'Silly because I've two pairs, but

Will surprised me with his invitation to eat out, and I didn't bring my handbag.' *Nah, shut it. You don't have to explain. Give her another twenty years and she'll be in the same boat.* 'I'll have the chicken breast stuffed with garlic mush—'

'Chips or baked?' she asked before Gail could finish about it being wrapped in bacon and served with barbecue sauce. Her mouth was watering already.

'Chips.' She sighed, sinking back on the bench and watching a vision of Cynthia in a sparkly angel costume complete with tinsel wings—she was getting angel and Christmas fairy confused—hovering just beneath the baby chandeliers, wagging a finger in disapproval. She flicked two fingers under cover of the cloth and hoped the chef didn't skimp on the chips.

Will ordered the steak. The waitress departed, and the business talk began, in the first five seconds of which it dawned on Gail that it was her lodger who was the most excited about the new endeavour. Apparently, he'd already drafted out an advertisement, which he'd get in the Echo for nothing as soon as she gave the word.

'I'm not sure. I haven't got your confidence,' she admitted. 'I'm off to the job centre again Monday, with Dilys.'

'That'll halve your chances,' said Will. 'Two of you, same age, same experience looking for work. Why don't you ask Dilys to be your partner?'

'I assumed you were going to be that.'

'Me? No. I'm only the ideas man.'

Gail chewed on her lip. 'It's scary, Will.'

'So's being on the dole.'

'Yes, but...' She couldn't think of any buts, and even if she had, they wouldn't have been voiced because, at that moment, two men were being led to a table by Blondie. They both wore suits. One was short and had dark hair and a moustache. The other was tall and slim with a head of grey hair and all his own teeth.

'Guy,' murmured Gail.

Will swivelled in his seat to see what had diverted his landlady's attention. He was in time to see two men sit at a small table. The taller of the two put up a hand and smiled in their direction.

'It's Mother's mechanic.' Gail felt she owed Will an explanation.

'Yes, he owns Chenwick Motors.'

'Owns?' So, he wasn't just a mechanic.

'Likes to get his hands dirty. I didn't recognise him at first. He's hardly ever out of his boiler suit. The other bloke's an estate agent.'

Gail let Will do the talking, especially once lunch had arrived and the chef hadn't skimped. The food was good, and she did it justice, savouring every mouthful. Eating and listening and yet Will, giving her a pep talk, trying to convince her that running a cleaning agency was child's play, finished before her. She'd noticed it in many men. How they could eat and talk at the same time.

The profiteroles begged her to rescue them from the sweet trolley, and as Will was having cheese and biscuits, she considered it only polite to join him.

She drained her coffee cup and popped a mint imperial into her mouth, wishing The Lion handed out chocolate mints instead.

'That's agreed, then,' said Will.

Over his shoulder, Gail's eyes met Guy's. She smiled, and he turned away. There was something about the man, something she didn't trust. Why was the owner of a successful business spending so much time with her mother?

'If you don't find a job or get an interview, let me know and I can stick this ad in the paper.' Will's voice stopped Gail drifting away.

'Yes,' she said to him, fingers crossed, hoping she was making the right decision.

7

'Your future is looking bright, but it's up to you to grab the opportunities on offer. Your ideal partner is right under your nose,' read Bradley from his daily paper.

What was that about her ideal partner? Gail was about to ask her boss to read it again when the unexpected happened. A customer walked in.

Professionals to the last, they both stood to attention, Bradley shoving the newspaper back in its hiding place at the same time as switching on his helpful smile.

Gail's smile was only half-formed. The other half didn't develop due to her recognising the customer. Sh...ugar. It was Blondie with the facial piercings. The waitress from The Red Lion, nose stone glinting under the fluorescent light tubes. She tossed back her hair, faced Gail and, like a loyal subject being presented to Royalty, gave a deep curtsey and offered up a bunch of flowers, much in the same dramatic way as Bradley had bestowed them upon Lexi.

'You left these,' said the girl, presenting the bouquet across the width of the counter.

'Funck you.' It was a deliberate cross between being polite—thank you—and what she really wanted to say, and when pronounced as if you had blocked sinuses, no one could accuse her of rudeness.

Blondie was deliberately trying to embarrass her but didn't know that what she was actually doing was upsetting Bradley.

'Yes, funck you,' Gail repeated, her face as scarlet as the centre tulip had once been and so hot you could have fried an egg on it.

Satisfied, Blondie retreated.

Gail used the flowers as a fan, waving them in front of her face, but they proved useless. 'S-s-sorry, Bradley.'

'For what?'

'These.' She jigged the flowers about, losing the heads of several in the process. 'They were outside in the bin, so I took them to the pub with me and left them on the seat.'

He was laughing. Laughing when she was trying to be so sensitive, trying not to hurt his feelings.

'It was my little joke giving them to Alexandra. Surely you knew that? Don't tell me you've spent the last fifteen years here and don't know when I'm joking?'

It was hard to tell sometimes. Gail shrugged. What could she say? And then, for the very first time, the full force of it hit her. It was like being mown down by an atomic-powered tank. All those years she'd been waking up happy, coming to work happy. Not many could say that. They were a team. They'd shared their problems, their divorce traumas—and they'd all had one. They'd laughed together and cried together. A lump the size of the Windsor knot in Bradley's tie leapt into Gail's throat and her eyes started to burn as hot as her cheeks. She screwed them closed. Mistake. She only succeeded in squeezing out a tear. A tear from each eye.

'Don't, Gail. Don't go all weepy on me.' Bradley held out his arms. She fell into them, and her tears fell onto his wide lapels.

'It's going to be so strange without this place,' sniffed Gail. 'So strange without you.'

He held her at arm's length, felt in his pocket and passed her a handkerchief, a huge white one with 'BJ' embroidered in the corner. 'Come with me,' he said.

Gail gave a little laugh. 'Oh, Boss. I'm going to miss you.' Instinctively, she flung her arms around him and stretched up to kiss his cheek, just as the door opened.

They sprang apart, Bradley rubbing at an imaginary speck of dust on the till, Gail collecting together the flowers from the countertop. When she dared raise her eyes, the sight of Guy searching through a rail of waterproof jackets sent her cheeks into egg-frying mode again. She'd never blushed as a teenager. Bugger the menopause.

It was Bradley who leapt to the rescue. 'Hello, sir. Can I be of assistance?'

Apparently, he was in the market for some working clothes. Bargain jeans, jackets, shirts, that type of thing.

Bradley slipped into salesman speak. 'Just the thing over here. Reasonably priced.'

And the door opened for the third time in five minutes. If only it had done that for the last six months, they would all be carrying on in their nice normal way. No midlife crises, job searches and sleepless nights. But it was only Dilys, complete with provisions from Kwik Save.

She made straight for Gail, whispering none too quietly, 'Who's that? I wouldn't kick him out of bed.'

'Sshhh. It's Mother's mechanic, and he'll hear you.' The two men were actually looking across at them. 'I think they both heard you.' There was more than a hint of panic in Gail's voice.

'Tough titties,' said Dilys, lugging her shopping be-hind the counter and into the staff kitchen. Gail followed her, not only to escape Guy but to cool off. She held her hands under the cold tap and pressed them against her cheeks. If she got any hotter, her head would explode.

'Here, try this.' Dilys produced a highly decorated tube from her handbag. 'What is it?'

'What's it look like?'

It was phallic-shaped. Gail didn't want to hazard a guess.

'Open it. It's brilliant. It certainly helped me.'

'Not a vibrator.'

Dilys laughed. Loudly. 'Mine wouldn't fit in there.' She giggled, taking the tube from Gail and twisting at the end of it. She poured out a long straw-coloured block and, with a flick of her wrist, changed it into a fan, plain one side and a badly painted picture of a couple Flamenco dancing on the other. 'Brought it back from Spain last year. It's great for hot flushes.' To prove her point, she began fanning Gail.

Gail sat down, closed her eyes and enjoyed the cool air wafting against her burning face. 'Oh, don't stop, that's lovely.'

'Keep it,' said Dilys. 'I'm over that stage.'

'Thanks.' Gail took it and gave a few final violent swishes before returning it to its package and slipping it in her pocket. 'Hi-ho,' she said.

Dilys wriggled into her tabard. 'Hi-ho, it's off to work we go. Never mind, I'll put the kettle on. It's nearly tea time, then it'll be going home time.'

And in another six weeks, it'll be the end of an era, thought Gail. *We'll be clearing the place out, and then what?* She pushed the thought aside. A hot flush was more than enough to be going on with. She didn't want a headache to accompany it.

Guy was putting a credit card in his wallet. He bent to pick up one of BJ's largest bags, bulging with a padded jacket. 'Good luck with your new lives,' he said as he walked briskly out.

'What did he mean by that?' Gail felt panic returning.

'Me going to Spain and you—'

'You didn't tell him?'

'I didn't know it was a secret,' said Bradley.

'Yes,' shrieked Gail. 'Mum doesn't know, and I haven't even told Dilys yet.'

'Sorry,' said Bradley, but she was already gone.

The cold air outside hit Gail's face. The sudden change of temperature made her worse. The heat crept down from her face, over her throat and under her sweatshirt. Hot pins stabbed her armpits, and she felt a trickle of sweat run down her cleavage. 'Guy,' she called. 'Guy.' The last thing on earth she wanted was for him to mention her new enterprise to her mother, especially as it wasn't even definite yet. Imagine the lectures.

As Gail ran to catch up with Guy, she had a vision of her mother in a judge's wig, daughter Tamsin, similarly dressed, sitting at her side. 'You are a stupid woman who has been led astray by evil men who encouraged you, a mere female, to enter the world of commerce.' Here, Pearl paused for effect, and Gail saw herself, black smudges on her face, her head a tangled grey mess on top of which sat ashes. The outfit she had chosen for her court appearance was a little number in sackcloth. As the twelve jurors began to twitch—Gail was sure she glimpsed her old headmistress in amongst them—Pearl continued, 'Stupidity is no excuse. You allowed a good man to slip through your fingers and instead consorted with—'

'Guy!' It was the last breath she could muster, and this time he stopped, turned and waited for her.

'You won't mention'—it was painful, the gasping and the stitch in her side—'anything to Mum'—she sucked in a mouthful of air and swallowed—'about me starting my own business.'

He stood there in silence. A silence Gail felt obliged to fill.

'Only, I haven't told anyone yet.' Another gasp, sucking in more air. 'Bradley and Will are the only ones who know.'

He wasn't going to help her out.

'It's a secret.' She held her side and tilted forward to relieve the stitch. 'I don't want anyone to know until...' *Until when? Until it's a reality? Until it's a success?* 'Until I've made up my mind that it's what I'm going to do.'

He spoke for the first time. 'Tittle-tattle isn't really my forte, so you don't have to worry your little hea d...'

Gail noted he missed out pretty.

'...about a thing. You're not the only one with secrets, you know.'

Disdain wasn't the word to describe the expression on his face. Superior? Amused? How about supercilious?

'Funck you,' she mumbled before doing an about turn and puffing her way back to BJ's. Her exterior may have appeared calm, but inside she was screaming.

Gail wasn't the only one pretending to be in control. Will fiddled with his ponytail. If Gina hadn't been in the office, it would have been his testicles.

The telephone call had started off normally enough but was rapidly approaching danger levels, and as he wasn't alone, he had to take care with his replies.

'Your wife and I had a nice chat today.'

'Oh yes, where was that, then?'

'I called into BJ's.'

'You what?' She was lying. Lexi would never have entered a place like that.

'And she told me I'd made a mistake.'

'A mistake?' Will began to sweat.

'She said you aren't married. I think you have some explaining to do. I'll expect you in five minutes.' The line went dead. Lexi wasn't a woman to mess with.

Will reached for his coat and his car keys. 'Got to go out, Gina.'

'Is there a problem?'

'You could say that.'

Gail, still angry at the way Guy had spoken to her, threw all her energy into clearing out half a dozen boxes of assorted tat. Guy, Mr Smarmy Whatever-hisnamewas, would never make her list of possible dream men. Not that she'd got an actual list. No, there weren't enough men to put on it.

'Hey, Dilys?'

'Yeah?'

'If you had to make a list of dream men, who'd be on it?'

Dilys tilted her head to one side and gave the question some serious thought for a full half-second. 'That bloke on the bins. All muscle and a great smile. And we've got a dishy new postman. And that mechanic your mother's going around with.'

'Guy? She's not going around with him. He just fixes that old car of hers and it's always going wrong. You don't fancy him, do you? He's horrible.' Gail tipped the last box upside down and began sorting the contents into piles. Junk, lesser junk, even lesser junk and junk you'd only meet in your worst nightmares.

'Who's on your list?' asked Dilys, dumping a pile of odd socks into a basket—there might be a one-legged person glad of them.

'That one who played Lovejoy, and Nigel Havers, though he could do with a bit more muscle, and the drop-dead gorgeous Swooney Clooney.'

They moaned together.

'Now there's a man who's improving with age,' said Gail.

'And he's a fantasy like the others on your list. You're hardly likely to meet any of them in the Co-op, are you? Now, how about making a proper list? One with real men on it. Men you know. You can fight me for my binman if you like.'

'I don't know many real men,' admitted Gail. 'Perhaps I feel safer with my fantasies.'

'It's about time you gave them up. Now, let's see, who do we know?' Dilys scratched, and smudged, an eyebrow. 'There's Will. And Bradley.'

'Our boss?' No. Bradley was definitely not the man of her dreams. A great mate, but no sparks there.

'No. I meant Fat Bradley from Flabfighters. He'd jump at the chance.'

It was time to change the subject. Gail sifted through the final items and triumphantly waved a scrunchie an inch away from Dilys's smudged left eyebrow.

'What is it?' asked Dilys.

'It's a scrunchie. For tying back your hair.'

'Oh.' Light was beginning to dawn. 'You mean one of those things to put round a ponytail?'

'That's right.'

'But your hair's not long enough for a ponytail.'

'It's not for me. It's a present for Will.' Gail dropped the scrunchie into Dilys's outstretched hand.

Dil peered at it. The scrunchie was fluorescent green and had a white sumo wrestler stitched to it. 'It's hideous,' she said.

'I know,' Gail said, laughing. 'He'll love it. And guess what? It glows in the dark.'

As she said it, a hint of aftershave wafted over them. 'What a bargain, madam. And with staff discount off sale price, it's all yours for the amazing sum of eight pence. Pay me next year. Now, what else can we do you for?'

8

First Officer William Bassett sat in the alien's vessel. His well-muscled body relaxed against the pale upholstery as the odourless, invisible truth serum began to work.

'I'm sorry, Lexi. I thought it safest to tell you I was married. When we first met, you had just buried your husband, and I didn't want you falling for me on the rebound. You were a vulnerable woman.' Christ, was that the truth? Even to his own ears, it sounded a load of pompous crap.

'Silly boy. I'm only the marrying type when there's a rich man around. Surely you knew I only wanted you for one thing.' Lexi was purring as she let her robe slip from her shoulders and slide, a mini snowdrift, to the floor.

The first officer leapt to his feet. If this wasn't an invitation for further exploration, he didn't know what was.

Ten minutes later, Will changed the script. This wasn't his alien princess. This was a newly discovered species whose sexual rituals were prolonged and intense. The female called the tune, and to Will's joy and despair, the tune appeared to be an astral "Hokey Cokey". Every time it got to *you put your doo-da in*, there was no time to follow instructions before it was *you take your doo-da out. In, out, in, out...* Except there was no in, only endless teasing with the alien's retreat to the opposite side of her ice cavern, well out of reach in order to *shake it all about* until he thought he was losing his mind, his self-control, his will to live.

Lexi leaned against the wall, watching him, her scarlet-tipped nails running up and down her thighs. Then she beckoned. With a grunt, Will rolled off the bed, caught his foot in the silk sheet and fell to the floor. On his hands and knees, he crawled towards her. Closer. Closer.

He was within reach of her foot when she laughed, stepped to one side and opened the door leading to the shower room. Her side-stepping caused him to crash headlong, head in the shower room, body in the bedroom. As he struggled back to hands and knees, he felt her foot. She was stronger than he'd ever expected. The kick delivered to his bare arse nearly lifted him into the air. The shock of it made him leapfrog forward. The door slammed onto the soles of his feet. Lexi's laugh and the click of the bolt coincided.

For a full ten seconds, he remained in position, hair hanging down his back and over his shoulders, head cocked to one side, like an overlarge puppy. Was this part of the game or the end of the game? Surely not the finish, not without the climax. This couldn't be happening to him. If she had hidden cameras and was capturing this, his humiliation... He scanned the glacial walls and ceiling. Thank fuck for that. He wouldn't have put it past the bitch to film all their encounters and send this particular gem off to *You've Been Framed.*

A quiet tap at the door.

Will wriggled around into a sitting position. 'Yes?'

'That'll teach you to mess with me.' Her voice was hard. 'Let yourself out and don't come back. This is goodbye, Mr Bassett.'

Will didn't need telling twice. At warp speed nine, he headed for the escape pod via the outer door of the shower room. Dragging on his clothes from the chest by the door, he hopped outside, stumbling as he mistakenly tried pushing both feet down one leg of his suit trousers. Never, never again, he promised himself. He hadn't appreciated how disturbed Reggie's widow was. He'd been too busy playing *Star Trek* to notice the danger he was putting himself in, and he'd been too sex-obsessed to recognise the fact that the partner in his fool's paradise could do with professional help.

'Lesson learned,' he said to the darkening sky. It was time to grow up. 'The next relationship I have will be a meeting of minds, not bodies.'

There was work to be done. Carrying the sheets to the washing machine, Lexi told herself she could live without her lover, though she might never find another man out there as considerate when it came to scrubbing his body, cleaning his nails and showering for ten minutes under needles of scalding water. He could stew for a week or two and then maybe she'd review the matter. Maybe she'd allow him back into her bed, maybe she wouldn't. In the meantime, he deserved punishing.

9

Saturday, 12 February

Darkness had arrived early. Barely four o'clock, and between the Day-Glo posters, car headlights flashed past in the blackness.

Another hour and a half. Ninety minutes and it would all be over. The customers were under the impression that it already was.

BJ sat on a rock, the sun beating on his curls, and stared out to sea. In reality, his craggy outcrop was a cardboard box filled with fingerless mitts, the sun an extra-fluorescent light tube switched on by Dilys, and the sea, sheer imagination.

His two girls, as he'd always insisted on calling them, were perched on high stools, staring into space. He remembered the time Gail had challenged him when he'd called them girls. 'I'm not a girl, I'm a woman,' she had told him huskily. As if he'd needed telling.

Dilys was filing her nails with an attachment of a Swiss army knife.

Gail was replaying the last week in slow motion. *This is the end of life as we know it.* She rehearsed the words in her head, but before they fell from her lips, the phone trilled. The three of them jumped.

'Bloody hell,' said Dilys. 'I nearly wet myself.'

'Good afternoon. This is BJ's, and this is the manager speaking.' Bradley covered the mouthpiece with his hand. 'Not impressed,' he said in a stage whisper. 'Says she'd sooner speak to you.' He held the phone out to Gail.

'Who is it?'

'Your Tamsin.'

'No prizes for guessing what she wants.' Gail took the receiver and grimaced at Tamsin's words. 'Actually, love, I'd rather not. I've got to work tomorrow. Can't you ask someone else?' She held the phone from her ear and waited for the tirade to stop. 'All right, then, as long as you're home before midnight.'

Dilys was rolling her eyes. 'Can't you ever say no?'

'She said no to me,' said Bradley.

'You what?' Dilys was suddenly wide awake and interested.

'He was messing about. He asked me to go to Spain with him.'

'And you said no? You want certifying.' Dilys turned to Bradley. 'You could try asking me,' she said.

'I know you too well. You'd say yes, then once we got there, you'd run off with some dark-eyed gigolo.'

'Oooh. Take me, take me,' begged Dilys, arms outstretched.

In two strides, Bradley reached her, wrapped an arm around her waist, clasped her hand in his and began waltzing her around the shop floor, expertly guiding her between the coat rails and oddment bins.

'*You had the last waltz...*' he sang in his beautiful deep voice.

Gail dabbed at her eye with a screwed-up tissue. She wasn't sure if she was laughing or crying. Bradley's voice had been known to move her to tears. Back in the Sixties, he'd been the lead singer in a famous pop group. Famous as long as you didn't ask anyone outside of Chenwick if they'd heard of BJ and The Boo-bop-a-loo-lahs. His musical tastes had broadened since then—pop, classical, jazz, hymns. He often sang as he worked and obliged his staff by singing requests during quiet periods. His rendering of "Rock of Ages" had once even stopped Pearl in her tracks.

'*The last waltz...*' he finished, bowing to Dilys.

He was heading towards Gail when the phone rang again. This time, she answered it.

'Mother.' This was followed by a lengthy silence. Conversations with Gail's parent were often one-sided affairs. Dilys's head swayed from side to side as she mouthed, 'Yak yak yak yak.' Bradley pretended to strangle himself, sinking to his knees, his eyes bulging.

'I... I... I,' attempted Gail. Finally, she managed some words edgeways. 'I can't on Monday. I'm going to the job centre. Sorry. Got to go.' Before her mother had chance to utter another syllable, Gail put the phone down.

'She wanted me to take her Christmas shopping in Birmingham on Monday,' Gail explained.

'Christmas shopping?' Dil's eyebrows disappeared so far up her forehead they were in danger of slipping down the back of her neck. 'It's only February.'

'She said the stuff that didn't sell in the January sales will be going dead cheap.'

'Hasn't she got anything else to do?'

'Apparently not.' Gail took a deep breath. Her prediction was coming true. Mother and daughter ganging up on her, demanding her time. She'd managed a no to her mother but not to Tamsin. She felt trapped. Suffocated. Squeezed in the sandwich again.

Spain sounded a good place to run away to, and she might have been tempted if Bradley's offer had been serious.

That evening, Gail stood by Will's side in the doorway of Tamsin's flat and wondered what he thought of it all. Meanwhile, Will wondered what Lexi would make of it—the toys strewn all over the fluff-balled carpet. The coffee table like a stall at a car boot sale. The drooping curtains with missing hooks. The over-flowing basket of washing waiting to be ironed, balanced precariously on top of a bandy-legged ironing board. Gail's old but well-cared for suite re-covered, not in Plumbs' made-to-measure, but in layers of newspaper. Unanswered post and saved junk mail.

'*Gwanny*,' cried Jack, appearing from behind the sofa and hurling himself at Gail's knees. 'It's my gwan-ny.'

Gail lifted the little boy up. All ginger curls and freckles, he clung to her neck, and she took a tenta-tive sniff. No, the faint odour of filled nappy hanging over the entire place was not on her grandson.

'Hello, Mum,' said Tamsin, holding the door wide. 'Thanks for coming.' All sweetness and light now that she wanted a favour.

'Hiya, Will. I didn't know you were coming too. Good job Gran's not here.'

Will was under no illusion as to what Pearl Proctor thought of him. A 'long-haired yobbo sponging off a stupid middle-aged woman' was how she'd once described him to her daughter, knowing full well that he was within earshot.

'Yes, a very good job,' he said, but his thoughts were more on Lexi than Pearl as he said it. Lexi would have a blue fit if she as much as peeped through the keyhole of this place. That or a field day scouring it from ceiling to floorboards.

Tamsin, in a stomach-churning spotted dressing gown—the recognisable spots being mascara, toma-to sauce, egg yolk and, hopefully, chocolate—scraped a layer of rubbish to the far end of the sofa. 'Sit down,' she said to Will.

Gail stacked a dozen of Jack's original wax crayon masterpieces together with a pile of the local freebie newspapers in order to clear a seat for herself. 'Will offered to keep me company. We've things to discuss.'

'What things?' Tamsin had never got the hang of subtle.

'Private things,' said Gail. 'Now, isn't it time you started getting ready?' What was the point in Tamsin asking her to be there for eight-thirty when she would take another couple of hours to bath, do her hair, decide what to wear and get her face on?

And as for Jack. He should have been in bed at least an hour ago, yet he was still wandering around in his day clothes. Whatever happened to routine? Tamsin was always complaining about her son being awake until midnight, but she was the one who let him play or watch television until he fell asleep on his feet. If she put him to bed at the same time every night, he'd soon learn what was expected of him.

'He's had his bath,' Tamsin said.

'So, why isn't he in his pyjamas?'

'I couldn't find them. They must be in the ironing.' She skipped off in the direction of the bathroom.

I asked for that one, thought Gail, standing up to search through the basket. The iron was already strategically placed, plugged in but not switched on. She rummaged through the clothes, which turned out to be mostly Jack's. With a shrug, Gail flicked the switch. What else were mothers for? She moved the basket to the floor, and a laugh escaped her.

Will, who had been trying to decide between a *Scooby-Doo* and a *Tweenies* video—he fancied himself as cool as Milo—asked, 'What's so amusing?'

'This.' Gail gestured to the ironing board. The cover on the board sported a picture of a naked man with an iron-shaped singe mark over his genitals.

'That's my daddy,' Jack informed them. He pointed a chubby finger in the direction of the singe. 'And that was his willy.'

Pity his willy wasn't annihilated before having the chance to get Tam pregnant, thought Gail. The little bugger hadn't been seen since, and Tamsin could have done with some help. She wasn't brilliant when it came to coping with housework and money. If only she could get her act together.

Gail worked her way through the basketful of tiny clothes. She'd supported her daughter when Jack was born, been there for her, and she supposed Tam had helped her when Roger walked out. Tam hadn't been very practical, but at least she hadn't ignored the situation. She sighed, remembering the time Tamsin had booked a hair appointment for her. 'Get a new look, Mum,' she'd said. 'My treat.' Trouble was, after Gail had been hennaed, trimmed and tousled, she'd had to cough up the money for it all, as Tamsin had conveniently forgotten to pay.

Gail folded yet another tiny T-shirt.

By the time Tam emerged, Will and Jack were entwined, deeply absorbed in their film, the basket was half empty and the clothes folded in a neat pile.

'Let Tamsin finish the rest,' the agony aunt said as she stared down at the ironing board cover. She was already too pink to blush.

Gail obeyed, putting the ironing board, complete with Daddy and his burned twiddly bits, out of sight in the kitchen broom cupboard.

'Thanks, Mum. You're a star.' Tamsin was wearing black trousers and a glittery top, both of which Gail had never set eyes on before. Her hair was piled on top of her head and her make-up was barely noticeable. All this in record time.

Gail stared at her daughter. 'You look lovely. Where are you off to? You didn't say.'

Tamsin's face lit up. 'His name's Jez. He's taking me for a meal. You'll like him.'

Gail had her doubts about that. Since the disappearance of Jack's dad, Tamsin had worked her way through a long string of unsuitable boyfriends. Not that Jack's dad had been suitable. Far too young and immature for settling down. No one who wore a back to front baseball cap should be allowed to father a child.

'He's older than my usual type and'—Tamsin searched for the right word—'grown-up. Mature.'

Panic bells rang in Gail's head. 'How old?'

'Thirtyish. And before you ask, yes, he's been married before, but she was a right slapper.' The look on her mother's face made Tamsin add quickly, 'He's got a good job. And he's teaching me how to use a computer.' She tugged at Gail's arm. 'Come and look.'

As Tamsin swung open the door to her bedroom, Gail's mouth dropped open in amazement.

'We did a makeover in here,' she explained. 'I thought it would surprise you.'

Gail's mouth was still open. Surprise her? The sight of the room nearly bloody killed her.

The walls had been painted a pale peach. The curtains and bedding, all new, were in the same shade. The head of the bed was adorned with cushions in deeper shades, instead of the usual discarded clothing. The carpet no longer had stains from spilled coffee. The drawers of the dressing table and the doors of the wardrobe were all closed. Not a thing out of place.

'Over there.' Tamsin pointed.

The far corner had been transformed too. Instead of cardboard and plastic boxes filled with God-knows-what, there was a mini office. Desk, chair and computer.

'A computer. How did you get that?' Gail had visions of being nominated guarantor for a loan at 1029.8 per cent interest to be repaid over ten years.

'It's Jez's old one. I haven't got time to show you now but I'm getting really good on it.'

'Playing games and surfing the net?'

'No, I could do that before.' Tamsin sounded horrified. 'I'm doing databases and spreadsheets.'

'Bloody hell.'

Gail felt a tiny hand grip hers. 'It's Mummy's 'puter,' piped Jack.

'Yes, and it's your bedtime,' said Gail, thankful for something to say. The bedroom, the databases and the other thing had completely floored her.

'We're going to tackle the living room next. Jez suggested a darker colour because of little fingerprints. What do you think of terracotta?'

Gail didn't know what to think and was saved from having to when the bell rang. Jack ran to the door and fumbled with the handle. From the other side, a voice wailed ferociously, 'Fee-fi-fum-foy.'

Jack giggled. 'It's Zez.'

And it was. The door crashed open. 'I smell the blood of a little boy,' roared the voice.

Jack raced across the room, throwing himself into Gail's lap. 'It's the giant.'

The giant, apparently unaware that Tamsin had company, galloped on all fours after Jack, reining it in when he came face to knee with his girlfriend's mother. 'Oops.'

For Gail, the name Jez brought visions of Alice Cooper to mind. Alice in his hey-day. Jez would have long black unkempt hair, a snarl instead of a smile, wear black, be thin and have at least one earring. Any Jez worth his salt would possess a guitar, his own kit for producing roll-ups and know his way around the DSS. Every Jez would, without a shadow of a doubt, have two-day stubble, bloodshot eyes and body odour.

Dark brown eyes with healthy clear whites, together with a waft of Calvin Klein, and her preconceptions fizzed away like aspirin in a glass of water.

Would the real Jez please stand up?

He did, brushing at the knees of his jeans before unfolding to a full six feet. His hair was short, almost the same colour as his eyes, and his smile was wide and easy. He swung Jack into his arms and hugged him. 'I left something by the door,' he said, setting him back on his feet. 'Will you go and fetch it for me?' Then he held out a hand to Gail. 'You must be Tam's mum,' he said. 'Pleased to meet you.'

Good looks, great aftershave, impeccable manners. Gail was impressed already. And that was before Jack returned bearing gifts.

The deep red carnations were for Tamsin. The toy bus for Jack. The Black Magic for Gail.

'Tamsin said you like dark chocolate.'

I like any chocolate, was what she would have said under normal circumstances. Under these, all she could manage was a mumbled, 'Thanks.' Not a funck you this time. Here was perfect son-in-law material, and if Tamsin didn't hang on to him, then Gail vowed she'd murder her daughter. Put her down as a hopeless case.

She was still dumbstruck when the couple waved goodbye, Jez promising to have Tamsin back well before the clock struck twelve.

Gail gave them a full ten seconds before dashing to the kitchen to check the pedal bin. As she'd suspected, balanced on top of its ageing contents was a dirty nappy. A disposable that hadn't been disposed of. Not properly. She carried the entire contents out to the dustbin, washed the pedal bin, sprinkled Tesco's own pine disinfectant in its innards, washed her hands and rejoined Jack and Will.

'Jez seems like a nice bloke,' said Will.

'Zez,' corrected Jack.

Nice bloke? An understatement. Gail didn't hold out much hope of him having an unattached father at home. That or a big brother. 'Yes, a nice bloke.'

As she struggled to get Jack into his *Fireman Sam* 'jamas, she pretended she was getting him into his pageboy outfit ready for his mum's imminent wedding. The mother of the bride wore a tangerine suit, size twelve and no elastic at the waist, with bitter chocolate accessories. She was escorted on this happy occasion by Nigel Havers. No, Harrison Ford. No. It had to be the best of them all. George Clooney. There again, as it was only a dream, she could invite all three. '*If you don't have a dream...*' she sang to the pageboy.

Jack settled between Gail and Will on the sofa to watch the last ten minutes of *Scooby-Doo*.

'Talking of dreams,' said Will, 'have you thought any more about the agency?'

'I've come to a decision.'

'And?'

'I'm going to the job centre with Dilys next Monday, and if we don't get anything, then it's all systems go.'

It was what Will had been hoping to hear. He knew more than most how many jobs were advertised. Not that many in Chenwick. Even fewer now that all the businesses on the retail park relied on kids working part-time to keep them going. It would be virtually impossible for Gail to find work. Her only other option was to work for herself, so he may as well pave the way. 'Have you thought of a name yet?'

'All I've come up with is Gail-Will,' she admitted. 'You know, our names together.'

'But I told you I wasn't your partner.'

'No, but you said you'd help with the advertising and that.'

'Gail-Will. Gail-Will.' Will rolled the words around. 'Almost,' he said, 'but not quite right. Your punters might expect Gail to turn up, and you won't be able to do that as your client list expands. You'll be sending your staff out.'

Gail wrapped an arm around Jack's body and drew him towards her. Whether it was to comfort him or her, she wasn't sure. Probably her. The thought of client lists and staff sent a chill through her. She decided to change the subject.

'It was awful today. Poor Bradley. I could have cried for him. For all of us.'

'Yes, and now life has to go on,' said Will.

Gail pretended not to hear. 'I'll miss that shop, the customers, the laughs we had.'

'You can laugh at this, Gwanny,' said Jack, without taking his eyes off the silly dog on the screen.

'Walls have ears,' Will whispered.

'I shall miss Bradley,' Gail carried on regardless, reliving those final moments of being in full employment. 'He said he'll miss us too. His actual words were, "I'll never find a couple of girls—"'

'Girls! That's it.' Will thumped his knee. 'Brilliant.'

Jack rolled into Gail's side and put his thumb in his mouth.

'That's what?'

'Not Gail-Will, but Girls Will. That's your new company name.' Will waited for a reaction but didn't get one. Unperturbed, he carried on, 'And your slogan can be, "Girls Will if you won't".'

'Won't what?' Gail felt she was missing something. A brain cell that was still awake for instance. All she wanted was to curl up with Jack and fall fast asleep. She wished now that she hadn't agreed to Will's suggestion of him accompanying her on her babysitting outing. She should have guessed that he'd had an ulterior motive but had been grateful for his offer of chauffeuring her to and from Tamsin's.

Will was on his feet and flapping his hand over the coffee table. 'Won't dust,' he said. He began stacking the clutter on the table into piles. 'Won't tidy up.' He pointed at the heap of folded clothes. 'Won't iron.' He dashed over to the kitchen door, gestured at the sink and proclaimed, 'Won't wash up. Girls Will if you won't.' His right arm swung across his body, and he bent from the waist in a theatrical bow. Presentation over.

Jack stopped sucking his thumb, giggled and clapped his hands. 'He's funny,' he said, referring to Will and not Scooby.

'Girls Will,' said Gail softly. It was like an omen. Something from the two men in her life. Girls from Bradley joined up with Will to produce a name for her new business. 'Girls Will.' For the very first time, the little worm of fear stopped wriggling and changed, albeit for a second, into a frisson of excitement. *If you don't have a dream...*

The television screen crackled into blackness. Jack bounced from his seat, picked up the remote control and, without looking at it, pressed the button for the video to eject. The screen flickered into life again. 'Do you like this one, Gwanny?' he asked.

Before she registered what was on, Will said, 'Brilliant.' He picked Jack up and made himself comfortable on the sofa, the little boy on his lap.

'What is it?' asked Gail, seeing what looked like foil-covered cardboard flying saucers dangling from lengths of string swing across a sequinned black cloth background.

'Ssshhh,' said the two boys together.

Zany Scrapes on Planet Zog. The title trembled mid-screen, the words seemingly carved into a sheet of paper so that the same black background showed through them.

'What the hell—' began Gail.

'Sssh.' The males had bonded.

Gail ssshed and reached for the Black Magic. She popped her favourite, Turkish Delight, into her mouth and held the box out. 'Want one?'

Will's large hand and Jack's small one reached into the box, felt around and took a chocolate each, their eyes never leaving the telly. The sofa the three of them shared vibrated from Will's laughter and Jack's shrieks of joy.

Gail sighed, made herself comfortable and, with the open box on her knee, settled down to Planet Zig or whatever it was called.

'The colour's gone off,' she hissed.

'Sssh. It's supposed to be in black and white,' Will hissed back.

'Oh, right.' In a strange way, Gail too became spell-bound by the sheer awfulness of Planet Whatever. Occasionally, the future, her future, interrupted her viewing. Girls Will. Gail Will. No, Gail won't. She won't think about tomorrow. She'll live for the moment. Her fingers searched the box for the chocolate with the swirl on top. The cherry filling made her mouth water. *Gail Will cope with her uncertain future. Gail Will not speak until this stupid programme is over.* She gave a chuckle. *Gail Will finish this box of chocolates in one sitting.*

Dilys found the remote control stuffed down the side of her armchair. She switched off the telly. *Zany Scrapes*, she knew, was totally idiotic, and she couldn't understand why it was on after the watershed, as it required the same IQ as *Teletubbies*. She would never have admitted it to anyone but she considered it the best entertainment on telly. Worth paying the licence fee.

She poured the remains of a two-litre bottle of diet coke into her glass, swigged it down and then, in surprise, noticed the empty jumbo-sized packet of full-fat salt and vinegar crisps on her lap. Dilys was comfort eating. And she needed it.

Next on her agenda was some serious research into Mars bars, established product versus frozen.

She took a bite of established. The chocolate coating cracked and the caramel stretched as she pulled off a chunk. Now, if she went to Australia, what would she say to Anne? Would she be welcome there?

She took a bite of the ice cream version. The chocolate coating cracked and the ice cream interior was soft and very sweet. Anne had sent her an invitation. There'd been no need for her to do that. It was the first move towards a reconciliation. Mmm, the ice cream version was excellent. Ten out of ten. Dilys took another bite.

Anne was her daughter after all, and whatever she'd done, even running off to Australia with Gail's husband... 'She's still my daughter,' said Dilys through the final mouthful of ice cream. She turned her attention to the solid bar. Crisps and chocolate had helped her come to a decision. If she didn't find a job on Monday, she'd spend part of her redundancy money on the holiday of a lifetime.

As she stood up, the empty crisp packet and the two Mars wrappers fell to the floor. The final fluttering from lap to carpet was a silver and white card with attached cherubs. The wedding invitation.

10

Sunday, 13 February

'No, no. Not yet,' moaned Gail to the alarm clock. Her flailing arm missed the button and sent the clock on a collision course with the floor, where its usual jangle was muffled by the shag pile bedside rug. Dragging herself to the edge of the double bed, Gail stared down at it. A series of blinks later and she could see that it was nine o'clock. Her lie-in was over, and it was time to rise and shine and get her arse down to BJ's.

Before she'd gathered the energy to emerge from the captivating warmth of the duvet, there was a tap on the door.

'Cuppa?'

'Mmm.'

Will entered with a tray, perched himself on the edge of the bed and held out one of the two cups to Gail, who was struggling into a sitting position. They sipped at their tea in companionable silence.

'*Could Will be the man of your dreams?*' asked a disembodied voice.

'No,' Gail answered without hesitation. 'For starters, he's fifteen years younger than me.'

'Lots of women have toyboys, and age should not be an obstacle to a relationship.' The disembodied voice slowly grew a body in the shape of her plump and smiley agony aunt.

'*Toyboys are fine for some, but I want a real grown-up man. Will's never going to grow up.*'

'*That could be fun,*' said the pink lady.

'*And it could be hard work. And what about Lexi?*'

'*A passing phase.*' The apparition nodded. '*He'll soon grow out of it.*'

'*So, he is going to grow and maybe one day become a real man?*'

'*I didn't say that.*' The agony aunt was hedging her bets. '*Tell me, Gail, what do you class as a real man?*'

'*Someone mature and wise. Someone who'll care for me, love me and—*'

'*Bring you tea in bed?*' The agony aunt pointed a pink-gloved finger at Will.

'*Point taken,*' said Gail. '*But Will's still not the one.*'

'Penny for them,' said Will, clattering his empty cup back on the tray and scaring away Gail's aunt.

'Only a penny?'

'OK. I'll do bacon and egg for your breakfast. And fried bread.'

'Lovely, but I'm still not telling.'

Happily loaded with calories and cholesterol, Gail stood at her front gate, staring across the fields opposite and down the hill towards the town. In the distance, she could make out the red roofs of the new buildings. Far away as they were, it didn't stop them from spoiling the view and knackering her income.

Behind the retail park, a cloud squatted on the horizon like a miserable grey mountain. Between it and the watery blue sky shone a band of silver.

As she closed the gate, she looked fondly at her mortgaged Victorian semi and wondered how many bricks she owned.

One to me, two to the bank. One to me, two to the bank. She speeded up her little chant, forcing her feet to keep up with it as she began the final walk to BJ's.

The streets were empty. As Gail passed St Andrew's, the bells began to chime.

'Eleven o'clock and all is not well,' panted Dilys, appearing from the church gates after taking her usual cheery shortcut through the graveyard. Together, they turned the corner and stopped. Outside the shop, two men were loading boxes into the back of a furniture removal van.

'I thought we were doing the packing,' said Gail. They hurried the last few steps to be met at the door by Bradley. Bradley as they'd never seen him before. In blue jeans and white T-shirt.

'Morning, girls.' His smile wasn't as wide as normal.

'Morning, Boss.' Theirs weren't either.

Bradley wrapped an arm around each of them and led them inside. 'Surprise, surprise.'

His girls stared in amazement. Most of the work had already been done. Was this why he'd suggested a late start? What had his exact words been? 'Be here for around eleven. Have a lie-in. It is the final day, after all.'

He must have been there since dawn.

Dilys was the first to recover. 'I'll put the kettle on, shall I?'

'That'd be smashing, love,' said the older of the two removal men. Dilys wound her way through the obstacle course of boxes. Gail remained where she was. As did Bradley's arm.

'The end of an era,' he said for the zillionth time since he'd announced he was giving up commerce. 'You can still come with me. It's not too late to change your mind.' His arm squeezed Gail tighter, closer.

'Tea or coffee?' Dilys shouted from the kitchen.

By lunchtime, the staff were waving the van and removal men goodbye, with Dilys blowing a kiss after them for good measure.

Bradley's smile was up to ninety per cent. 'I never thought I'd get rid of it all,' he said, beaming. 'It's on its way to a big warehouse in Birmingham. Job lot.'

'What, even the gas masks?' asked Gail.

'Even the gas masks.' Bradley nodded, holding the door open for them to go back in. 'Now, I'm off to get us a little refreshment and then we'll clean up and go home.'

For good, thought Gail.

Bradley ran across the road and took the front steps of The Red Lion two at a time. Five minutes later, he reappeared with several brown paper bags, three glasses and a bottle. 'Sandwiches. Hot roast pork with stuffing and a bottle of celebratory plonk,' he said, setting it all down on the table in the kitchen.

Dilys raised a wobbly eyebrow. 'The second time you've treated us to lunch this year, Boss. It's time you retired.'

Bradley managed the final ten per cent of his smile, filled the glasses with sparkling wine and, raising his, proposed a toast. 'To all of us,' he said. 'To our futures.'

'Our futures,' murmured Gail. 'The farthest I can see into mine is an early night.' She didn't mean to sound miserable and wasn't sure why she felt as bad as she did. 'Don't mind me. I'm tired. It was nearly one by the time I got home from Tamsin's, and I'm hoping that being a permanent babysitter isn't my entire future.'

Dilys bit her lip and blinked hard. It was highly unlikely she'd ever be asked to sit for a grandchild of her own, and she daren't ever suggest looking after Jack.

Gail drained her glass and carried it through to the kitchen. There was work to do. As she waited for the mop bucket to fill, she thought about Dilys's daughter, who was unlikely to produce an offspring.

Roger wouldn't want one at his age. Dilys would most likely never be a grandmother. Gail's thoughts drifted back five years.

I had it away with my best mate's dad. As a confession story, with photos, it would have fetched in around three hundred quid from one of the popular weekly women's magazines. They could have had a picture of her and Dilys together. *'We're still best friends,' said Gail Lockwood (seen left), whose husband Roger deserted her for the daughter of her pal, Dilys Lloyd.* Then there'd be a picture of Tamsin and Anne glaring at each other. *'Unfortunately, the same can't be said of our daughters.'* And they could finish the whole lot off with a quote from her own mother, who would in all probability insist on a full-length centre spread of herself, leaning against her Jag-uarr, wearing an ensemble suitable for a Royal Garden Party. *'Roger was the perfect husband until he was lured away by that little hussy. Like mother, like daughter is what I always say,' said Pearl Proctor, the doting mother-in-law.*

Gail tipped Flash into the bucket and heaved it out of the sink.

'Do a good job, girls,' said Bradley. He was wiping the shelves down himself. 'The new owner's hoping to move in asap.'

'The new owner?' Dilys and Gail squealed together. It was the first time Bradley had mentioned the shop being bought. Gail had thought it would be leased, probably to another charity. No one wanted shops in town anymore.

'We only signed the deal yesterday,' said Bradley. 'His name's Charles... Charles...'

'Bronson,' guessed Dilys.

Bradley shook his head.

'Haughtry? Aznavour? Windsor?'

'Henderson,' said Bradley. 'He's opening a gentlemen's outfitters.'

'Oooooh. Sounds posh.' Dilys laughed. 'Bit different from this place.'

'Just a bit,' said Bradley, 'and before you ask, there aren't any jobs going. He reckons he's going to run the place single-handed.'

'He should manage that easily enough,' said Gail. 'It's what you could have done for the past twelve months.'

Bradley grimaced and attacked the shelf as if it were one of the poncy councillors who, rumour had it, were all driving around in brand new cars donated to them by the hierarchy of Chenwick's latest superstore.

By mid-afternoon, they were on the last leg. '*Smile though your heart is breaking...*' sang Gail as she dropped the contents of the kitchen cupboards into a black bag.

'Is it?' asked Dilys, walking in on her.

'Is what?'

'Your heart breaking, and if so, why?'

'It's only a song,' said Gail, with her head under the sink. By the time she emerged, the words had been changed to suit the occasion. Mopping the floor as she reversed out of the kitchen, she sang, '*Smile though your legs are aching.*'

'*Smile though your back is breaking,*' Dilys joined in.

'As you're both that knackered, I've ordered taxis,' said Bradley. He shuffled his feet, watching them in fascination as he talked to the floor they were shuffling about on. 'Thanks. Yes, thanks, both of you. I'm... er... very grateful. Yes, very grateful. I'll never forget either of you. And... um... well, you'll see how grateful. Your redundancy money should be in your accounts by tomorrow and... um... there's a bit extra too... to show how... how—'

'Grateful you are,' Dilys finished for him, and Gail was glad of it. Seeing Bradley so stuck for words and struggling to express himself was torture.

'Yes,' he said, raising his head yet still managing to avoid eye contact. 'I'll fetch my car round and stick this lot in the boot.' He gestured towards the bags of mugs, tea and coffee, cleaning fluids and dusters that leaned against the selection of mops, brooms, buckets, bowls and vacuum cleaner, but before he could leave, a taxi blasted its horn.

'It's for you, Dilys,' he said, dashing at her and pecking her cheek. 'I got you one each, as you live opposite ends of town.'

'You are pushing the boat out. Bye, Boss. It's been fun. Don't forget to send us a postcard.'

'I won't,' said Bradley, following her to the door.

'See you outside the job centre. Nine o'clock sharp,' Dilys shouted back to Gail, and then she was gone.

'I'll get the car,' said Bradley, following her.

Alone, Gail wandered the empty shop and discovered a copy of the Echo's monthly magazine under the till. Folding it up, she stuffed it in the top of her bag to read during her first week of retirement. A nicer word than unemployment. Her fingers ran over the bare shelves, stroked the counter and patted the top of the till, as if it were a dog's head. She was going to miss all this. She felt as empty as the shop looked. It was as if a big piece of her insides had been ripped out, and if it felt like that for her, what must Bradley be feeling?

Sheepish and guilty were two words that sprang to mind on his return. 'What's up?' Gail asked, trying to see beyond the bowed head and into Bradley's face.

'Umm...'

Not more umming and ahhing.

'I didn't order you a taxi,' he blurted, still staring at the floor.

'That's OK. I can walk.'

Bradley slowly raised his head until he was looking directly into her eyes. 'No, I wanted to give you a lift. There's all this stuff.' He brandished a mop. 'I thought you could use it, you know, in your new business.'

'If I start it.'

'You will.' He sounded certain.

Together, they loaded the boot of his car. In silence, Bradley locked the front door and posted the keys through the letterbox. Without a word, he held the passenger door of his third-hand BMW open.

They didn't speak again until he pulled up outside the house in Rosehill Avenue. Bradley shot out of the car to open Gail's door and help her out. He emptied the boot, stacking everything inside the gate, and then stood, hands in the pockets of his jeans, looking lost.

'Goodbye, Bradley, and good luck,' she said, stretching to kiss him. She felt his warm cheek beneath her lips and suddenly his arms were around her and their lips somehow met. Breathless, she broke away first.

11

Monday, 14 February

Valentine's Day. Normally, Gail ignored it, but this time around it was different. When she'd transferred BJ's offering from her front path to the shed, she'd discovered a sealed envelope with her name written on it in Bradley's handwriting, hidden between the brooms and brushes.

'Must be my redundancy cheque,' she told herself, ripping it open. There was no cheque, but there was a card, all hearts, flowers, glitter and pink ribbon. Her hand shook as she opened it to see what Bradley had written. 'Missing you already.' And there was a kiss. She wondered if Dilys had received the same.

It was probably the card that had given her a sleepless night in which she'd watched the action replay of the kiss with Bradley in slo-mo. *And the darkest hour is just before...* four-fifteen, said the illuminated dial of the alarm clock on her bedside table. Bradley would be airborne, on his way to his new life in the sunshine. Perhaps he had really meant it when he'd asked her to go with him. Now she'd never know.

She lay on her back and stared at the ceiling. In the darkness, pinpricks of light began appearing across it, like those luminous stars she'd bought for Jack's bedroom. But these weren't stars. They were miniatures of Bradley.

Bradley rearranging the monster knot of his tie. Bradley beaming at a customer. Bradley drawing smiley faces on pink Day-Glo posters.

A pink poster shimmered and turned into her pink agony aunt. '*Have you allowed the man of your dreams to slip through your fingers?*' *she asked.*

Gail rubbed her eyes and stared harder. As the pink poster shrank, Bradley grew until above her bed loomed wall-to-wall-Bradley, wagging a finger at her. 'Your ideal partner is right under your nose,' his voice boomed.

No. No, it couldn't be. It couldn't be Bradley. He was her second-best friend, after Dilys.

'Fucking hell, Gail. You don't know what you do to me.' Those had been the last words he'd said to her.

Gail's lips moved. *Fifteen years and now he tells me.*

Flinging herself onto her side, she thumped the pillow, or was she dreaming she was thumping the pillow?

It was D-Day as well as Valentine's. Decision Day. At nine o'clock sharp, a bleary-eyed Gail stood outside the job centre, waving to a slowly approaching Dilys.

'God, you look terrible. It must have been one hell of a good night, or a bad one,' said Dilys, plodding up the steps.

'Bad,' said Gail. 'The second one in a row. If it goes on like this, I'll be spending my redundancy on plastic surgery.' She patted gently at the bags beneath her eyes.

'Come on. Let's see what they've got.' Dilys stood tall, lifted her chin, slipped her arm through Gail's and marched at the job centre doors.

The swish they made did nothing to lift Gail's spirits. What was the point in going in? It would be all minimum wage and no-hope ageism, but Dil didn't know that. This was her first visit and maybe, just maybe there'd be a job available. Correction. A couple

of jobs going that would suit them. Gail sniffed. She
was very close to tears. *Shit. What's happening to me?
I'm not usually like this.* For some unknown reason,
she thought back to the final morning she'd gone to
BJ's. There'd been a cloud over the retail park. A cloud
with its silver lining on show like a slipped petticoat.
Today, all she could see was cloud. Another correction. She couldn't see it. She could feel it because the
whole damned black heap was sitting on her head.

'What do we do now?' Dilys wanted to know.

'Play with the computer. It tells you what jobs are
going.'

So, they played and, to their surprise, got the hang
of it.

Press, press, went Dilys. 'What's a sous-chef?'

Gail fished her glasses out of her handbag. 'You're
looking at the catering vacancies. Washer-upper.
That's the only one we could do.'

Dilys wrinkled her nose and continued her search.

Gail scanned what was on offer half-heartedly.
Nothing new and exciting, well-paid and suitable for
an ageing woman.

'*And what would that be, exactly?' asked her agony
aunt. 'Sensible mature woman to escort rich elderly
couple on world tour? No qualifications necessary.
Dream on.*'

'Here's one,' squealed Dilys, stabbing at the screen.
'Chalet maids required for popular Swiss ski resort.
Cor. I've read about those randy ski instructors and
all that how's-your-father in front of roaring log fires.
I'm up for some of that. How about you?'

Gail's smile was more ski slope temperature
than log fire. She pointed out the final words
with her index finger. 'It says eighteen- to twen-
ty-five-year-olds only.'

'Shame. I could almost feel those flames burning
my bum, the fur rug underneath me and the ski in-

structor on top.' Dilys gave a shiver of delight to go with her raucous peal of laughter. 'What next?'

'We could try asking over there.' Gail gestured to where Harry Potter sat at his desk, watching them over the top of his little round spectacles.

'Oh, isn't he sweet?' cooed Dilys.

Gail almost felt sorry for him as her friend marched over to his desk and sat down.

'What have you got for a good-looking, hard-working woman?' were Dilys's first words.

Master Potter seemed to shrink, but his magic wasn't strong enough for him to disappear altogether. 'H-h-housekeeper?' he stuttered.

So, Cherie hadn't found a suitable candidate.

'Is that all?'

'There may be some temporary vacancies nearer Easter.'

'Like what?'

'Stacking shelves, collecting trolleys.'

'You what?' Dilys was beginning to realise how few her opportunities were.

Harry repeated the possible job offers.

'I was thinking more nightclubs than supermarkets,' said Dilys sweetly. A warning sign to Gail. 'More along the lines of pole dancers for their Grab-a-Granny nights.'

The lad squirmed in embarrassment.

'You could come with us.' Dilys winked. 'We could teach you a thing or two.'

Harry spluttered. Before Dilys could put him off women for life, Gail took hold of her arm and dragged her towards the exit.

'Bar staff or bog cleaners. No thanks. Been there, done that. Let's get coffee.' Dilys flounced out of the building, Gail in her wake. They practically power-walked their way to the romantically named Central Cafe, hesitating only once, and that was for a mere second, outside an empty shop that had already had its sign taken down. BJ's was dead. Long live Chas Henderson, quality gentlemen's outfitters.

'Hot chocolate,' gasped Gail, plonking into a window seat. She was still out of breath when Dilys returned with the tray.

'You sound like a dirty old man,' said Dilys, offloading cups and teapot and sliding the tray onto the neighbouring table.

Gail wheezed her thanks and looked questioningly at Dil's purchases. 'What, no cake?'

'No, I'm on a diet, and this one's going to work.'

Gail was getting her breath back. 'What is it? Calorie counting? Cabbage soup? The twenty-eight-day plan?' They'd tried them all.

Dilys leaned across the table. 'It's the C-Food diet.'

'Not that old one?' Gail wasn't in the mood for prehistoric jokes. 'See food and eat it.'

'No,' said Dilys earnestly. 'I'm not going to eat anything beginning with C unless it's fruit or a vegetable.'

'So, cauliflower's all right?'

'Yes, and so's cabbage.'

'And carrots?'

'Yes. But not the other foods. I was thinking about it in bed. And the diet.' Dilys giggled. 'Most fattening foods begin with C. Chocolate, crisps, cheese, chips, cake—'

'Cream, croissants,' added Gail.

'Yeah, you've got the idea. And if you say cookies instead of biscuits and candy instead of sweets...'

'Hey, that's a good one.' Gail was impressed. 'It should work considering everything we eat seems to begin with C. I might join you. After this.' She spooned the spiral of Cream, generously sprinkled with Chocolate powder, from the top of her hot Chocolate.

'Pig,' said Dilys, pouring pale green tea into her cup. 'Think of Laxi-Lexi and what giving up chocolate did for her.'

'Made her skinny and stupid,' suggested Gail.

'Stupid? Oh, yes, she thought you and your lodger had been down the aisle together.'

For several minutes, they sipped their drinks in silence, deep in their own thoughts. Gail was reminding herself to ask Will if he had any idea why Mrs Lexi Camberlege thought he was married, then she switched to wondering how to broach the subject of Girls Will and a possible partnership to her mate. Meanwhile, Dilys was trying not to choke on her disgusting herbal brew and searching for the best way to tell Gail she'd made up her mind to go to the wedding.

They summoned the courage at the same time. 'I've got...'

'You first,' said Gail.

Dilys happily abandoned her healthy cuppa. 'My redundancy money,' she began. 'I've made up my mind. I'm using it, some of it, to go to Anne's wedding.'

'Good for you.'

'You're sure you don't mind? My daughter and your ex-husband?'

'That's history.' As she said the words, Gail realised she was speaking the truth. Roger was the past. She'd got a whole new set of problems now. 'How long will you go for?'

'Dunno. It could be six weeks or six months depending—'

'Six months?' The colour drained from Gail's face. Even her blusher faded. She sucked in some air.

'Why don't you come with me?' Dilys asked cheerily, not noticing the ghost sitting opposite.

Bradley had asked the same thing. First, he'd gone, and now Dilys was making plans too. Gail felt tears creeping up again. By the end of summer, her life would be empty of good friends. She sniffed. What the hell was up with her? Turning into a wimp when she needed to be brave.

'I can't. Roger wouldn't be too pleased with me turning up, and anyway, I've got other plans.' She stopped, a lump blocking her throat.

'Sounds mysterious,' said Dilys. 'Come on, you can tell me.'

'Will started it. He said cleaners are always needed, and somehow we came up with the idea of Girls Will.'

'Girls will what?'

'Clean houses. Maybe do a bit of everything. Shopping, dog walking. You could help me. We could be partners.'

'Bloody hell, Gail. It's a big step. Have you thought it all through?'

'No,' said Gail. 'It's too scary to think about.' She was out of puff again. 'I'm just going to jump in at the deep end.'

'Been running a marathon?' asked Will.

'It feels like it,' panted Gail. She'd left Dilys to catch the bus home, and as she was passing the offices of the Chenwick Echo, she'd risked calling in to see if Will could spare her five minutes.

Will pulled out a chair. For the first time in her life, Gail felt like an old lady as he helped her to sit. 'What on earth have you been doing to get like this? I'm going to call the surgery, see if they can see you now.'

Now? How naive could men get? Everyone knew you had to wait a month or more for an appointment. Gail didn't have the breath to explain the facts of surgery life to him, she didn't listen to what he was saying on the phone and, for a moment, didn't take in what he said to her as he put the phone down.

'Gail? Did you hear? I can take you round now.'

Stuffing hell. Next time she wanted an urgent appointment, she'd get a man to make the call. She was obviously the wrong sex to persuade the receptionist—Cat-Woman, as she and Dilys had christened her—into being human.

Cat-Woman smiled like a real person as Will led Gail in. God, his fussing was making her age a year a minute.

'Mr Bassett,' purred Cat-Woman.

Gail sighed, sagged and stared. The receptionist must use a cement mixer to get all that slap on every morning. Thick orange foundation, at least three shades of blue eyeshadow, finger-thick eyeliner in coal black flicking out from the outside corners of her eyes, giving her the cat-like appearance that had brought about her nickname. And to finish off, long curled eyelashes, black and clotted like the dirty bristles of a broom that had been used to sweep a mucky farmyard.

'And this is?' Cat-Woman looked pityingly at the baggage Will had ushered in and was half holding up.

'Mrs Gail Lockwood.'

'Aaah.' The purr was more interested now. 'Are you a relative, Mr Bassett?'

'No, Mrs Lockwood is my landlady.'

Cat-Woman's eyes glinted. Her lilac claws spread themselves on the appointments book. Gail, in her elastic-topped comfy trousers and thick coat that made her look a good XL, felt big and old and faded against this thirty-something feline. Like a, like a... Rottweiler.

That's it. I'm a Rottweiler, and she'd better watch out. This cat looking down her snooty snout. Rottweilers have been known to savage cats. They've probably eaten them. Except, according to Dilys's diet, I can't 'cause cat begins with C...

'Dr Holliday will see you now,' purred Cat-Woman. *So, clear off and leave this Bassett fella to me*, is what Gail imagined she left unsaid.

'Do you want me to come with you?' asked Will.

Gail shook her head. *No, stay where you are and play mouse.*

Doc Holliday—an inappropriate name, as there was not a holster or six-shooter in sight—was a busy man. Extremely busy, efficient and fast. Gail had seen him before and knew what to expect. He didn't disappoint her. As she walked into his room, he was there, as always, at his desk, pen poised ready over his prescription pad. Gail hovered.

'Sit down,' he commanded without raising his eyes. 'What can I do for you?'

Grab them with your opening line, Gail had once heard a comedian say when interviewed on television, so that was what she did.

'I'd like a sex change.'

She had his full attention. He even dropped his pen. And because she felt guilty about her lie, Gail told him everything. Breathlessness, insomnia, hot flushes, being weepy, losing her job and her best friends. Absolutely everything. The gates had opened, and she and the good doc were set to drown in the flood.

He gave her 'a good going-over', as Pearl would have called it. He was even sympathetic.

'A touch of asthma,' he said. His voice was soft, and Gail was beginning to warm to him. He had nice eyes, grey with dark lashes, and his all-grey hair suited him. 'And when you had the hysterectomy, your ovaries were left in. They've probably been producing some oestrogen but...'

The man of her dreams? He could be, and then he blew it.

'...you have to face facts,' he said. 'They are now well past their sell-by date.'

'So, the doc reckons it's asthma?' said Will, switching on the kettle. He'd driven Gail home and insisted on getting her settled, as he called it, before returning to work.

'You're my lodger, not my carer,' Gail told him, but she was grateful for his concern and even more grateful for the tea. 'Now, get back to work and see that my advert goes in this week's issue.'

'Sure about that?'

'Of course.' The medication would soon work, and the doctor had said it was stress-related, so all she needed to do was get on with life and get rid of the stress.

'You won't go rushing about as soon as my back's turned?'

'Don't think I don't appreciate what you've done but piss off, Will.'

'Have you got everything you want? Shall I pass you your bag?'

'So I can sit with it on my knees like some geriatric? Yes.' The yes was because she'd remembered his present. Her bag was where she'd left it after her brief and final encounter with BJ. She tipped out the contents on the kitchen table and handed Will the tiny brown bag. 'Pressie for you.'

'What is it?' He opened the bag and pulled out the fluorescent green scrunchie. He touched the sumo wrestler attached to it. 'That's fantastic,' he said, exchanging the elastic band holding his ponytail together for Gail's gift. 'I love it.'

'Thought you would. Now go.'

Finally alone, Gail carried her tea and the magazine through to the living room. Before her backside touched the debt-laden suite, the phone rang. It was Dilys.

'How are you? You looked awful this morning. Talk about one foot in the grave.'

Gail explained about the visit to the doctor and the asthma diagnosis, but it didn't end there. That was what was good about having a friend of the same age and sex. She could tell Dil everything. Well, nearly everything. 'He thinks my oestrogen levels are low, so he sent me to the nurse for a blood test. Maybe that's what's causing me to be weepy.'

'Weepy?'

'Yeah. I might be cheerful in company, but once I'm on my own'—she swallowed hard to stop the approaching tears—'it feels as if I'm falling apart.'

'No, not you, Gail. You're the one who keeps us all going. You can always see the bright side.'

Gail didn't respond to that. 'If the levels are low, he suggests upping the HRT a bit.'

The chat lifted her spirits but left her tea cold. She made a fresh cup and sat with her hands around it, enjoying the warmth. If the phone rang now, it could go stuff itself, even if it were little Harry offering her the job of escorting George Clooney on a full-time basis for ten grand a week. If the doorbell rang, she'd ignore that too or shout bugger off at the top of her voice depending on her stress levels or her hormone levels. If the house caught fire, she'd bloody well go down with the sinking ship. Whatever happened, she was going to drink a whole cup of tea in peace and at her own pace.

What she hadn't taken into account was her own thoughts. Bradley's copy of the Chenwick Echo's monthly magazine sat on the coffee table in front of her. It was supposed to amuse her for half an hour once she'd finished her drink. There were a few decent articles amongst all the advertisements. *New Furniture Store for Retail Park*, screamed one ad. *Bradley Jones*, screamed the entire thing. Bradley had paid for it, carried it into the shop, read it, no doubt filled in half of the crossword using the easy clues and left it under the till.

Poor Bradley, thought Gail. If she was suffering from stress, it must be worse for him, having to get rid of his business, his home. He'd even arranged for his BMW to be sold.

'*But Bradley will soon be sunning himself on a beach while you're inhaling Ventolin and panicking about Girls Will,*' said her agony aunt from the centre spread of the magazine as it lay open on Gail's lap.

'*Mmm, but I've got my friends and family here with me, which is more than he has in Spain, and he doesn't speak the language. Bradley's is real stress.*'

She put down her empty cup, snapped the magazine shut, leaned against the cushions and closed her eyes. Yes, Bradley had to be under an awful lot of strain to say the things he had. To act like he did. Of course he'd miss her. She'd miss him too. Over the course of a week, they'd spent more time together than any married couple. No wonder he'd got confused about their friendship.

The magazine slid to the carpet as Gail's eyes closed. *Need to get some energy from somewhere*, she thought, snuggling into the cushions. *I'll add it to my to-do list.* Get job.

Sort out family relationships.

Pay off the suite.

Do roots and nails.

Get man, get laid.

Her agony aunt had escaped the glossy pages and was standing in front of her. 'I'll add "find energy" to the top, shall I? Without it, what hope do you have of achieving any of the rest?'

12

Tuesday, 15 February

'I was on my way to the hairdressers,' said Pearl, 'and I thought I'd drop in to see how you're getting on.'

'Fine,' lied Gail. It was early. She hadn't even had breakfast.

'The trick is to keep busy. It helps keep your mind off your problems.'

'I don't have any problems.' Gail crossed her fingers behind her back.

Pearl shuffled towards her awkwardly. Probably due to the oversized silver shell suit she was wearing. It matched the silver hair that straggled from beneath a sweatband topped by a turquoise bobble hat. Self-consciously, she put an arm around her daughter's shoulders. 'I know you still hurt over Roger.'

'I do not,' screamed Gail. 'Mother, when will it sink into your head that I do not miss Roger, do not love Roger, do not want Roger?'

'Now, now, don't get upset. One day, you'll find someone else.'

Gail pulled away from her mother's caress and began shoving dirty laundry into the open mouth of the washing machine. 'And I am not interested in Will either. He's my lodger. We have an agreement. He pays me to cook and clean for him, do his washing, and that's all.'

'I should hope so too', agreed Pearl, shuffling over to the kettle. As she switched it on, Gail tried to switch off by humming.

"Bridge Over Troubled Water" only partly blocked out the lecture on The Proper Role of a Respectable Landlady, which Pearl was delivering. It was rather like listening to the ten commandments. Each rule was a 'do not'.

Do not allow your lodger to leave items of clothing or personal belongings anywhere other than his designated room.

Do not allow your lodger to eat or drink in his room.

Do not allow your lodger to entertain in his room.

Do not allow your lodger to see you in your night attire.

Do not address him by his first name...

Gail, trying hard to shut out the continual drone of her mother's voice, concentrated her attention on the washing machine. Through its porthole door, the sight of the laundry swirling around was soothing as opposed to listening to Pearl's never-ending list. But she wasn't the only one watching the washing. From beneath the Adidas sweatband, Pearl's beady eye latched onto the porthole.

'Disgusting', she spat.

'Disgusting? What?'

'That.' Pearl's hand trembled in consternation as she pointed at the round window.

'That?'

'Don't play the fool with me, my girl. You know very well what I'm on about, and you should be ashamed of yourself.'

But Gail didn't know. She bent so that her head was on a level with the automatic's window, her eyes circling in time with the washing.

Pearl put one gnarled hand to her forehead and used the other to support herself. A dramatic faint was on the cards. From long experience, Gail knew what was expected. Just in time, she dragged a chair behind her mother's sagging knees. Pearl collapsed onto it.

'Oh, Gail. How could you?'

Matricide was on the cards. Gail placed her hands together as if in prayer and took a deep breath.

'How could you?' Pause for effect.

Light suddenly dawned. All this because...

'How could you put your underwear in with his?' Pearl's shudder should have registered on the Richter scale.

At that precise moment, a pair of the lodger's Darth Vader boxers performed a tango with Gail's best red Wonderbra, and Pearl did an excellent impression of a death rattle before recovering enough to shoot bolt upright and announce, 'It's practically fornication.'

Gail gave yet another sigh. Now was definitely not the right time to reveal her future plans to her mother.

'Another day, another diet,' announced Dilys.

Gail stood at the self-service counter behind her friend. 'Make mine a herbal tea,' she said. 'I need something to soothe me after Mother's visit.'

'Mango and monkey pee,' said Dilys. 'For two.'

'You what?' The spotty girl, fresh out of school and soon to be out of Central Cafe as soon as her modelling contract came through, didn't look amused.

'Herbal tea,' explained Dilys.

'Oh, is that what it's called?'

Dilys grinned. The kids of today... they knew nothing.

'Monkey pee stuff? Ugh. Don't fancy it meself.'

'You should try it,' Gail informed her. 'We get it direct from the zoo and have been drinking it and washing in it for the past—'

'Seventy years. And not a drop of water touched my face.' Dil lifted her face ceilingward and stroked her cheek as she'd seen the eighteen-year-old advertising anti-wrinkle cream do on the telly. 'Yeah, must be seventy 'cause we started using it when we left school,' she finished.

The girl showed interest for the first time, staring at them both. 'Wow. Cool. Looking good.'

They were giggling like schoolgirls when they sat in their favourite window seat.

'Wow. Cool,' Dilys imitated.

'Poor girl. She'll be in the Echo next week for breaking into the ape house.' Gail dunked her teabag in and out of the water.

'And the RSPCA will be after her for forcing chimps to sit on potties.' Dil gave her cup a good stir, the string from the teabag twisting itself around the teaspoon. 'I managed to get an appointment with Sharon so we can go get our roots done together.'

'Great. Shall we treat ourselves to lunch first? A nice plate of sh-sh... shit! Look at that.' Gail lunged forward, pointing through the window and nearly falling through the plate glass.

The yellow Jag was sailing slowly past. Slowly enough for them to see that Guy was driving it and Pearl was in the passenger seat, but that wasn't what the pointing and lunging had been about.

They stared wide-eyed at each other. Dilys's mouth opened but nothing came out.

'Her hair. Did you see my mother's hair?'

Dilys nodded and hoped she wasn't smirking. 'Talk about bloody buttercups. Do you think it's supposed to match the Jag?'

Perhaps because urine had formed a large part of their conversation since meeting in the Central, it came to mind when Gail tried to describe the acid yellow of her mother's new look. 'It's like dog piss on fresh snow,' she wailed.

'Do you think she's trying to impress that bloke from the garage?'

That was one thing Gail had never considered. 'My mother? Impress him? Gorgeous Guy?'

'You might not think he's so gorgeous when you hear how old he is. That fat woman from Flabfighters was telling me only yesterday at the bus stop.'

Gail bit back a reply about managing to be ageist and sizeist, if there was such a word, and waited for further information. Dilys didn't disappoint.

'Seventy,' she said with a flourish.

'No, you've got to be wrong.'

Dil's fringe swung back from the violent shake of her head. Beneath it, like a couple of caterpillars, lurked one thin eyebrow and one fat one. 'Nearer your mother's age than yours. I wonder if he's still got a bit of lead in his pencil.'

'He must have been washing in monkey pee.'

They dissolved into giggles.

Side by side, Gail and Dilys sat, waiting for their colours to take. Lunch had been difficult. The C-food diet wasn't as easy as they'd first thought. Cheese salad wasn't allowed. Ham salad wasn't fancied. Chicken had caused another problem. Gail had insisted that it was fine with the skin removed, but Dilys stuck to her guns. It began with C. Eventually, the waitress in Harper's, a tiny wine bar tucked behind the library, suggested their Slimmers' Special. A platter of salad arrived with a huge dollop of cottage cheese on the side.

'We should have stuck with ordinary cheese,' Dilys had moaned. 'This Cottage Cheese is two Cs. Three if you count Crappy.'

Afterwards, there'd been a slight disagreement over the choice of pudding until Gail had declared emphatically that the Chocolate, Cherry and Cointreau Confection was actually a Gateau and therefore allowed.

'You ladies want anyfing to read?' cooed Sharon—Shaz to regulars and friends—indicating a tottering pile of tattered magazines.

'Got anything from this century?' asked Gail, mopping at a trickle of red dye with the sensible black towel draped around her shoulders.

'Don't fink so,' said Sharon cheerily, just before her smile slipped. 'Oh Gawd, I'd forgotten. You're Pearl Proctor's daughter, aincha?'

Gail didn't dare move her head and set off a haemorrhage of dye.

Shaz didn't want an answer. She simply carried on. 'Got nice 'air, she 'as. Did 'ave.'

'You did it?' Gail couldn't believe it. Sharon was good at her job. Had a successful business. She'd been doing Pearl's hair for years and managing to keep her happy. Sharon had perfected the art of backcombing and spraying Pearl's straggly locks until they stood out around her head like a dandelion clock.

'It worn't my fault. She came in 'ere demanding apricot, and I said to 'er, "Not on top of that silvery white, it won't take", but did she listen?'

Does she ever? thought Gail, picturing the scene.

'I didn't wanna do it, but she forced me. I warned 'er. I just 'ope she won't sue. I shoulda got 'er to sign a disclaimer.'

'She loves it,' said Gail.

'Loves it?' screeched Sharon and Dilys together.

'She must do. Think about it, Dil. What, apart from the hair colour, was different about my mother this morning?'

Dil thought and shook her head, causing a mini avalanche of black streaks, which Sharon dabbed at with a fistful of cotton wool.

'She wasn't wearing a hat,' said Gail triumphantly. 'She had her hair on full display for all the world to see, and that can only mean one thing.'

'She loves it,' screeched Sharon and Dilys together.

Later, as Sharon rinsed off Dilys's black, she went into hairdresser-speak. 'Planned your 'olidees yet?' It was that time of the year when she was never sure whether to ask about holidays or, 'Get anyfing good in the Janu-ery sales?' Her smile twinkled like fairy lights when Dilys went into full details of her planned trip to the wedding in Australia. Good stuff for Shaz. A holiday and a wedding for the price of one.

Later again, as she rinsed off Gail's red, she got more than she bargained for. Gail told her all about her plans for Girls Will. Gawd, she'd got a lot to tell 'er customers. Keep 'er going for the rest of the week.

'Girls Will if you won't. That's good, that is. You couldn't do my 'ouse for me, couldya? I never gets time meself. Too busy 'ere.'

'When can I come around and take a look at it?' asked Gail, not believing her luck. A customer already, and the ad didn't come out until Friday.

13

Dilys stood at the bus stop, feeling guilty. She should be helping Gail out, not swanning off to Oz. It was like being torn in two. Loyalty to her best friend dragged her in one direction and a desperate desire to be at her daughter's wedding in another. If only she could do both.

'That's it,' she said aloud, making the girl with the baby buggy move a few yards further up the shelter. *I can help deliver leaflets, get organised, get her some custom.*

'Anyone want a cleaning lady?' she asked the queue. 'Good, honest, reliable.'

They all shuffled further along the shelter.

Dilys looked at her watch. The bloody bus wasn't going to turn up, and she wasn't about to hang around for the next one, not when she could be drumming up custom for Girls Will. She could try Fred in his Friendly Fry-up and that nice lady at the library.

The nice lady in the library still lived with her mother. Poor cow. 'Mum does all the cleaning,' she said. 'It keeps her occupied.'

Dilys's face dropped along with her adjective. Nice.

'You could put up a card on our noticeboard. Here, I've got a few empties.' She handed three postcards over. Plus a felt-tip.

Dilys restored her smile. 'Thank you. Thank you,' she said. What a nice lady.

'Girls Will if you won't,' she wrote. 'Reliable cleaning agency. No job too big or too small.' That always sounded good. She finished off with Gail's phone number and then repeated the process on the other cards.

The entire noticeboard was three deep in ads and posters. Dilys spent a happy ten minutes trying to look official and disposing of out-of-date information about Christmas fayres, various items that had been for sale and must have been sold by now and yoga classes that had begun in early January, so newcomers wouldn't have a chance of catching up. She stood back to admire her work. Everything was pinned in slightly wonky lines, leaving the best position on the board free. With a bright red pin, Dilys stuck the Girls Will postcard at eye level and centre stage.

'Brilliant.' She picked up the discarded information and screwed it up into a ball, which she tossed into a waste bin outside the automatic exit doors.

Dilys caught Friendly Fred preparing for the teatime rush. He put a bucket of raw potato chips on the pristine floor. The chrome range gleamed under the spotlights. Dil checked her new hairdo in the tiles on the wall.

'I don't suppose you want a cleaner, do you? This place is spotless already.' Damn, she'd answered the question for him. 'How about for home?'

'Sorry, the wife does the polishing an' all that.'

So, while he consorted with the cod, there was a little lady at home waiting for his return carrying the remainders of the day. Probably not such a little lady, then. 'Who's the cleaner? You?'

'No. It's Gail. She's starting her own business.' Didn't that sound grand?

'Got any cards? I'll stick one in the window for you.'

Two down and one to go. Dilys dithered outside the old shop. There was the new sign above the windows. Chas Henderson. Gentlemen's whatsit. There was one sign on the window. 'OPENING SHORTLY'. She still couldn't see what was going on inside though. Bradley had used a patchwork of Day-Glo. This Chas had opted for long net curtains.

Dilys did her usual—bust out, chin up, smile on—and marched in. Almost marched in. Bust and chin came into contact with the locked door. 'Firkinell.' She pressed her hands against the door to lever herself away just as Chas Henderson, proprietor of the gentlemen's outfitters, opened it to see what was going on. Dilys fell into his arms.

'We've got to stop meeting like this.' She smiled up at him, then did a double take. 'Firkinell. George Clooney.'

'No, Charles Henderson, but you're not the first to notice the resemblance.'

He's so up himself, thought Dilys as she pulled herself together and Chas, like one of the gentlemen he outfitted, waited for her to speak.

'I used to work here,' she said, 'and now I don't work, but that doesn't matter because I'm going to Australia to see my Anne get married. That's my daughter, and she's marrying Roger, who used to be married to Gail, who used to work here with me, but now we don't and...' She drew breath.

Chas, eyebrow lifted, lips curved, concentrated on his impersonation of Mr Clooney. When Dilys drew breath and didn't continue, he tweaked his eyebrow up another centimetre. It was that tweak that transported Dilys from dreams of Hollywood back to Chenwick's dying town centre. As far as she was concerned, he'd blown it.

'Dilys Lloyd,' she said. 'Calling on behalf of Girls Will.' She held out the final card. 'Give us a call if we can be of assistance.'

With satisfaction, she noticed how far away from his eyes he had to hold the postcard to focus on it.

'This may be what I'm looking for,' he said. 'Are you the owner?'

'No, that's Mrs Lockwood.'

'Tell Mrs Lockwood she can expect to hear from me.'

'Thank you very much,' said Dilys. She held out her hand to shake his and managed to stifle her reaction.

'The silly sod was wearing nail polish. That clear stuff, but it was definitely there,' Dilys told Mrs Galleon as they waited at the bus stop.

'Well I never. Do you think he's one of these New Men?'

'Dunno,' admitted Dilys. 'S'pose that's better than an old one, but give me a Real Man any day.'

Mrs Galleon's nudge almost knocked her sideways. 'What's your name, love? I can't keep saying that little Welsh woman from Flabfighters.'

'Dilys. Dilys Lloyd.' She lifted a Rimmel stripe as Chas had done. Not that his eyebrows had been painted on, though they could have been. Dil didn't know where a man who painted his fingernails might draw the line, so to speak.

'Nesta Neate,' Mrs Galleon introduced herself, much to Dil's delight. Now she didn't have to reciprocate with, 'And I can't keep saying that big fat woman.'

'Don't say a word. I've heard it all before,' said Big Nesta. 'It's a daft name, but it suits me.'

Did she mean because she was daft?

'Neate by name, neat by nature. That's me.'

'Really?'

'Yes. Tidying up and cleaning. That's my passion. I'm not much of a reader and the telly doesn't interest me.'

'Not even *Zany Scrapes*?' Dilys couldn't believe that there was anyone on the planet who disliked the adventures on Planet Zog.

Mrs Galleon... Nesta Neate shook her head. 'Never heard of it.'

'My mate, Gail—'

'Is that the redhead?'

'Yeah. She's starting her own cleaning business. I don't suppose you'd be looking for a bit of part-time work?'

'Could be,' said Big Nesta, producing a crumpled paper bag from her pocket. 'Caramel?'

'No thanks, it begins with C, but I'll have the paper off yours.'

The big lady shrugged and popped two into her own mouth.

As the bus pulled up, Dilys scribbled Gail's number on the sweet wrapper. 'Give her a call. She might have something for you.'

They had to sit on separate seats, as Nesta's bulk filled a double without any help. Dilys left her chewing her sweets and sat two seats behind, parking her shopping bag by her side. She felt like a prize Brownie. She'd done her good deed for the day. Several. With luck, Gail would be getting at least two phone calls. Feeling inside her bag, she pulled out a small box. The bloke in the shop had sworn it was a good one and it was pay-as-you-go. A gift for her best friend. Gail would make good use of a mobile phone.

Pearl called it the futility room because it was futile trying to find anything in there. In one corner, the washing machine was topped with yellowing newspapers waiting to be recycled. Clothing, waiting to dry, hung from several washing lines strung across

the room. Boxes around the four walls were filled
with tins, bottles and jars waiting to be taken to the
recycling centre. Silver paper and foil waited for a
caller from any charity wanting them. Large corners
torn from envelopes and holding stamps waited for
the next *Blue Peter* appeal.

It's more of a waiting room than a utility room,
thought Gail as she made her way through it en route
to her mother's kitchen. An ironing board with a safe
tartan cover toppled towards her like a randy drunk.
She shoved it back against the wall. Her mother could
do with a cleaner, not to mention a rubbish skip and
someone brave enough to chuck the lot out of the
window and into it.

Gail was trying not to breathe too deeply. Pearl's
central heating was on full blast, causing the contents of the row of saucers on the futility floor to
ripen more speedily. The cat flap clattered as a monstrous ginger tom forced his way inside. Testicles
intact and in proportion to the rest of him, he swag-
gered towards Gail, an overstuffed orange cushion
on legs. Gail stepped back, right into a saucer. The
fragrance of fetid fish and rancid rabbit rose up to
surround her.

'Bollocks,' she cried. 'Sorry, Arnie, no offence.'

'Meow,' wailed Arnie as he chewed his way through
the contents of a saucer.

'Is that you, Arnold?' called Pearl from the kitchen.
He'd been named after Schwarzenegger.

'Yes,' called Gail. 'I mean, yes, it's Arnie and me.'

'What do *you* want?' Mother, the hostess with the
mostest.

'Honestly, anyone would think I never came to see
you.' Gail followed her mother through the kitchen
and into the parlour.

'You don't very often.' They both knew it was a lie.
Pearl was in a long purple silk dressing gown. The

fluffy slippers on her feet and the feather boa around her neck were peony pink. Beneath the bare light bulb hanging from the centre of the ceiling, her hair looked radioactive.

Bare light bulb? 'Where's the lamp shade?' asked Gail. 'Sorry, chandelier.' It had been a cheap pressed glass creation, made to look more original and colourful by the paint daubed on it by Pearl. As a child, Gail had seen it sport every colour of the rainbow, plus thundercloud black, and there'd been that time when it had hung above the dining table and Pearl had sprayed it with glitter for Christmas, only the glue had come unstuck from the heat of its light bulbs and the *Snow White and The Seven Dwarfs* candles beneath. The gentle snowstorm it had produced had given their turkey a unique crispy coating.

'It was a dust gatherer.' Pearl turned her back to close the long velvet curtains. 'I got rid of it. Now, what did you want?'

It was brusque, even for Pearl. Gail would have preferred her mother to be in a good mood but couldn't wait that long. Too many people already knew about Girls Will, and there would be hell to pay if Pearl found out about it from Sharon or anyone else.

'Sit down, Mum,' she said. 'I've got something to tell you.'

Pearl lifted a tabby off the seat of her chair and sat it on the arm. It matched the one already sitting on the other arm. 'You're not pregnant, are you?'

'Bit late for that,' said Gail, and gave her mother an edited version of what she was about to undertake. 'I'll be a company director,' she concluded, but Will's title for her cut no mustard with Pearl Proctor.

'Girls Will? Sounds like a brothel. You'll have all sorts of perverts phoning.'

Gail resisted the urge to reply to that. She shoved her hands into her pockets. They'd suddenly grown a life of their own, a life that had one aim—to throttle elderly ladies with glow-in-the-dark hair.

'Cleaning agency. Nobody pays to have a duster put round. It's a silly idea. Doomed to failure,' prophesied Pearl. 'Why can't you get a proper job?'

'Because there aren't any bloody jobs.' It was rare for Gail to swear in front of her mum, but Pearl was enough to drive a saint to distraction.

'Of course there are,' said the woman who didn't know what Situations Vacant meant. 'A young girl like you could get work anywhere.'

'I'm not young, Mother. Not for the job market, anyway. I'm fifty bloody years old.' She'd done it again. Sworn.

'You can't be.'

'You should know. You gave birth to me.'

'Not when I was thirteen, I didn't. Listen to me, my girl, don't you go around telling people I've got a daughter in her fifties. You do the same as me and knock ten years off pretty sharpish.' She patted her fluorescent locks.

'You're passing yourself off as sixty-three? Have you thought that if the four generations of the family all knock a decade off it'll make our Tamsin fifteen and poor Jack minus seven?'

'You always have to be awkward,' said Pearl, bending to pick up a black and white kitten and unknowingly risking a bash on the head with a blunt instrument.

'Yes, always awkward,' said Gail, making for the kitchen. Time to go before the lust for violence or the bad language got stronger.

'Use the front door,' said Pearl. 'You can see yourself out.'

'Goodnight, Mum.'

In the hall, Gail stopped. The furniture was missing. 'Mum.' She put her head around the door. Pearl was stroking the kitten. 'What's happened to the hat stand and the bureau?'

'Got rid of 'em,' said Pearl. 'Dust gatherers.'

'Right,' said Gail, and then to try to please her, 'by the way, your hair looks...' She couldn't think of a suitable word. She didn't have to.

'Gorgeous,' said Pearl. 'Now, thank you and good-night.'

Tamsin opened the door an inch. 'Mum, what are you doing here?'

I'm not winning any popularity contests tonight, thought Gail.

'You can't come in,' said Tamsin. 'Jack's in bed and I'm busy.'

'Just called to tell you your gran wants you to knock ten years off your age, and I'm starting my own business. Girls Will. My advert will be in the paper this Friday.'

'That's cool, Mum. I'm pleased for you. Now, I've got to go.'

The door closed. Gail wanted to kick it. Tamsin was so selfish. She hadn't asked why her gran wanted her to be fifteen or what sort of business her mother was starting.

'It's a brothel,' shouted Gail through the keyhole. 'Specialising in black leather and cream cakes.'

Behind her, a man juggling with a six pack of lager, a strongly scented bag of chicken balti and the keys to the flat opposite, struggled to tap Gail's shoulder.

He grinned at her. 'Got a card handy, love?'

14

Picking up a hitchhiker was a new experience for Gail. The person concerned had seen the car, staggered to the edge of the pavement wagging a thumb, and then, as Gail's Clio had slowed, they'd waved a bottle of wine before hitching up their skirt and flashing a thighful of cellulite.

'Hiya,' said Dilys, getting into the passenger seat. 'I was on my way to see you. Got a pressie and some news.'

'Did you say news or booze?'

'Got both,' said Dilys. 'Where've you been?'

'To hell and back.' It was said in Gail's best John Wayne voice. 'Let's stop at a pub, shall we? I don't want to go home. Will's there and he'll want to talk business—have you been to the bank? Got your printing sorted? Phoned the other agencies to see what they're charging?—And I can't be doing with it.'

She drove out of Chenwick, towards the Birmingham road. A quiet pub was called for. They found one by the river. It was all red brick from the outside and all olde worlde inside. Posters hung from the beams, declaring its first anniversary.

'It looks really ancient,' said Dilys, giving it the once-over. 'Look at the beams. They've got little holes all over them. Woodworm.'

'Probably paid some kids on a job scheme to make them with a drill,' quipped Gail, getting out her purse. 'What are you drinking?'

As the only drinks they could come up with beginning with C were Champagne, Chardonnay, Cider or Cointreau, they were spoiled for choice. Dilys ordered vodka and lime.

'I'll have Coke,' said Gail. Damn. It began with a C. 'Diet Coke, please.'

Morning tea, lunch and now evening drinks. Their redundancy money wouldn't last long if they kept this up.

Gail told Dilys where she'd been and Dilys told Gail what she'd done.

'That Chas,' she said. 'He's a stunner, but don't let that fool you. He thinks he's God's gift. I bet you he undresses in front of a full-length mirror.' The idea of doing that was unthinkable to both women.

'He said he'd phone?'

'"Tell her to expect a call," is what he said. And that reminds me.' She fished in her bag and hooked out the mobile. 'You'll be wanting one of these. It's your pressie.'

Instantly, the tears were there, queuing up, spilling over and splashing onto the Orange box. Gail sniffed, choked and searched for a tissue.

'It's only a phone,' said Dilys. 'Not the answer to all your problems. Bloody 'ell, talk about mood swings. From murder to misery in thirty minutes.' She reached over the gnarled oak table and patted Gail's hand just as two men, all beery breath and big bellies, bent over them.

'Fancy a drink? Fancy a bit of whatever you fancy?'

'Piss off,' spat Gail. Her pendulum swinging back to murder.

'Please,' added Dilys.

'Lesbians,' said the prize-winning paunch owner. 'Been 'aving a lovers' tiff?'

Together, Gail and Dilys stared at their intertwined hands and burst out laughing. Gail's pendulum had looped the loop.

'Fancy chips?' asked Dilys after her second drink.

'Chips begin with C,' Gail reminded her.

'Oh bollocks. Fancy French Fries, then?'

They took their chips back to Dilys's house and ate them out of the paper, adding more salt and vinegar and wrapping some up in slices of bread and butter.

'More wine?' asked Dilys, shaking the second bottle over a large empty wine glass to get the last drip. It was empty. 'Never mind. I've got more where that came from. Co-op special offer.'

It was cold, white and fizzy. *Harmless stuff*, thought Gail, until she tried to stand up.

'You'd better stop the night,' said Dilys. 'You can have the spare room.'

She was too late. Gail was already sleeping, her feet drawn up beneath her on the sofa.

Dilys crawled up the stairs, dragged a blanket from the airing cupboard and flung it downstairs before tottering carefully down behind it. 'Here y'are,' she said. 'G'night.' She tucked the blanket tightly around Gail, pulling it down over her feet and up to her chin, only to discover her feet were then sticking out again. 'S'all right,' she decided, and set off to tackle the uphill climb to her own bed.

Gail dreamed she was lying on a beach, wrapped in a sack that restricted all movement, which was a shame because she was desperately thirsty and a long cool drink with clinking ice cubes and baby parasol sat on a table by her side. The sun beat down on her head. She was getting hotter and hotter. Struggling to extricate herself from the sack, she only managed to bind herself more tightly. A trickle of sweat ran down her chest, between her boobs. The back of her neck was damp. The sun was so bright she couldn't make out sea from sand from sky. So hot. Like an ice cream, she was going to melt.

How am I going to get out of this one? she wondered.

Right on cue, her agony aunt appeared. She was holding a long cold drink and sitting beneath a full-sized parasol. 'You need a hero,' she cooed, flinging her arm outwards to indicate to Gail that one was on his way. His face wasn't visible because the brim of a large white sombrero cast a shadow over it.

'Guess who?' Her agony aunt sipped her drink. 'I'll leave you two alone, shall I?' Without waiting for an answer, she disappeared, together with drink and parasol.

The hero was dressed in a white suit and a maroon frilled-fronted shirt, and he was riding a donkey. A large straw-filled donkey with a price tag still hanging from its ear. Gail squinted to read how much it cost, and there in felt-tip were the words, 'Final Day!!! Massive Savings!!! Bargains!!! Bargains!!! Bargains!!!'

'*Bradley*,' she squawked, and crashed onto the living room floor, still rolled in Dil's spare throw. Her hero? The man in her dreams? What the hell was in that fizzy stuff?

Quietly, she made her way to the bathroom to strip down to her undies and sponge away the night sweat.

After downing two glasses of water, she went back to her makeshift bed and spent the next hour staring at the invitation propped on the fireplace. Two silver cherubs, wings overlapping. It was the one subject she and Dilys hadn't even touched upon. She hadn't liked to ask. If her friend wanted her to know any of the details, such as exactly when in the autumn the wedding was, she'd have told her, wouldn't she? Two silver cherubs swinging on a golden heart. Anne and Roger.

Finally, Gail succumbed. Two steps and the cherubs were in her hand. They separated to reveal one heart beating beneath their wings. Beating? No. It was Gail shaking.

The silver print was a blur. She had to search her bag for her glasses and then she couldn't be sure of what she saw. She opened her eyes wide. Blinked. It was still there. The date. The fourth of March.

No, no. Not that soon. Next month. Of course. Their autumn's our sodding spring.

The shock was so great she couldn't rustle up a swear word bad enough to suit.

Carefully, she replaced the invitation in the exact spot she'd taken it from, then let out a stream of every swear word she could think of and gave the cushions a bloody good thumping.

'I don't mind you getting married,' she told a plump square one adorned with a ring of cross-stitched pansies, 'but why the hell did you have to choose now to do it? Trust you, Roger. You always were an inconsiderate bastard.'

It was mid-morning when she arrived home to find a large sheet of paper stuck to the fridge door with a collection of *Dr Who* magnets, gifts from Will.

The block capitals at the top of it shouted at her. 'WHERE HAVE YOU BEEN?' Will sounded like a husband. 'You've had two phone calls,' it continued in quieter print. 'Charles Henderson and Tamsin.' There followed a list of questions. 'Have you seen the bank manager about your business and opening an account? Made an appointment with the accountant? Got your printing sorted? Phoned the other agencies to see what they're charging?'

'Yes, yes, yes, no, but I'll do it as soon as I've had a bath.'

That one pound ninety-nine plonk didn't agree with her. Her head felt too big and heavy for her neck to hold up. She poured herself a mug of orange juice and carried it up to the bathroom. It was one of those days when she had a hankering for a long soak in her good bath foam. Ylang-ylang. There was an inch left in the bottle. Extravagantly, she tipped it all into the tub.

'Oh, balls,' she screamed as the plug gave a burp and lifted. Gail made a grab for it, but the water was boiling. There was nothing she could do except watch the expensive bubbles gurgle down the plug-hole. It would have to be the electric blue stuff from the pound shop. She stripped off, checked the water temperature, added cold, which made the window and mirror grow instant coats of fog, and slid into the tub.

'Mmm. Bliss.'

Beep-beep, beep-beep.

'Whoever you are, you'll have to wait,' she shouted at the phone. Slipping further into the strangely sweet-smelling water—it reminded her of Dolly Mixtures—she consoled herself that whoever it was could leave a message.

It was Charles Henderson. 'This is the second time of calling.' The voice had a slight Scottish twang to it. 'Would you please call me back? My number is...'

Bugger. It was going to be one of those days. Gail dialled the number immediately.

'Good morning. This is Gail Lockwood of Girls Will, returning your call. How may I help you?'

'Charles here.' She hardly took in what he said. If he looked as good as he sounded, she'd help him all right. How had Dilys described him? A stunner? 'Perhaps you could meet me at the shop sometime next week and we could go to my house from there. Five-thirty on Thursday the twenty-fourth?'

'Five-thirty Thursday,' repeated Gail. She put the phone down and panicked.

'*What are you going to wear?*' her agony aunt asked before disappearing as suddenly as she'd arrived.

Probably startled by the phone ringing again. Gail answered immediately.

'Oh good, you're there. Did you see my list?'

'Yes, Will, and by the time you get home, it'll be covered in ticks.'

'Good girl.' He sounded like Bradley. Gail sat down. 'Where did you spend last night, or shouldn't I ask? Tell me you pulled.'

'It would be a lie. I was with Dilys.'

'Have you answered your calls?'

'Tamsin, no. Charles, yes. I'm off to see what he wants doing and give him a quote next week.'

'What are you goin' to wear?' The same question her agony aunt had asked a minute before. 'You could do with a smart suit. Look the part. Got to go. Bye.'

A smart suit. One with trousers and a skirt so you could mix and match. That was what she wanted.

The phone rang. Again.

Dilys didn't give Gail a chance to speak. 'It's me. I was a coward last night. I was going to tell you to your face and then couldn't bring myself to do it. Sorry. The ticket for Australia. I've got it. Went back to the travel agency yesterday and everything's sorted, and I fly—don't get upset, Gail—I fly from Heathrow tonight. Last night was meant to be a goodbye drink. Well, it was, but you didn't know that. Sorry. Deserting you in your hour of need, that's what I'm doing.'

Gail's first thought was, 'Yes, you are deserting me, and I'd never do that to you.' But would she if things were the other way around?

With tears in her eyes, she said, 'Don't be daft. If it were Tamsin getting married, I'd go to the moon for her. You go and enjoy yourself. Are you all ready? Packed and everything?'

'Yes. I thought I'd go early. Anne might need some help and then I'll stay a while after the wedding, but I'll be back by the end of March.'

'Is there anything I can do for you?' The line went silent. 'Are you still there, Dil?'

'There is one thing, but it sounds stupid. You couldn't record *Zany Scrapes on Planet Zog* for me, could you?'

Another fan. 'Of course I can. Have a wonderful time, and give my love to Anne and Roger. Bon voyage. Send me a postcard.'

'I will,' sobbed Dilys, and the line went dead.

That was it, then. No Bradley and now no Dilys. It didn't bear thinking about. Gail shook herself. If she kept busy, the time would soon pass. Dilys would be back. And Bradley... Bradley would be settled. It wouldn't take him long to find some leggy, well-preserved blonde with an all-over tan to keep him company at night, and during the day he'd be swiping at golf balls.

She picked up the telephone directory. She'd call the other agencies and pose as a prospective customer to find out what they were charging. Then she'd call Sharon at the salon and see when it would be a good time to take a look at her house and check what was involved.

Half an hour later, she was ticking the final item on Will's list when she heard, 'Gwanny!' and a scrabbling at the door.

'Hi, Mum.' Tamsin walked in and kissed her, pocketing her spare key.

Jack produced a flowerpot containing miniature daffodils. 'It's for you, Gwanny. Zez said.'

'Jez said?' Gail took the pot and looked questioningly at Tamsin.

'Jez said I owe you an apology for last night. He says I should have let you in, but we were in the middle of doing the living room, and I didn't want you to see it until it was finished.'

'Zez is doing mekuvvers,' announced Jack. 'Wiv paint.'

Tamsin crossed the kitchen and reached for the kettle. 'I'll make tea, shall I? And you can tell me all about your brothel.'

'Broffull, broffull,' sang Jack as he dropped to his knees and zoomed a police car across the tiles.

15

Wednesday, 16 February

Bradley couldn't be bothered to go for a walk on the beach. He couldn't be bothered to go to the golf course or even the bar. He sat on the balcony of his third-floor apartment and watched all the retired Brits wandering aimlessly beneath him, and he knew that he didn't want to be one of them.

He slumped, as much as was possible, in the plastic fake-wrought-iron patio chair. *A midlife crisis, that's what I've had. A bloody midlife crisis of astronomical proportions.* Other men had them and got through in one piece. They left their mistresses and returned to the loving arms of their families, they climbed some nameless mountain in the Himalayas or walked from John O'Groats to Lands' End and got it out of their system. But he'd had to go and make a right pig's ear of his. Sell all his worldly goods and start a new life in the sun.

'Why didn't I revive The Boo-bop-a-loo-lahs if I wanted a change?' he asked the unnaturally blue sky. 'No, nothing sensible for you, Bradley, boy. You had to move here permanently when a week's holiday would have done.' Give him seven days away and he was always glad to go home. He'd arrived Monday and now it was Wednesday. He'd never cope with a lifetime of this. There was only so much idling about a bloke could do.

He was conscious of a big hole inside him. Not in his heart. More in his stomach. Like hunger. The shop had always filled that gap, but this was more than the shop missing. He wasn't actually longing for customers or suffering withdrawal symptoms for a bit of stock control. No. What he missed was the girls' company, the shared laughter and fooling about. The afternoon singsongs, the endless cups of tea and banter. And, Christ, he missed Gail. This self-imposed exile was turning into a colossal bout of homesickness. Worse than homesickness. It was more like a bereavement.

Hippos wallowed in mud. He was wallowing in self-pity. Give it time and he'd settle in, get used to a life in retirement. 'Mud, mud, glorious mud...'

His song was interrupted by a ring on the bell. His chair fell over backwards in his rush to greet the visitor. A welcome interruption in a long boring day.

There was a smile on his face as he opened the door. It remained stuck there. False like everything else about this corner of paradise. What was it he'd said about welcome? 'Brenda!'

'Brad, darling.'

Brad. He'd never asked her to call him that. He held his breath as she pushed past him, reeking of perfume and suntan oil. It was eighteen degrees outside, but sunscreen and a bikini? She was tanned, scrawny and dressed as if she were about to perform the dance of the seven veils—or scarves, to be precise. The scarves were all long floaty ones in varying shades of blue and green. One was tied around her pinky-blonde hair like a bandana, another wrapped around her neck. Bradley had seen beneath this one when she'd removed it before plunging into the pool. She wore it to disguise the deep lines around her throat. Her scraggy neck reminded him of the strangled necks of the chickens whose bodies hung from hooks on the market stalls. There were signs of scarring too, as if she'd undergone some terrible surgery. Did they do head transplants? The remaining scarves were tied around her breasts and hips, covering a white bikini, and the smallest of them all was knotted around her left wrist, between a bonanza of gold bracelets.

Brenda sprawled on the sofa, her bare feet resting on the coffee table so that she could admire her fuchsia-painted toenails and the narrow gold chain around her ankle. 'The gang wanted to know where you were. Aren't you coming out to play today?' she asked huskily. 'Or shall we stay in and play, the two of us?' She let a scarf slip to reveal her bikini top. White with orange staining around the edges. Fake tan.

Bradley was terrified of her and hadn't got the foggiest idea of how to get rid of his unwanted admirer. Brenda and Pearl could have been sisters. Sisters who eternally argued over who was the younger and the most attractive, and, like Pearl, he guessed Brenda wouldn't respond to subtle hints. Any other problem he would have

welcomed into this new empty life, but not this one. It would take sledgehammer tactics to dislodge Brenda from his side, and he knew he was incapable of them. Never in his life had he been intentionally rude to a woman, and it was too late to start now.

'I was on my way out as you arrived,' he lied. 'Come on, let's not waste the sunshine. Don't want to keep the gang waiting, do we?' No siree. There was safety in numbers.

As he quick marched his way to the tennis courts, he composed the following day's postcard to Gail. *Wish you were here to rescue me. I am being pursued by a man-eating nympho. Love BJ (Bleeding Jittery).*

'*Saturday is shopping day,*' sang Gail to Jack as they took the escalator to the first floor. She didn't want to risk the stairs and have Tamsin see her struggling for breath or having to take her asthma medication.

'One, two, thwee, jump,' shouted Jack as they reached the top. The three of them jumped, landing on thick, deep carpet. Ladieswear. Coats and jackets, dresses and suits as far as the eye could see.

'You're bound to find what you want here,' said Tamsin as they walked into the maze of clothes rails.

Handley and Lanyon's wasn't where Gail normally shopped. Kays Catalogue was more like it. But this outfit was important. It would be no use frightening off prospective clients by looking like some posh tart. On the other hand, frumpy wouldn't do. She had to get the right balance between smart and casual.

'Does madam require help?' An elderly assistant loomed, clad in black from head to toe, her hands clasped as if in prayer. Her balance definitely wasn't right. She was a sort of upper-class shopgirl crossed with retired nun. She gave a little bow. Definitely leaning more towards the nun side.

'S'not madum. That's my gwanny.' Everyone ignored Jack.

'Only browsing at the moment,' said Gail.

The nun reversed, as if she were in the presence of royalty, and disappeared behind the Aquascutum macs. Gail and Tamsin headed for the suits.

'What size, Mum?'

'Twelve, if it's generous and got an elasticated waist.'

'And if it hasn't?'

'Fourteen,' hissed Gail, 'but I'd sooner have a twelve.'

'How about this nice beige one?' Tamsin held up a shapeless skirt and oblong jacket with brass buttons. That was the trouble with getting older. People expected you to choose beiges and greys. Invisible colours for the invisible age group of women. Well, Gail wasn't going to be invisible.

'Definitely not beige,' she said. 'Nor fawn or neutral or any other variation on it. Not even grey.'

Twenty minutes later, Gail was all for giving up and going home. This was nothing like turning a few pages of mail-order. The choice was vast. Separate sections of the first floor were given over to different manufacturers, and as the floor was the size of several football pitches, dying of starvation before they'd seen everything available seemed a distinct possibility.

'I'm hungwy,' said Jack. He would be after pushing his car the distance between two goal posts.

'So am I,' said his gwanny. 'I haven't had any lunch.'

'Excuse me.' The nun materialised. 'We do have a coffee shop on the floor above.'

'Sounds good to me,' said Tamsin.

'You go. I'll catch you up.' Gail had spotted a red suit on a nearby rail. She waited for her daughter's and grandson's legs to vanish from view on the up escalator before turning to the female version of Peter Cushing and asking, 'Have you got that suit in a generous twelve?'

The skirt was a narrow fit, the jacket short. It came with trousers as an optional extra. The colour was tomato red.

'Very nice, madam. The colour suits you.'

Gail did a twirl in front of the long mirror. Yes, yes, yes. She re-entered the changing cubicle to replace the skirt with trousers. Oh, yes. Perfect.

The price ticket definitely wasn't one of Bradley's. For a split second, she dithered, then, 'Wrap it up,' she said. It would be worth it. The cut and colour gave her confidence. It was exactly what a company director of a small but thriving business would wear.

OK, she was the workforce too, but not for long. Girls Will was going to take off. It had to.

She could see herself, like Wonder Woman, changing from cleaning clobber to smart suit as she twirled around in a phone box. Or was that Superman?

16

Wednesday, 23 February

Gail had stared at the red suit hanging on the back of the bedroom door for a week. A week in which she'd told her mother and daughter, her lodger and Shaz, her first client, that she was ill. She had asthma and low oestrogen levels and needed a rest. Once again, she looked at the suit. All that money down the drain. Perhaps if she took it back, she could get a refund. What had she been thinking? She couldn't run a cleaning agency. She couldn't cope with her own daughter or her own mother. She hadn't been able to keep hold of a husband or a job.

'I'm absolutely useless,' she told the pillow.

'Rubbish.' *Her agony aunt had never shouted so loudly. 'If you tell yourself that, you'll soon start to believe it. You can do this.' She flounced onto the bed and spread her long, silky pink dress across the duvet. 'Now, take your new strength HRT pill, and you'll soon feel better.'*

Gail had forgotten her new medication. No wonder she was on the verge of blubbering again and feeling so sorry for herself. She turned to thank her agony aunt, who'd said something useful for a change, but she'd already disappeared.

It's all right for some, thought Gail. Disappearing was a great gift to have. Then she remembered Dilys, who would be having the most fantastic time on the opposite side of the world. So busy enjoying herself that she hadn't had time to phone. Bradley too. So much for all that 'missing you' stuff. He hadn't even bothered sending her a postcard. She was out of sight and out of mind as far as they were concerned.

'*Rubber ball come bounce right back...*' The Everly Brothers' old number leapt into her head. Life was like a rubber ball. You bounced back because you had to, but as you grew older, it got harder and harder to do it.

'I'll bounce back,' she whimpered, 'after I've had a little sleep.' She wasn't seeing her first client until five-thirty. Huh. Big deal. One client wasn't going to keep the wolf from the door.

Dilys had been alone in Australia for a week. She sat in the primrose room, on the primrose bed, and stared at her bare toes wiggling above the primrose carpet. You could take colour coordination too far. Talk about a primrose prison. And it was all her fault.

She'd been so proud of herself, getting not only halfway around the world but from the airport to her daughter's bungalow on the outskirts of Sydney. A solo voyage. And she'd never forget the look on Anne's face when she'd opened the door. It wasn't supposed to be like that. It was supposed to be like a telly advert for plane travel. The family waiting to welcome you, all hugs and kisses. Tearful reunions. Tears of joy. A reconciliation between mother and daughter. She'd forgiven Anne for having an affair with Gail's husband, and Anne should be mature enough to understand why she'd been so angry and why she'd kicked her out and thrown her belongings out of the bedroom window. Dilys thought they'd come some way towards forgiveness and under-standing through their letters and phone calls. She'd been mistaken.

Anne's palatial four-bedroom bungalow put South Fork to shame. After the official guided tour, Roger had stood, arms folded above his beer belly, his hair glowing the same blue-black as his fiancée's, and broken the news. No room at the inn.

'You can't stay here. We've got guests coming for the wedding.'

Dilys didn't know how she'd managed to keep her gob shut. Guests? What the hell did they think she was?

Within an hour, she'd arrived back in Sydney, booking into this Pissing Primrose Hotel.

Anne had driven her to the hotel in a huge and expensive open-topped car. All baby pink and chrome. There'd been a similar one in baby blue parked alongside it outside their massive bungalow. His and Hers. Anne's and Roger's. They'd certainly landed on their feet, down under.

Dilys had stood, like Gretel lost in the forest but without Hansel for company, in front of the huge reception desk.

'How long will you be staying?' asked the competent, young and beautiful receptionist.

Dilys chewed her lip and fiddled about with the tag on her suitcase.

'Sixteen nights.' Anne made the decision for her. 'There's no point in you hanging about after the service because we're going on honeymoon. To New Zealand.'

Honeymoon? It was laughable. They'd lived together for five years and now they were making it legal and having a flaming honeymoon. What for? Roger was old enough to remember the way it used to be. Marriage first, followed by the honeymoon and then you moved in together.

'We're going out with friends tonight,' said Anne. 'I'll be in touch.' And she was gone, leaving her poor mother standing all alone in a hotel foyer, in a strange country. Anne hadn't offered to pay for the hotel and hadn't asked if Dilys could afford it.

'Room 103,' said the receptionist, handing over the key.

Dilys had taken her case, her jetlag and her swollen ankles up to her room. The screw at the top of the zero on the door number was missing, so the golden zero had swung downwards. Ominously, what was left was thirteen. Unlucky for some.

After having had all day to get ready, Gail had left it until the last minute. Well, thirty minutes. She sat, staring at the wall, her hands spread on the kitchen table in front of her. The second hand on the wall clock edged towards the twelve for the fifth time. Her five minutes were up. If her Viva Vermilion nail polish wasn't perfectly dry now, she'd sue that bloke on the market for selling dodgy products. Lifting her hands to her face, she blew on her nails, for luck, and cautiously touched a glowing red thumbnail with her index finger. Dry. And they looked bloody fantastic.

'Bloody, at any rate,' she heard Pearl's voice say in her head. 'What've you been doing? Skinning a rabbit?'

'Get lost,' hissed Gail, reaching for her slap-bag and the magnifying mirror she'd taken to using. Not that a mirror was necessary. She'd been putting on make-up every day—if you didn't count the week after the hysterectomy—since she'd left school. Discreet today, she told herself, picking out the palest of her large selection of bronze eyeshadows. Discreet colour but still tons of mascara. And the lipstick? There were several reds to choose from. Gail opted for the newest, which still retained a bit of moisture. She re-fluffed her hair and gave it another good squirt of concrete-hold hairspray before running up the stairs to put on her new suit.

'Oh, Dilys. I wish you were here,' she said aloud as she twisted and turned in front of the dressing table mirror. 'Do you think these dark tights are OK, or should I go for the mink ones?'

'*Dark, definitely.*' *It was her agony aunt.*

'Dark, definitely.' It was Will.

'Bloody hell, Bassett. I nearly jumped out of my skin. What are you doing here?'

'I left work early to wish you luck, but you won't be needing it. You look'—his eyes roved from the black stilettos to the concrete hair—'fantastic. I could fancy you if you weren't my landlady.'

It was the suit that did it. Gail not only looked but felt like a new person in it. If only she could stop shaking. The dress rehearsal had been yesterday. Now she was due to play the lead in some reckless play with no script and no supporting cast. She was a one-woman show.

'I've got you a good luck gift.' Will handed her a box the size of a large handbag.

Gail tried to open it, but her hands wouldn't work. 'Can you do the honours? I don't want to chip my nail varnish.'

Will did the honours.

'Oh, Will.' She couldn't say any more in case the huge reservoir of tears she'd acquired over the past week decided to overflow again. Who'd have thought she'd ever use a briefcase?

Lifting out the burgundy case, Will clicked open the clasp. The lid shot up, and he held the case up to display its contents, just like the models did when showing the prizes that could be won on quiz shows. 'I collected your printing for you,' he said, handing it to Gail.

Business cards, letter-headings, invoices and a large pad with 'Girls Will if you won't' printed across the top put Gail's mascara in serious danger. Will had thoughtfully added a collection of pens and pencils too.

'It's the best present I've...' She bent to close the case, a good ploy for hiding her crumpling face. The best present since Dilys had given her the mobile phone or she'd discovered exactly how much Bradley had paid into her bank account.

Will ignored the fact she was upset. 'Now, you know what to do, don't you?'

A sniff had to suffice.

'Walk around with the pad in your hand and jot down *exactly* what the client wants. There may be items they don't want you to touch, like computers, personal stuff. There might even be rooms they don't want you to go in.' He was thinking of Lexi's white chamber. 'Make sure you write it all down. You can't rely on memory. Act with confidence. Your clients won't know you haven't done this before. They'll look to you for guidance because in all likelihood they won't have done it before either.'

'The blind leading the blind?' suggested Gail.

Will clasped her shoulders and kissed her forehead. 'Go, knock 'em dead.'

In the beginning, it had been any old shop. Now it was his. It had taken four days and a large part of four nights of hard work, once the painters had left, but it was ready now. Charles would open in the morning. First thing.

He'd done well, even if he did say so himself. The shelving was neatly stacked, the shirts not only in size order but also filed in colours, and shades of colour, the deepest hues at the bottom, palest at the top. It looked good. Suits lined the rails, their polished coat hangers all facing north. Separates were to the left and knitwear to the right.

He'd invested in the most attractive dummy with superior nylon wig and expressive countenance, according to the brochure, and he'd clothed him and propped him in the window. All that remained was to take down the long net curtains and reveal his new world to the discerning shoppers of Chenwick.

The sign on the door said 'Closed'. Above it, he hung the specially printed 'Open Tuesday' sign. He fetched the steps and unhooked the nets, stowed the steps back in their cupboard—a place for everything and everything in its place—and meticulously folded the nets.

From his position behind the main counter, he surveyed his world. It was all admirable, especially as he'd had no help from she who claimed to be the one with the taste. He'd show the bitch he could manage without her. What had she said? 'You won't last five minutes without me.' Huh. It had been five weeks, and what had he achieved? He'd got his own shop. She could keep that poxy little place in Brum. He'd got his own house. It might be small but at least he didn't have to share it with her. She was sharing their detached five-bed, two en suites, integral double garage, large gardens, in desirable area with the man who'd cut out her verruca. Shacked up with a chiropodist. They were welcome to each other.

'I'm perfectly capable,' he muttered. 'I don't need you, Avril, apart from one thing, and you weren't much use at that.'

Charles checked his watch. There was still half an hour before Mrs Lockwood was due. He would wait in the kitchen, away from prying eyes. Opening the drawer, which had held BJ's assorted tea towels less than a week ago, he took out a bottle of nail polish remover, a bag of cotton wool balls and his faithful leather zip-up manicure case. All the unpacking and stacking had played havoc with his cuticles. Thirty minutes of TLC wouldn't go amiss.

At five twenty-five, he finished his manicure and re-entered his little Eden to run his fingers down a column of shirts. Pink for tomorrow, to go with the grey suit? The shade? One towards the top end of his spectrum. Pale. He chose one in what might be called Tea Rose and placed it in its cellophane packing in his briefcase.

At the door, he stopped and turned to survey his world, his empire, his creation for the final time that day. Yes, it was very good. He'd go as far as to say excellent.

Outside, the sky above The Red Lion was tinged in a pink very similar to the new shirt he had chosen.

'*If my friends could see me now,*' sang Gail as she headed towards town in the Clio, her shiny new briefcase on the passenger seat.

'*You haven't done that for days,*' said her agony aunt, *settling herself into the passenger seat, sitting atop the briefcase.* '*It's because you've finally got something to do. Please, let this mood last, at least until you've seen Sharon and this Charles Henderson, the one Dilys reckons is drop-dead gorgeous.*'

'*But right up 'imself. That's what she said. I'll soon find out.*'

Gail looked at the clock on the dash. It said five-fifteen. She took a left, taking her the long way around. *Don't want to get there early and look desperate for work.*

As she slowed for the junction at the bottom of the hill, Guy's garage came into view, and there was Guy himself, at the petrol pumps. His was the only place left for miles where you didn't have to serve yourself.

Gail slowed down. Dilys must have been wrong. He couldn't possibly be seventy, and anyway, if he was, wouldn't he be retired? The Clio came to a standstill at the junction. Checking that there was nothing behind her, Gail sat and watched. There was nothing wrong with her long vision. She saw Guy smile at the woman he was serving, saw his hand touch hers as he gave her change from the pocket of his boilersuit when she paid for her fuel. The woman waved as she drove off. It wasn't until the forecourt was clear that Gail saw the sign. 'Business For Sale'. It hadn't been there when she'd given her mother a lift to pick up the Jag. Perhaps Guy was old enough to retire after all. Not seventy, but sixty-five. He still looked ten years younger.

A horn beeped. It was a car behind her, and whoever was in it was obviously in a hurry. In her interior mirror, she saw the male driver flap his hand in a shift-your-arse gesture. Quickly, Gail checked the road and pulled out. As she drove past the front of the garage, she saw Guy again. He was lifting a piece of furniture off the back of a truck.

'*Isn't that your mother's bureau?*' *asked her agony aunt.*

17

Thursday, 24 February

Dilys sat, soaking her feet in the bidet, praying for her blisters to miraculously disappear. She'd walked that many bleeding miles around Sydney she could get a job as a tour guide. But what else was there to do when you had to be careful with your money? She hadn't counted on paying for a hotel or buying all her own meals, not that she'd had much appetite since the plane had landed. Some days, all she'd eaten was the breakfast the hotel supplied.

Anne had phoned her once to tell her how busy they were, but before Dilys had chance to offer her services as a wedding planner, or even a lowly assistant, her daughter had ended the call. Dilys had called Anne several times, but the phone was never answered.

She picked up a primrose towel and carefully patted away her tears and then dried her poor feet. She had to go and see that nice young man at the travel agency, the one who was rearranging her flight home. She could take yet another walk around the shops after that.

Gail squealed to herself as she parked on the double yellow lines opposite what used to be BJ's and was now shining with new paint and declaring itself 'Chas Henderson, Gentlemen's Outfitter'. The squeal was for the proprietor himself. He was standing in the doorway and was the spitting image of George Clooney. The man of her dreams.'Drop-dead gorgeous,' she mumbled. As she flung open the car door, the little Clio rolled another foot along the kerb. 'Get a grip,' Gail warned herself, leaning back in to pull on the handbrake. 'Don't mess this up.'

Her knees, which she often thought looked like bags of jelly due to water retention, were acting as if they'd actually turned into bags of jelly. All pudding knees, nerves and stiletto heels, she wibble-wobbled over the road, wishing she'd had a wee before leaving home.

'Mrs Lockwood?' How did romance writers describe their heroes' voices? His was black treacle, and it had only taken two words for her to stick in it.

Gail made a quick and conscious effort to close her mouth and stiffen her knees, hoping she didn't come over as a goldfish clicking its heels and standing to attention. Goldfish? Heels? Get a grip. Get a grip. Love at first sight? Pull yourself together.

'Henderson. Charles Henderson.' He took her hand.

Clooney. George Clooney. Girls Will. Girls Will if you won't. That was what she should have been saying. Gail Will and Gail would, given half a chance.

His hand was large, warm and sunburnt. She finally managed to look him in the eyes. So brown, so... so... shut up.

'Gail. Call me Gail,' she said.

He let go of her hand and gave a smile to set her teeth chattering.

'What do we do now?' he asked.

Make love in treacle. No. 'How exactly can I help you?' How could she sound so normal? She hadn't been this turned on in years. Not since Roger had swept her off her feet with his brooding eyes and Elvis quiff.

'It's at the house,' he said. 'I'll show you. Would you like me to drive you, or will you follow in your own car? I've moved to the new estate, near the retail park.'

'I'll follow,' said Gail. *Careful, or you're going to blow this.*

'Mine's the Toyota Land Cruiser.' It meant nothing to Gail. Fortunately, he pointed to it. The one she'd almost hit by leaving her handbrake off.

'Right.'

They crossed the road together. Gail hadn't locked her car door. Charles held it open for her, and it wasn't an excuse to ogle her legs. He was a real gentleman. Gail hoped she could get that grip on herself before they reached the new estate.

'Who's acting like a silly schoolgirl? Her passenger was back, wearing a pink jacket, which clashed with Gail's red one. 'You're not going to make a fool of yourself, are you? Think about it. Why would he give you a second look? He only wants you for one thing. Cleaning.'

'Go away. I need to concentrate on my driving. I don't know this part of town.' Gail blinked away her agony aunt.

Chenwick Council had christened the new housing development The Orchards. The name seemed appropriate enough, seeing as that was what the land had once been until they'd seen fit to replace row upon row of apple trees with red brick executive dwellings and bare earth. In a few years, once the gardens got established, there might once again be blossom and colour.

Charles's Land Cruiser turned into the gravelled driveway of a small detached house. Gail parked on the road. Her knees, restored to flesh and blood, if not bone, managed to carry her across the Cotswold stone slabs to the front entrance, where Charles waited with his key.

'Coffee before we start?' he asked.

'That would be nice.' Gail attempted demure and polite when, in reality, her blood was boiling and her bosom heaving with passion. Like a heroine in a romantic novel. She was still struggling to come to terms with the fact that this Chas Henderson was having the same effect on her as Paul McCartney had produced circa 1963, and Roger a few years later.

Warm air rushed to meet her, and she prayed it didn't bring on a hot flush. The hall smelled of fresh paint and new carpet.

'This way.' Charles ushered her from the foot of the stairs and through a door into an immaculate kitchen.

'Instant all right?'

'Fine.' They were turning into a coffee advertisement.

As Charles filled the kettle and opened cupboards to reveal regimental arrays of crockery, Gail looked around. There wouldn't be much work here if the rest of the house was this clean and tidy.

The two cups and saucers matched the tray Charles stood them on. 'Come into the lounge,' he said, and Gail followed, willingly.

The walls were cream, the curtains navy blue, the carpet was cream and the suite navy with a huge assortment of expensive gold cushions. Gail surreptitiously glanced back to make sure her shoes hadn't marked that exquisite carpet, the one she was sinking into. Resting in a white marble fireplace were the makings of a real fire. Real coal, wood and paper. Gail shivered.

'Cold?'

He'd noticed. 'No, not at all.' *I was thinking of making love on this carpet and in front of that fire. No, no.*

Red alert. Thoughts like that would bring on a hot flush and that would mean a beetroot face.

'Shall we sit down?' Charles gestured towards an armchair and set Gail's coffee on a small table next to it. He took the sofa.

Gail put her briefcase on the floor and picked up her cup. She took a sip of coffee and wondered what to say. *Are you married? Will the wife be home soon?*

'You've made it very nice here.' *Bloody hell. Is that the best you can come up with?*

'Yes,' said Charles. 'No arguments this time about colour schemes and choice of furniture.'

Gail cocked her head to one side and gave him a puzzled look. It worked.

'The last time we had a new house, my wife argued over every little detail,' he continued. 'But this is mine. I chose the lot.'

Gail waited a second, but no more information was volunteered. 'And she didn't mind?' she said.

'Not at all.' The full force of his film star smile rattled the coffee cup in her saucer. 'She didn't come with me.'

'Oh, I'm so...' *Relieved. Overjoyed. Ecstatic.* 'Sorry.'

'No sympathy, please. I'm sure we're both happier. I know I am.'

Gail leaned back on the gold cushions and tried not to look too Cheshire Cat-ish. 'So that's why you'd like the services of Girls Will.' That was more like it. More business-like. She was in the market for work, not a relationship. No, that was wrong. One or the other would be good. Both would be glorious.

'Your friend, Dilys, told me this is a new business venture for you.' He leaned forward, legs apart, elbows resting on his knees, hands either side of his face. His nails weren't varnished. Dilys must have made that up. 'That means we have something in common.'

Gail's breath was beginning to stutter. It was as if she were a balloon and someone had untied the knot and was letting the air out in tiny bursts. The bloody Ventolin was in her bag in the car. *Don't panic.* 'I hope we'll both succeed.' She deserved an Oscar. 'But'—now it was her turn to lean forward—'if you don't mind me saying, Mr Henderson—'

'Charles. Chas to my friends. Call me Chas, please. Gail.'

God. Asthma, hot flushes, wobbly knees and, if he said her name in that soft treacle again, wet knickers. What a combination to have to put up with. Where was she? 'Umm, oh yes, your home is immaculate, and I can't see you as the type who needs a woman to follow you around tidying up behind you.' She put down her empty cup.

'You know me already, Gail, and what you say is true. I can do everything for myself.' He stood up.

'Then why did you call Girls Will?'

'I can do everything for myself, except for one thing.'

To all her other symptoms, Gail added palpitations.

'Allow me to show you.'

'Of course,' bleated Gail, and like a trusting little lamb, she gambolled up the stairs behind him. *What are you? Baaa. Thick or something? Asking for it? Well, funny you should say that.* No, he wouldn't try anything on. She'd known him long enough to fall head over heels, so she knew she was safe. *Tell me I'm safe,* she begged the ceiling.

The bed was king-sized, its cover silk and in the same burgundy as Gail's briefcase. Gail hesitated by the door. She'd read the books and seen the movies, and it wouldn't take three guesses to know what was going to happen next. Or perhaps it would. Take three guesses. She wasn't in a book or film. She was not starring with George Clooney. She was with

Charles Henderson, who no longer lived with his wife and who could do everything for himself. Apart from one thing.

Chas beckoned.

Baaa, baaa, went Gail.

'I can't go on like this,' he said. 'It's been five weeks since my wife and I parted, and I simply can't manage any longer. Your card said, "no job too big or too small", so I was hoping... Avril used to do it once a week, but she wasn't much good at it, so please say you will.' He picked up an Ali Baba basket and tipped the contents onto the bed. Gail allowed her mouth to drop open and her knees to sag.

'There are thirty-five shirts there, all washed but waiting to be ironed. I've been taking a brand new one out of my stock every day. I can't go on like this.'

'Oh, oh.' Gail's laugh started at her troublesome knees, rattling its way up and up, past the heaving bosom and the loudly beating heart. 'Oooh.' She tried to stop but couldn't. It was back to red alert for the hot flush and no hope for the mascara as tears sprang to her eyes. She pointed at the mountain of pastels and stripes, the deep shades and the checks, the collars and cuffs. 'Oooo, oooo, I'm sorry.' She brushed at the tears with the back of her hand and through leaking black lashes saw Chas laughing too.

'Here, take this.' He offered a handkerchief, which Gail couldn't see for mascara. Gently, he took her by the shoulder and turned her to face him. 'You will take the job, won't you?' he said, drying her eyes for her.

If Dilys had been there, Gail would have given her all the glorious details, but she wasn't, so Sharon from the salon had to do.

'Wot I wanna know is did 'e shag ya or didnee?'

She came a very poor second.

'No, I just told you, we were in his bedroom, and he patted my eyes—'

'Patted ya what?'

'Eyes. I'd been crying, from laughing, and he took his hanky and... and... it was a bit like *Brief Encounter*.'

'Brief an'... what? You mean it was a quickie?'

Gail gave up. 'Let's forget it, shall we? Now, what did you want done, *exactly*?' She took her pad and pen from the briefcase and followed Shaz from room to messy room. It was mostly a case of, 'Dust and tidy and ya know...'

Back in the kitchen, Shaz rinsed a couple of mugs under the cold tap. 'Fancy a coffee?'

'No thanks.' *Not until I've blitzed your kitchen for ya... you.* 'I've got to get back, but what I suggest is a thorough spring clean to begin with and then for Girls Will to come in twice a week for a couple of hours and see how we get on.' It sounded as if she had an army of workers to call upon, and she could have done with an army for a few hours to get this place straight, but once it was put to rights, a weekly visit might do depending on whether Shaz would keep it tidy or let it revert to its current state. Strange because the salon was always spotless. Perhaps the house was such a tip because Sharon didn't have the time or energy to spend on it.

'You'm a Gawdsend,' she told Gail as she followed her out to the car.

Gail got in and was about to drive off when Shaz tapped the half open window. 'Whassat lot in there?'

The Ali Baba basket on the back seat had tipped over, and its contents were spilled on the seat.

'Chas's clothes,' said Gail without thinking.

Sharon tapped again. This time louder. Gail reached over and fully wound down the window.

'You'm tellin' me you didn't 'ave a shag but you've got all 'is clothes in the back of your car? That's what I call kinky.'

'It's what I call ironing.'

'Ya don't do ironing an' all? Ya couldn't do mine, couldya? Bloody Gawdsend, that's what y'are. If you 'ang on a mo' I'll get it for ya.'

It was like a dressing-up game. Gail took off her red suit and hung it in the wardrobe, then she wriggled into her jeans and dragged on a sweatshirt. One minute the boss, the next a worker.

As she ran down the stairs, Will was struggling in with part of the mountain of Sharon's ironing. What Gail hadn't known was that Shaz had a live-in boyfriend. From the number of his shirts, Gail deduced he must be an office worker. Shaz had certainly kept quiet about him.

'I've set the ironing board up in front of the telly for you,' said Will. 'Do you want a cup of tea before you start?' He gawped at the overflowing Ali Baba and the four well-stuffed black binbags. 'And at regular intervals through the night?' He frowned. 'Can you manage this, Gail?'

Gail gave the biggest smile he'd seen for weeks. 'Good, isn't it? And the paper hasn't come out yet.' She lifted out a moss green shirt with button-down collar. 'I can do two or three of these while you make that drink.'

Will made a dash for the kitchen. Gail lifted the shirt to her face. It still held a faint scent of Chas's aftershave. 'Anyone who had a heart...' she sang. She'd do his first because he was the first customer. At least, that was what she told herself. The truth was the sooner she got all the shirts done, the sooner she'd be able to return them and see Chas again. Carefully, she finished the first shirt and picked up the second. If confidence could have been measured on one of those Test Your Strength machines you saw in old-fashioned fairground scenes, she'd have taken the hammer, and the force of her confidence would have not only rung the bell but sent the thing into orbit.

18

Friday, 25 February

Gail's living room looked like an explosion in a menswear factory, with shirts hanging from, or draped over, every available surface. By mid-morning on Friday, the new edition of the Chenwick Echo, the one with her advertisement in, had been out for hours and the phone hadn't rung. Her wrist ached and the iron was playing up. Instead of a confidence machine, Gail could see a deep and slippery-sided pit, the walls adorned with crumpled clothing. A gigantic tape measure running from the edge of the pit and down into its black depths registered not inches but misery, starting with A Bit Low, proceeding to Want To Cry, which Gail had slipped well beyond. She'd seen Bloody Miserable, Fucking Awful and was in danger of reaching the next sign, which declared in blood red, Suicidal. Her feet were slipping past the monstrous S when she heard, 'Cooeee. It's only me.'

Mother.

'It's cold out there.' It must be. Pearl was in her *Doctor Zhivago* outfit. Long boots, long coat with big fur collar and matching Russian-style hat. She flounced in and sat down. On a pile of ironed T-shirts. Not that there was anywhere to sit without damaging Gail's production line.

Gail pulled at her mother's fur muff, which dangled around her neck from a black velvet ribbon. 'Gerrup, Mum.' It was a definite scream.

Pearl stood. For the first time, she took in the state of Gail's living room. 'What's going on?'

'Work, that's what.'

'Don't tell me this is what a company director does all day. Presses somebody else's smalls? Handles the vests and underpants of total strangers?'

Gail pulled a face. Forget Suicide. Think Murder. She could plead insanity due to hormonal imbalances and be out in a couple of years.

'This agency lark, Gail, are you sure it's not just another of your little fantasies, along with marrying Paul Lennon or that Ringo Whatsisname? You're not sixteen anymore.'

From the confines of her muff, Pearl produced a torn sheet of newspaper. 'You're going to get into trouble about this, you mark my words. "Girls Will if you won't." There was many a time when your father was alive and I wouldn't. If I'd seen this advert back then, I'd have given Girls Will a call, and they could have... you know what I'm talking about.'

Gail knew but didn't want to think about it.

'I tell you what, Mum, if I get any dodgy offers, I'll give the callers your number and you can deal with them.'

'You do that, and I'll give them what for. At least I can do that for you, but count me out when it comes to dusting and polishing.'

Gail wanted to tell her mother she was the last person she'd call on. Pearl wasn't programmed for housework. An occasional tidy-up was all she managed, though she was the first to drag a finger over anyone else's sideboard in search of dust.

'Just be careful, Gail. I'm only telling you for your own good. I'd be failing in my motherly duty if I didn't warn you of the pitfalls. Don't come crying to me when it all goes wrong, and it will, you know.'

The phone rang. Both women ran to reach it, but as she'd inserted her hands back in her muff, Pearl lost the race.

'Girls Will,' said Gail.

Pearl glared at her.

'Dog walking. Yes, we do dog walking.' Gail picked up a pen and wrote down details on the pad. 'Yes, I'll call this evening, and thank you.'

'It'll be a gigantic, slavering, child-eating Doberman,' warned Pearl.

'It's an ancient spaniel, actually.'

'I bet it smells.'

Maybe she'd get a lenient judge who'd give her community service or a suspended sentence. Gail prepared to bare her teeth and attack. Unaware of the danger, Pearl made a U-turn and flounced out. The front door shook on its hinges.

Gail switched off the iron. A rest, caffeine and chocolate were called for. She filled the kettle, ladled Nescafe and sugar into a mug and allowed her hand to hover above the goodie tin. Her fingers dipped in, tightened around a biscuit and began tearing at the wrapping.

'That's Chocolate,' said her agony aunt, placing a pink-gloved hand on the lid of the tin. 'You can't eat that. It begins with C.'

'No, it doesn't. It's a Twix, now bugger off,' shouted Gail.

The hand and remainder of the pink-clad woman evaporated.

Gail flopped into a chair, put her feet on the kitchen table and concentrated on the chocolate biscuit. It wasn't easy. Thoughts, ideas and worries bombarded her like machine gun fire. She pulled the pad and pen towards her, got comfortable again and started making lists.

Buy a rail to hang the ironing on, and coat hangers.

A new iron—and keep the old one for backup.

A new ironing board wouldn't go amiss.

But what if there was no more ironing? It would all be a waste of money. No, *don't think like that. Do a good job and you'll get seven shirts a week from Chas and God-knows-what from Shaz and who knows how many more.*

But there'd only been one phone call and that was dog walking. What about a poop scoop? Should she add that to her list? And how was she going to get all this ironing back to the clients without creasing it. Hanging on a rail in a van? Perhaps she could part exchange the Clio? Guy might do her a deal.

'Guy. The question is, can he be trusted?' she asked the empty Twix wrapper. What was he doing with her mother, and what was he doing with her mother's furniture? Was he really conning an old lady out of her belongings? He didn't look the type.

The phone rang for the second time that morning. *Please let it be another customer.*

'Oh, Will, it's you.'

'Don't sound so disappointed. I only wanted to know if you've seen the paper?'

Gail hadn't for three reasons—she'd been too busy ironing to go out and get one, she was frightened of missing a call if she did go out and, last but certainly not least, the one available copy had been in Pearl's mitts. Or muff, if you wanted to get technical.

'I'll bring one home for you at lunchtime,' said Will. 'Do you want a bag of chips to go with it?'

She'd already had chocolate, so may as well start the diet again tomorrow.

'Yes, please.' He usually had lunch in town. It was good of him to think of her. One day, he'd make someone a lovely husband. He was thoughtful and caring and kind. What a pity he was Will.

'Chips first, before they go cold,' he said, passing a paper parcel to Gail, who felt a tiny twinge of guilt at abandoning her C-food diet.

She wasn't the only one with a guilt twinge. 'Throw in a nice piece of cod,' Will had said ten minutes earlier to Fred. Will knew the way to get around Gail was through her stomach. He made sure the Chenwick Echo stayed well away from her, on his side of the table. If she was full, she'd be in a better mood, though even that was debatable the way she'd been behaving recently. She'd left the advertising side up to him, and he knew his job. He'd done her proud really. He could only hope that she'd see it that way too.

'Only one call,' said Gail, licking her fingers.

'Give it chance. Most people won't be reading the paper until the weekend.' 'I suppose so. Let's have a look, then. Pass it over.'

Will hesitated for a second. Too late now. Time to face the music. He opened the Echo to the relevant page and handed it to Gail.

'Oh, my...' Her face, which had been flushed from ironing and eating, suddenly looked as if it had been swiped with a whitewash brush. 'What the hell is all this, Will?' She put the paper on the table and jabbed at the article about Girls Will. It came complete with a photograph of her head and shoulders and an enormous advertisement. 'I asked you... I paid you to put in a small ad. This is nearly half a page. It must have cost a fortune, and what's all this?' Her finger circled around the page. 'And this, and this?'

Will gave a little-boy-in-trouble grin.

'All these adverts from satisfied customers wishing me well? I haven't got any customers.'

'I know that, you know that, but Joe Public doesn't. Some mates owed me favours, and they don't mind what they endorse as long as they get their names in the paper. All I did was ask them if they wanted to be involved in an advertising campaign for a new business, special rates, and told them that if they used your cleaning services, they'd get a good discount.' He didn't tell her that it had also made him feel better about involving her in the story he'd fed Lexi, the one about him being a married man.

'But, Will, this is all lies.' Gail was reading the feature about her company. Whoever had written it had made it sound as if she were multinational, established since the beginning of time, when she'd followed Adam around, washing his fig leaf, polishing the apple and giving the serpent a good dusting. 'No wonder Mother was having a go about it.'

'It's called publicity, and it'll bring in the work, I promise you.'

The portion of fish and chips had been an extremely generous one, and after eating it, Will didn't fancy an afternoon's work. Sitting at his desk, he thought what he could really do with was an afternoon nap. Once or twice during his stint as advertising manager, he'd gone off in the early afternoon on the pretext of visiting a possible new customer and ended up having a snooze in an out-of-town lay-by. It was what he wanted to do now, but he wouldn't because of Gail.

'Only one call. We'll see about that,' he said, pulling the phone on his desk towards him. He'd soon drum up business. Gail deserved to be a success. She worked hard and life hadn't been easy for her. All that was required was a good boost to her confidence. He tapped out one of the numbers from the reduced rate ads surrounding Gail's.

'Tommy, it's Will here.'

Slowly and methodically, he worked his way through the endorsers of Girls Will, trying to persuade them that they couldn't do without office cleaners or someone to help out at home. A couple promised to phone Gail.

'This afternoon would be good,' he said to Martin, who owned a wine bar and had a harassed wife and three children under school age at home.

'OK. OK. I'll do it now and surprise the missis. If I get her some help, she might not use the old excuse so often. "Not tonight, Mart. I'm too tired."'

They both laughed. 'Thanks,' said Will, 'you're a pal.'

He was about to put the phone down when Martin asked, 'What's this Gail to you? Trying to get in her knickers, are you?'

'Certainly not,' said Will. 'She's my landlady.'

'Whatever you say, old man. Whatever you say.'

Why did other men always think you had an ulterior motive if you tried to help a woman? Will was at the end of his list. He yawned and thought of bed. And as thoughts do, bed made him think of the white bed in the white room in the white house. And Lexi.

'Lexi. Why didn't I think of her before?'

'You talking to me?' asked Gina. She looked as tired as Will felt.

'No, love. You tired?'

Gina gave a weary nod.

'Why don't you go out for half an hour? Get a cup of coffee, do some shopping. Get some fresh air.'

Gina didn't need telling twice. She grabbed her jacket and made a run for it before Will changed his mind.

Will turned his attention to the phone. Surely no one in the world warranted help with their housework more than a woman with a compulsive cleaning disorder?

'Alexandra Camberlege.' The voice at the other end of the line was so refined.

'It's me, Will.'

'Fuck off.' Not so refined now.

Will rubbed his ear. The force with which Lexi slammed down her phone sounded like a bomb blast.

By five o'clock, Gail knew Will had been right about his advertising campaign. There'd been half a dozen calls enquiring about house cleaning, one about babysitting services and one from Nesta Neate asking if Gail had any vacancies. She wrote Nesta's address down in her diary and promised to see her as soon as she could manage. Her diary was beginning to fill. The ironing had been carefully folded and packed into plastic boxes, ready to load into the car, the two invoices written, and she had time to bath, change and do her hair and make-up before returning Chas's shirts. He'd be home by then, and so would Sharon. She could drop her stuff off on the way.

Gail's imagination hadn't been playing tricks on her. Chas Henderson was as good-looking, charming and amusing as he'd been in her dreams and action—or should that be no action—replays.

'That was quick,' he said as he helped carry his shirt collection into the house, 'and very efficient.'

'We'—that was the fictional *we* of Girls Will—'aim to please.'

A lift of the eyebrow. The appearance of the slow, lazy smile, and Gail was sinking into those brown eyes.

'You do?' It was a question. 'Then perhaps you'd consider pleasing me by agreeing to stay for dinner.'

Yes, yes, yes, yes, yes, she was about to scream. Then she remembered Mrs Southgate and the smelly spaniel. Damn, damn, damn, damn, damn. Work or pleasure? It was going to have to be work, but would he think she was playing hard to get?

She took a deliberate look at her wristwatch. 'I'm so sorry,' she said. 'I would have loved to but I've another client to see.' Yes, she certainly would have loved to, and she couldn't believe what she was saying, what she might be turning down. Bedclothes, for instance. No. She hadn't had sex for five years or more, and she didn't know if she ever wanted to have it again. Fantasy men were fine by her. You could have all the adventures you wanted, sexual or otherwise, and no complications. If she was ever going to hop into bed with a real flesh and blood man, she'd need plenty of notice so she could go on a strict diet and do those pelvic floor exercises.

Hang on a minute. The man had only suggested dinner.

Chas seemed genuinely disappointed. He'd probably never ask again. She'd blown it.

Gail, in a spangly costume and gold lame tights, cartwheeled into the circus ring. 'And now, ladies and gentlemen, here is the star of the show, the world-famous contortionist, who is about to...

'Kick her own backside,' said Gail, performing the feat to rapturous applause. 'How long will this client take?' asked Chas. 'You could come back afterwards. It would give me time to cook.'

Gail resisted the urge to throw her arms around him. At the same time, she managed to control her smile so that it didn't quite split her face in half. 'Half an hour. Three-quarters.' *Don't sound too keen.*

'Perfect,' he said. 'You can help me celebrate my first day's trading.'

She waited until her little car was around the corner before thumping the air with her fist. 'Oooooh, yes. Oooooh, thank you, God. Thank you.'

The spaniel didn't smell, and Mrs Southgate was a sweetie who had arthritis and couldn't give her pet enough exercise. 'Short walks around the block I can do,' she explained, 'but Perry's piling on the weight. Could you manage a run in the park a couple of times a week?' Gail pencilled Perry in her diary and hoped jogging across the park would help both of them get trim.

Twenty-five minutes later, she parked at the entrance to The Orchards housing development. She'd give it another ten minutes before arriving at Chas's. Take things slowly, that was what she had to do. She was out of practice at the dating game. In the past five years, her only relationships—she scoffed at the word—had been dinner with Ken from next door, and that was because she'd felt sorry for him when his wife ran off with the bloke who came to fit the new carpet, and a couple of disastrous dates with Desperate Dudley, who'd fixed the washing machine. 'You're safe with me, darling. I'm impotent.' She'd never forget the wrestling match in his van when he'd wanted to show her his harmless hosepipe. She wouldn't fall for that one again in a hurry.

Time to go before memories of Dud the Stud put her off men completely.

The flickering candle flames reflected on the polished mahogany tabletop. Sweetly scented freesias in sherbet colours stood in a pretty glass vase.

'I've opened the wine,' Chas called from the kitchen. 'Pour yourself a glass.'

Gail filled both glasses. She was raising her own in a silent plea for Dutch courage when Chas walked in carrying two pasta bowls.

'I hope it's all right,' he said, leaning very close as he placed hers on the table. 'Penne with mushrooms, broad beans, French beans, a bit of this and that. Olive oil, shavings of Parmesan.'

'It looks wonderful,' said Gail, shivering as his body almost touched hers.

And it was wonderful. Not just the food, but the company, the surroundings, the way he'd bothered with candles and flowers, the way he talked as if she was special. How many years since anyone had done this for her? Had any man ever done this for her? The answer was no. Will bought her chips and they had an occasional meal out. Roger had taken her out at the beginning of their relationship, but once married, he'd expected his dinner on the table when he got home from work and couldn't have found the kitchen without the aid of a map. This, being fussed over, was a new experience, and you didn't get many of them once you were over fifty.

Gail relaxed. She was going to enjoy every mouthful and every second. And thinking of seconds, she wondered what was for pudding.

Chas stood up to refill her glass for the third time.

'Are you trying to get me drunk?' she asked, leaning back in her chair so that she could gaze into his eyes. *Bloody hell, Gail, you're actually flirting with this man, and you thought you'd forgotten how. There's that sexy eyebrow lift again. Is he flirting?*

She watched, dreamily, as he poured the wine, his tanned hand around the bottle. His fingers were beautiful. Yes, beautiful. Long and narrow with well-shaped nails. Piano fingers, Pearl would call them. Well, she wouldn't mind being the keyboard and having them romp over her, practising scales. Now, where was middle C again?

'Fresh fruit salad?' he asked. 'With Greek yoghurt and honey?'

'Honey? Yes, please.' Honey.

He opened what Gail took to be a second bottle of wine. It wasn't until he suggested a brandy with their coffee that she counted three empty wine bottles on the table.

'There'sh no way I can drive home.' Even to Gail, her voice sounded slurred. What she wanted to add was, *So I'll have to stay here, with you,* but the wine hadn't flowed enough for her to become that brazen.

'Don't worry,' said Chas, his voice soft, or was his slurred too? 'It's early yet.'

So, did he want her to stay? That's what he was saying, wasn't it? She wasn't one hundred per cent sure. Play it cool.

They'd moved to the lounge, where Gail fell onto the navy-blue sofa. She tried straightening herself so that she was leaning seductively against the gold cushions. It wasn't an easy manoeuvre, especially with the contents of her glass mysteriously swishing about and the message from her brain to her out-of-condition stomach muscles telling them to hold it all in, getting lost along the way. When Chas sat next to her, more muddled messages hurtled up and down her spinal cord. The most persistent one encouraging her to be like Arnie, her mother's cat, and pounce on her prey. But she couldn't do that. She was one of the generation who expected men to make the first move.

Chas had the brandy bottle in one hand, his glass in the other. He sloshed a little more into Gail's glass. 'Here's to you and your new business,' he said. 'And to you and yoursh,' said Gail, and gulped it down in one.

Chas relaxed against the cushions. 'Did I tell you about my wife?'

Gail's eyes widened. *No, not that, please. Not the my-wife-doesn't-understand-me routine.* She tried to concentrate on Chas's lovely face, but his features, the straight nose and strong jawline, were as slurred as his voice. She kept quiet as she attempted to focus

more clearly, which she did by widening her eyes
even further, until they hurt.

He didn't wait for an answer. He told her, starting
with his first sighting of Avril on the silk tie counter
in Handley and Lanyon's, and finishing a lot later with
her flinging his personal tie collection, 'like a handful
of fish food', to the Koi Carp in their ornamental
pond.

Gail didn't take in the entire tale. Her eyes kept
closing and her brain taking little naps. Politely, she
regained consciousness as he was concluding.

'And here I am,' he said.

*OK, he's not a cheerful drunk, but I'll give him the
benefit of the doubt. The wounds are still fresh, but who
wants to be his bit on the rebound? Not me. Liar, liar,
bum's on fire.*

'I'm shorry, Chash. Been there myself. Know how
you feel.' *Actually, I don't know how you feel. Give us
a feel, and I'll rate you from one to ten.*

'I'm sorry too,' he said. 'I'll call you that taxi. Leave
your keys, and I'll drop your car to you in the morning.' He went to use the phone.

'You're not as shorry ash I am,' she hissed.

She stared at the gold silk cushion she'd been cud-
dling, tracing her finger along the basketweave pattern, and then she hurled it across the room. He was
calling a taxi for her when she was drunk enough to
agree to anything. Anything? Was that the truth? She
stood up, wobbled and made a grab for the sideboard
to steady herself. A huge black and white photo of
Chas himself gazed directly at her.

'A kish wudabin nice, or a little bita shlap and tickle,'
she told the paper version. 'I think I might be ready.'

19

Saturday, 4 March

Dilys should have been happy. Her hair was immaculate. Her eyebrows were just like a normal person's. There wasn't a zit in sight. The lilac dress was a little loose. So, there was an upside to this wedding fiasco. What had they talked about at Flabfighters? Falling in love or having a loved one hurt you—the two ways to guarantee weight loss. The way Anne was treating her hurt like hell, but when she'd had the miseries before, her cure had been to comfort eat. All those lovely C foods. This time, she'd gone right off her grub.

She pushed her feet into the violet shoes, picked up the tiny clutch bag and let herself out of the primrose room. All that primrose, lilac and violet. It was like being part of a painting on the front of an Easter card. All sugary sweet when, to correspond with her mood, it should have been underripe lemons and vinegar.

A morose teenager in an ancient pick-up truck collected her from the hotel. It was the insult of all insults. *The bride's mother was driven to the marriage service in a shitty old banger. By the time she jolted and bounced her way to the church, the bruises on her backside coordinated beautifully with the lilac and purple outfit, which happened to be the most expensive she'd ever bought.*

Dilys dithered at the entrance to the church and took a deep breath. *Come on, Dil, you can do this. Imagine Gail's by your side.* She smiled at her imaginary friend and did what they always did when they wanted to make an entrance. Stood tall, chin up, stomach in, breasts out. With her spine like a broom handle, she walked proudly down the aisle and took up position in the front pew, on the opposite side of the aisle to Roger, who was resplendent in grey top hat and tails. He didn't acknowledge her. The *Wedding March* began to play. The congregation stood to watch the bride glide down the church in a designer wedding dress which, while pretending to be sarong-style, looked for all the world like a fluffy white bath towel.

To the strains of the *Wedding March*, Dilys's fingers, inside her dinky little handbag, methodically destroyed the wedding present she'd planned to give the happy couple.

'I, Zoe Anne Lloyd, take thee...'

Zoe. It was the name Dilys had chosen for her. If her baby had been a boy, Dilys would have called him Jamie or Frazer. Jamie after *Doctor Who*'s sidekick or Frazer after the actor who played him. Frazer Hines. But she'd given birth to a girl and named her Zoe, after the girl in the series, the one who had stowed away in *Doctor Who*'s Tardis.

Dilys allowed a tear to slip down her cheek. It was nothing to do with the wedding and the old-fashioned words of the service. It was all to do with the past. The bride shrank and became a tiny dark-haired baby who smelt of Johnson's powder and beamed up at her adoring public. But Dilys couldn't keep her like that. The adorable baby sprouted into a toddler who kept her daddy twisted around her little finger. The toddler shot up and became a teenager who blamed her mother for her father running away with Sally from the fish counter. The teenager blossomed into a young woman who flirted with Gail's husband and announced one night that she was going to live in Australia with him.

Where did I go wrong? Dilys asked herself.

She missed the exchanging of rings and the signing of the register during her quarter century flashback. Suddenly, music was blaring and, arm in arm, the smug newlyweds were strolling down the aisle and out into the sunshine.

As the congregation followed, Dilys undid the catch on her bag and scooped out the contents.

There was laughter and cheering as friends of the bride and groom presented them with lucky horse-shoes, black cats and kisses. Some threw rice, others fragile and tiny paper shapes in rainbow colours. Traditional confetti.

Dilys pushed her way through all the noisy strangers. It gave her immense pleasure to shake her wedding present over those identically inky dyed heads. She had ripped the one thousand pounds cheque she'd made out to them into minuscule pieces. Homemade confetti.

Photographs in Australia were the same as every-where else. They took ages. Dilys was called over once to take position between her daughter and new son-in-law-cum-best-friend's-ex. The photograph-er, working at a snail's pace, snapped every possi-ble variation of guests before the party was finally allowed to leave in a convoy of assorted cars and a rumbling of hungry stomachs.

She was the invisible woman. No one was intro-duced to her and no one made any move to talk to her. Anne's friends were all as self-centred as she was herself.

Dilys slipped away from the rowdy reception at the posh country hotel and asked the snooty receptionist if she could use the telephone. She dialled a company who'd taken out a full page in the directory. 'That will be perfect,' she said. 'Thank you.'

Thirty minutes later, her taxi arrived.

'Anne.' Dilys didn't give her daughter time to ignore her, following her into the ladies loo. 'I don't know why you're treating me like this, and I can't take any more. I'm off home.'

'You don't know why?' Anne threw back her shoulders and made a quick grab at the top of her dress. 'You all treated me like a leper when I fell in love with Roger. *You.* My own mother. *You* should have been on my side.'

'Gail's my best friend.'

'And I'm your daughter.'

'And Roger doesn't deserve either of you. He's been with half the women in Chenwick.'

'Only because he was searching for the right one.' Anne flicked at her fringe. 'And now he's got me.'

Dilys pressed her lips together so firmly that they disappeared completely. She wanted to say, *God help the pair of* you. Instead, she rearranged her mouth into as much of a smile as she could muster and said, 'I hope you'll both be very happy. I did have a big fat cheque for you as a wedding present, but once I got here, I changed my mind and ripped it up.'

That certainly got Anne's full attention.

'If you and Roger follow me outside, you can see what I've replaced part of it with.'

She felt like The Pied Piper as she led the pair of inquisitive rats out through the main entrance. A white stretch limousine was waiting on the drive outside, its engine purring.

'Oooh,' and 'Aaah,' gasped the rats.

'Dilys, it's so generous,' said Roger.

Anne shoved him to one side. 'Mum, you shouldn't have,' she gushed, embracing Dilys in a theatrical show of love and gratitude. 'Is it to take us to our honeymoon?'

'No,' said Dilys, picking a piece of ripped cheque from Anne's hair. 'It's to take me to the airport.' If she lifted her chin any higher, her head would fall down her back. She stepped briskly to the limo, where the chauffeur waited to help her in. Sitting in state, she watched the shocked faces and open mouths of the bride and groom. They wouldn't be forgetting this in a hurry. As the car pulled away, Dilys, in a passable imitation of Elizabeth II, gave a regal wave, and Zoe Anne, in a less passable imitation of a blushing bride and more of a horse being pestered by a swarm of angry bees, gave chase.

Dilys squirmed around in her seat and waved through the rear window. It didn't take lipreading lessons to know what her daughter was screaming. As she galloped behind the car, Anne lifted her huge and colourful bouquet of exotic blooms above her head. It was a mistake. The stretching movement was too much for the bath towel sarong. Her left boob popped out like a baby's bald head.

Oops. Twins.

Anne took advantage of the unexpected freedom of movement and, like an Olympic javelin thrower, swung back her arm and hurled the bridal bouquet. It bounced off the limo's boot before sending up a shower of dust as it hit the ground.

Dilys burst into tears.

20

Monday, 6 March

'Gwanny.' The little voice floated up the stairs.

Gail, up to her chin in Radox Original, groaned. Not now. She loved her grandson to bits but not now, when she was making mental lists of things to do. Mental because she hadn't got a spare roll of wallpaper to write them all on. It had been a busy time for her, working alone.

Her agony aunt came to her assistance, reciting what she needed to do before bedtime. 'Walk Perry. Blitz Sharon's. See Nesta. Do a bit of detective work about Guy. Check to see if any more of Pearl's furniture has gone walkabout.'

She did her invisible act on hearing Jack shout again.

'Gwaaanny.' This time with a note of impatience.

'I'm in the bath. Give me five minutes.' Gail stood up and reached for her wristwatch while the bubbles slid down her body and into the hot water. The hot water she'd been looking forward to lying in for a quarter of an hour. The treat she'd promised herself after getting up at six to finish off another ironing job.

'God, Tamsin, it's only half past eight. What've you done? Wet the bed?' Gail shouted from the bathroom.

'Will you have Jack today?' Tam shouted back.

'What did you say?' Gail wrapped herself in the bath towel and listened for a repeat.

'Thanks, Mum.' The back door slammed.

'Gwanny,' shouted Jack urgently.

Shivering, Gail ran down to him.

He was relaxed enough about being abandoned, sitting on the floor, his back against the enormous rucksack his mother humped around containing toys, nappies, drinks, a change of clothes. 'Mummy's gone,' he said, ripping open the post.

'I can bloody well see that.'

'That's a naughty word.' He handed a picture post-card to her. 'That's pwetty.'

Deep blue sky and deep blue sea merged, and beyond a strip of gold stood a line of white buildings. Gail turned it over.

'Hi, Gorgeous,' she read. 'Come, be my companion, my golf caddy, my drinking pal, dancing partner, bed warmer. My saviour from a life of debauchery. Yours forever. Bored in Spain.'

Trust Bradley. No news about how he was coping with retirement or how his apartment was or if he'd made new friends. No news at all unless he was telling the truth about being bored. Her smile was wide even though she had to blink back a tear as she put the card on the table. Bradley, her link to a safe and secure past.

'And a bwown one,' said Jack, handing her the gas bill. 'And one fwom Mummy.'

'If you want me, call my mobile.' Short and not so sweet. Gail placed the scrap of paper with Tam's mobile number on top of the other post. *Reminds me. I must tell Will about my mobile.* He'd used the home number on the paperwork. The list grew longer.

'Where's Mummy gone?' asked Gail.

'Wiv Zez. Got zams.'

'Got what?' She understood the Zez bit. While she was about to rush around all day with a three-year-old in tow, her flaming daughter was swanning off with the latest boyfriend. But what or who or even where was zams?

Jack sighed. 'Zams,' he repeated. 'Zams.'

Gail unzipped his coffee-table-size rucksack and marvelled at how Dick Whittington had managed to pack all his gear into a spotted hanky on a stick. Dragging out an assortment of toy cars and emergency vehicles, she asked, 'Will you be a good boy and play while Granny gets dressed?'

'But I'm hungwy,' he wailed.

Tamsin hadn't given him breakfast. Typical. Gail got a dish and the Weetabix and milk and hopped from one foot to the other while she waited for him to sprinkle on his own sugar. She was in the bedroom pulling on her jeans before the first spoonful of cereal had touched his lips and back down again, dressed and hair brushed, as he scraped the bowl. She poured a mug of juice and, while he drank it, slapped on some moisturiser and lipstick plus a bit of hair wax and scrawled her own mobile number on the bottom of a note to Tamsin. 'Working all day. You'll have to phone me to find out where I am.'

Jack helped her carry her cleaning kit out to the car. She'd pretend everything was a game.

'We're going to do a makeover,' she told him as she drove to Sharon's. It was the day of the big spring clean.

The game lasted nearly an hour. Jack helped make the bed and dust anything below the height of Gail's knees. Gail rushed to get as much done as possible before boredom set in. She rushed so much that Shaz's bedroom was soon transformed with the aid of Mr Sheen and Ventolin.

'Don't want to play anymore,' Jack announced. 'I wanna go to the park.'

'Good idea,' said Gail. 'We could take a doggie for a walk.' *We can split the day up. Walk Perry, come back here, visit Nesta, come back here, see Pearl, come back here.* A pattern was emerging.

Sedate was a good description of the elderly spaniel. He plodded happily along, making an occasional scurry into the long grass bordering the path. Jack, in red wellies found in the rucksack, ran over the wet grass and kicked every blade in the park. Gail kicked a few as well. To her, they were Tamsin's arse.

'Broffull, broffull,' sang Jack. 'Zams, zams.'

'I wish I was three again, or even thirteen,' said Granny Gail, and immediately regretted it. *Be careful what you wish for*—her mother rounded a privet hedge—*because you might get it.* Surely not. Time couldn't possibly have reversed. But there was Pearl in an outfit straight from the Sixties, when Gail had been thirteen. Long and tight white PVC boots covered her bony kneecaps but still left a gap between their top and the hem of the lime green mini coat.

'Gwanny Pearl,' squealed Jack.

Mother, screamed Gail in silence.

'Guy,' squealed Jack, and set off towards them. Gail and Perry had no option but to follow.

DI Lockwood, taking over Gail's body, approached the suspect with caution. Well-known businessman. Huh. How many of them had she come across in her illustrious career? Villains hiding behind a respectable veneer, or was that facade? The gangster's moll twisted nervously at the bleached kiss curls on her rouged cheeks. Her arm linked through his, she gazed adoringly into...

Bloody hell. Adoringly. She was and all. Pearl was dressed like a teenager from the Beatles era, and she was about as lovestruck as any teenager could be.

'Fancy seeing you here,' she simpered. 'Guy was keeping me company on my daily constitutional.' The moll fluttered her eyelashes as she lied through her teeth.

Constitutional? She was as fond of exercise as the pope was of condoms. Gail's analogy brought a smile to her lips, if not her eyes. 'We were giving Perry, the slavering Doberman, his constitutional too. *And getting paid for it.*' The last few words with emphasis and a sly glance at the villain to see if he knew she was having a dig at him taking advantage of a defenceless old woman. Probably bleeding her dry. Scrub defenceless, Gullible was more like it. 'Sorry, we can't stop and chat.' And she was away with Perry attached to one hand and Jack to the other.

It might have been the cops and robbers fantasy that made her do it, while she was still in character, so to speak. As soon as Perry was safely returned to Mrs Southgate, Gail broke the speed limit all the way to her mother's house for a quick bit of breaking and entering. Not that it was breaking, seeing as she had a key, and not that it was entering. Surely if you were in possession of a key given to you by the house owner, the entering of that house was not illegal, even if you were creeping about and whispering as if it were. Stepping out of DI Lockwood's skin before she got a headache, Gail convinced herself that what she was doing was all in a good cause.

Jack followed her.

'It's another game,' she lied. 'We have to find Granny Pearl.'

'Is she hiding?' asked Jack.

'Yes,' said Gail, stepping over a saucer of cold tea. Arnie was partial to a drop of Typhoo.

The cats closed ranks as they made their way through the kitchen, twisting around Gail and Jack's legs, mewing for food. They'd be mewing a lot louder than that if Guy bunked off with Pearl's life savings and pension book. The cupboard and bank balance would be bare.

Nothing wrong with the kitchen. Gail crept into the living room. All OK apart from the bare light bulb where the chandelier should be. 'Do you think she's upstairs?' Gail whispered.

'Yes,' shouted Jack at the top of his lungs.

They checked Pearl's bedroom first. It was the same as ever. Huge mismatched wardrobes—new, second-hand and rescued from skips—lined the walls and encircled the bed, which was the only other piece of furniture in the room. Lying in that at night, Pearl must have dreamed she was in the centre of a wooden rugby scrum. Fans, photos, feathers and old ribbons and rosettes from Christmas presents past adorned the doors leading to her vast clothing collection. Gail's tensed shoulders relaxed, dropping from around her ears, back into the correct position. Nothing appeared to be missing.

Jack dropped to his knees and crawled beneath the bed. 'She's not there,' he said. He crawled back out again, shunting an ancient rose-garlanded chamber pot in front of him. 'I've found Gwanny Pearl's sweet-ies,' he informed Gail.

Gail peered into the depths of the pot. It was a miniature chemist's shop. Tablets for indigestion, constipation, headaches, rheumatism and sore throats jostled for space alongside cold cures and cough sweets. Sticking from one side was a pair of spare spectacles and a tatty paperback. Gail pulled it out. *Homeopathic Remedies for Cats and Kittens.* Gail pushed it back.

'Can I have a sweetie?' Jack was looking at her while brushing balls of fluff from the knees of his trousers.

'They're not sweeties, darling. It's medicine.'
Enough to wipe out an army. Certainly enough to
dispose of a comfortably off old biddy.

Gail saw a scene in which her mother reclined
lopsidedly on a sofa, rather like she'd done herself
at Chas's. But instead of having her wine glass filled,
Pearl was already well and truly sozzled and allowing
Guy to feed her Dolly Mixtures and Diazepam.

'Let's try the other rooms,' she said to Jack, swiftly
erasing the picture.

The other rooms were empty. Empty of Granny
Pearl. Empty of furniture. Even the carpets and curtains had gone. Inside her tights, Gail's feet began to
prickle and break into a sweat that travelled like an
upside-down waterfall which, in an instant, reached
her head. And, as the hot flush swept north, her
stomach plummeted to the south.

By the time she'd fastened Jack into his car seat,
she was out of breath again.

'Gwanny Pearl's gone,' said Jack.

'I know where she might be.' With luck, his search
of Sharon's house would give her enough time to get
another bedroom and her thoughts into order.

His foot was on the first stair when he burst into
tears. 'Wannagohome,' he wailed.

Gail picked him up, sat on the stairs to cuddle him
and admitted that was what she wanted too. 'But we
can't. We've got to finish the makeover.'

'Noooo,' he yelled, burying his face in her shoulder.

'Tell you what,' said Gail, 'be a good boy while I do
some work and we'll go and have a burger.'

Cajoling and playing hadn't worked. Now bribery
failed. What else remained? Gail had to finish the task
she'd begun. A hairdresser talked to people all day,
and those people could be future clients if Sharon
sang the praises of Girls Will loud enough. But if Gail
didn't stick to her part of the bargain, which, if her

memory served her right, was, 'You won't recognise this place when I've finished with it', then a disillusioned Shaz could manage a lot of badmouthing. With a palpitation and a cold sweat, it dawned on Gail that Sharon could literally make or break her. The brutal truth was simple. Jack had to go.

She carried him out to the car, strapped him into his car seat, gave him her last Rolo and opened her briefcase. On top of her beautiful stationery lay her mobile phone and the scrap of paper with Tamsin's number on it. She squinted at the numbers on the phone, held it at arm's length so she could focus and called Tamsin.

'Sorry, the person you are calling is not responding.'

Balls. What now?

Her agony aunt came to the rescue, rolling out a long sheet of wallpaper adorned with pink roses. Gail's mental list of work to be done was written on it in invisible ink. Clad in a pink apron, the agony aunt's index finger hovered above one word. Nesta.

'Nesta is your only hope,' she said. 'With her help, the work will get done and Jack will be kept occupied.'

Gail fastened her seat belt and headed across town.

Jack was happy again. All it had taken was a plateful of bread soldiers spread with a cheese triangle, crisps on the side and a goldfish, swimming in clockwork circles around its lonely bowl, to pull faces at.

Gail sat balancing a plate of homemade fruitcake on her lap, hoping it was an omen. If Mrs Galleon—*mustn't call her by the nickname*—Nesta Neate had time to piss about making fruitcake, then it was time she found something more constructive to do with her time.

'So, you're stuck,' said Nesta.

Gail answered with a nod and kept on chewing. *Galleon's Gourmet Fruitcakes.* If Nesta started up her own business, she'd make a fortune. Hadn't Will said that about a fortnight ago? And here she was interviewing her first potential employee. If you could call it an interview.

Gail swallowed. 'I can't promise regular hours.'

'But you can promise me this afternoon and cash in hand?'

'Yes.'

'I'll take it. Finish your lunch and we'll get going.' She swigged down her tea, strapped on a flowery apron as big as a single sheet and tucked some pink Marigolds into the pocket. 'Ready when you are.'

Stately as a galleon... The lyrics running through Gail's head had to be restrained. She watched as Nesta rubbed polish on the dining table. The woman was more like a battleship the way she attacked Sharon's long-postponed housework.

As she lifted dusty crockery from the wall unit and carried it to sit in a sink of Fairy bubbles, Gail sneezed.

'Bless you,' said Nesta. 'Have one of these to suck. It'll help keep the dust down.' She fished out a crumpled white paper bag of pear drops from her apron pocket and offered them to Gail.

'Thanks,' said Gail, taking one. 'You know Guy, from the garage, don't you?'

Mrs Galleon, Nesta, popped two pear drops into her mouth and carried on shining. 'Guy Reeves. Yes,' she said. 'Fancy him, do you?'

Gail blushed and sneezed. The character witness continued without help.

'You must remember his wife.' Nesta squirted Mr Sheen on one of the dining chairs. 'The one with the long dresses. Always carried a wicker basket over her arm.'

Gail had a vague recollection of a woman who walked around Chenwick as if she'd escaped from a Regency painting. Wife? 'So, he's married?'

'You are interested.' Nesta tipped the chair upside down, as if it were made of balsa wood, and gave its bottom a good wipe. 'Well, he's available. His wife died a few years back. Treacle toffee?'

How many bags of sweets are secreted in that apron? 'No thanks. How's he off for money?'

Nesta stopped long enough to shake her duster and frown at Gail. 'Didn't have you down as a gold-digger.'

'No, I'm not. I don't want him or his money.'

The mobile gave a muffled ring. Saved by the bell. Gail rushed to answer it. She didn't want Jack disturbed. He was curled up on the sofa, fast asleep. If he'd only stay asleep, then they might, just might, get done before Shaz returned from her long stint with the perming curlers.

'Mum, it's me.' The long-lost daughter. 'Where are you?'

'At bloody work,' hissed Gail. 'Where are you? And where have you been all day?'

'Tell you when I see you,' said Tamsin. 'Can you come and pick me up?'

'No. Can you catch a number thirty-two bus?' She gave her Shaz's address.

There were no apologies when Tamsin finally arrived. No thank yous. 'Hiya, Mum. Wait till you hear what I've been doing. You'll be so proud of me.'

Oh, yeah? Gail didn't trust herself to speak.

'Aren't you going to ask me?' Tamsin looked so animated, Gail was tempted, but no.

'I'm too busy at the moment,' she said. 'Nesta and I have this place to spring clean before five-thirty.' She checked her watch. 'And it's nearly four already.'

'Can I help?'

That was a first. Tamsin offering assistance. The downstairs cloakroom was a rest home for spiders, a haven for germs. Mutant life forms frolicked around the U-bend. There was a chance of the whole room collapsing at the first sight of bleach and a bog brush.

'You can clean the lav,' said Gail.

Tamsin went off with a grin. No moaning, no refusals. Gail almost felt guilty.

Together, Nesta and Gail tackled the bomb-damaged kitchen.

'Shall I do the hall as well?' called Tamsin.

'Do anything you see,' Gail yelled back.

As Nesta carried mops, buckets and brooms out to the car, Gail walked through the house, room by room, doing a thorough check. Tamsin was in the dining room, reading.

'That's my bloody diary.' Gail snatched at it.

Tamsin swung away from her. 'Hey, Mum. You're doing well. Talk about busy. Surely you can't manage all this on your own?' She closed the diary and dropped it into the open briefcase. 'Impressive notepaper.' Her smile was angelic. 'You could do with a secretary. Gis a job.'

'You've got to be joking.' The very thought of it was appalling.

'No. It's what I'm training for. Office work. Computers and that. It's where I've been today. Taking exams.'

Zams. Of course. 'How come? You don't go to college.'

'Private tuition. From Jez. It's what he does. Runs his own business, training people in office skills. Did you like him, Mum? Only, I think he's the one. You know. The One.'

Gail often imagined she was standing in her own tunnel at a point where lots of others converged. They were labelled Work, Love Life, Home Life, Money and so on. Today, her mother's tunnel had darkened, but a light had just appeared at the end of the one with Tamsin's name above it. It must have been the euphoria that caused her to say yes. 'But you'll have to help out with all sorts of work. Cleaning, dog walking, shopping. It won't be sitting on your bum all day, typing and filing your nails. And if that cloakroom's not up to scratch, you can forget the whole thing. OK?' It was a straw for Gail to clutch at. If there was so much as a smear on the tiles, Tamsin would be out before she'd begun.

There wasn't. Gail checked the plughole of the basin, half hoping it would be blocked with gunge. It shone. Bloody hell. Could this transformation of her daughter be down to one thing? Love? Or was it simply that Jez was working miracles? An archangel on a mission.

With perfect timing, Jack awoke, opening his eyes and rolling off the sofa in one movement. 'Wannagohome,' he wailed.

'Right. Let's go,' said Gail.

In the car, she was generous with her thanks, as Bradley had always been after a good day's work. 'You've both been brilliant. I don't know what I'd have done without you. Thank you.'

She dropped Tamsin and Jack off first and then drove to Nesta's. There was enough cash in her purse to pay her star performer.

Nesta chomped on a fresh pear drop. 'Call me anytime,' she said, bending to speak to Gail through the driver's side window, which left her ample backside denting the privet hedge bordering her front garden.

Gail waited for her to let herself into the house, then she leaned back in the seat and drooped, as if she were a doll made from her own dusters. The relief. Oh, the sheer relief. It was done. Shaz's Tip was now Sharon's Palace.

'*Didn't we do well?*'

'*We?*' queried Gail.

Her agony aunt ignored that question. '*One tiny thing,*' she said sweetly. '*You forgot to make out an invoice. That's not the way to run a business—do the work and not ask for payment.*'

'*Point taken.*'

Gail reached for her briefcase. If she made out the invoice, she could drop it in to Sharon's on her way home.

She folded it, inserted it in an envelope, which she placed carefully on the passenger seat, and turned the key in the ignition. Rain clouds were gathering, and it was beginning to drop dark. Gail flicked the switch for the headlights. Their beam cast a spotlight on a tragic figure trudging along the pavement, shoulders hunched, head down. The picture of misery lugged a huge suitcase that banged into its side at every weary step.

'Dilys.' Gail was out of the car and running towards her.

Dilys looked at Gail through panda eyes. Her face was pale, her hair a mess, her eyebrows missing.

'What the...' Gail was terrified.

Dilys dropped the case and stood, arms at her sides. Even in the twilight, her tears were visible. They splashed like thunder raindrops, marking the flagstones.

Gail tripped over the suitcase in her rush to throw her arms around her best friend. Dilys toppled backwards into the hedge with Gail clinging to her.

'Whatever's the matter? Why aren't you in Australia? I wasn't expecting you back for at least another fortnight.'

'Got deported,' sobbed Dilys, making a heroic attempt at humour. And then the tears came again. So many that if any passing Chenwick councillors had witnessed them, they'd have put out a flood warning.

21

Tuesday, 7 March

'I should have gone to Spain to see Bradley. He'd have made me welcome.' Dilys took another swig of wine.

They were sitting on the pay-later suite, a plate of sandwiches, a box of tissues and a couple of wine bottles and glasses on the table, within easy reach.

'Of all the stupid, thoughtless, idiotic...' Dilys reached for another tissue and dabbed at her swollen eyes. 'If only I hadn't had a kid in the first place. Anne's always been trouble, and I was stupid enough to believe she'd changed.' Another tissue, another swig of wine. 'Why? When all we've done over the past five years is exchange half a dozen letters and a phone call at Christmas.' Swig. Sniff. 'Fancy not phoning to let her know I was going to the wedding. How could I be such a stupid cow?'

'Life will look better in the morning,' said Gail, wishing she'd kept her mouth shut. What a pathetic thing to say.

'Will it?' Dilys howled. 'I've no family, no job. I'm all alone in the world. What am I going to do?'

'The same as me. You'll bounce back.'

As Gail tucked her into the spare bed and kissed her goodnight, as if she were Jack, she said, 'Dilys, I've survived, and you can too. First thing tomorrow morning, we'll make you a to-do list.'

What'll go on it? wondered Gail as she fell into her own bed, suffering from exhaustion.

'*Don't ask me at this time of night,*' *said her agony aunt, standing by the door in a pink nightdress and matching negligee.* '*I need my beauty sleep, and so do you. Goodnight.*' *She went, leaving Gail to think about her own to-do list.*

Getting a job had been her first priority, and she'd done that by making one for herself. Pay off suite was one she hadn't got around to. Get a man. Could she tick that? Was Chas her man? And sort out the family. That was the biggie to go on Dil's list. Perhaps Dilys could write to Anne, explain how she wanted to fix things. There was something else too. Something she needed.

Oh yes.

'Energy.' It came out as a cross between a groan and a snore.

Lexi, in her white robe, lay flat on the floor in front of the fake coal fire with real gas flames. Her head rested on a cushion, her legs were straight and together, her arms out wide, at shoulder height, the palms of her hands open and facing upwards, exactly as Joan Collins had recommended in her book, *My Secrets*. Except Joan had recommended ten minutes for relaxation and Lexi had been there all day. Ever since she'd weighed herself. It had been fifteen days since she'd seen Will, and she'd put on two pounds.

She'd never been absolutely sure if Will had been spinning a yarn—whether it was fact or fiction, that spiel he'd given her about weight loss in relationship to sexual activity—but her bathroom scales had persuaded her that he had been telling the truth.

The relaxation, the warmth from the fire made her languorous. And sexy. She roly-polyed across the carpet until she could reach the phone, pressed out a number, heard it ring twice.

'Will,' she purred into the mouthpiece. 'I want you now. And, oh, Will, that scientific survey you were telling me about... You didn't lie to me, did you?'

Off to seek out new life and new civilisations, Will was on his way to Hill House. Anything had to be an improvement on staying at home with Gail creeping around as if someone had died and loud sobs coming from the spare room. Gail's pal, Dilys, had paced up and down all night and refused to leave her room all day.

Will approached his mistress's planet with caution. What was all that crap about a scientific survey? What exactly was Lexi on about?

It hit him like a meteorite. A wayward piece of space flotsam that sent him hurtling down a black hole and into the past.

The first time they'd met. The meeting about her dead husband's business empire. Lexi licking her lips, crossing and uncrossing her legs. Will wanted to be sure he wasn't misreading the signals, so, skilfully, he'd guided the conversation from newspaper advertising to newspaper reports about health and fitness and eventually dropped in the one vital piece of trivia that he'd hoped would seal the deal.

'This new scientific report states that every bonk burns off five hundred calories,' he told her. It wasn't an out and out lie. He was sure he'd read it somewhere but had a vague notion of it being three hundred and fifty. Never mind. Best to err on the generous side.

What a master stroke, telling a woman she could have her cake and eat it and simply work off the calories by way of an energetic leg-over. It had been a sure-fire way into Lexi's knickers. Talk about a merry widow. Her enthusiasm had been the reason he'd fabricated a marriage. It was his safety precaution.

Dilys had refused food and hadn't slept since arriving home. Shut in her room, she'd spent the entire day trying to compose a letter to Anne. Gail couldn't sleep for worrying about her.

Counting sheep was supposed to work, wasn't it? Cocoa certainly hadn't. She closed her eyes, relaxed her aching limbs and tried visualisation. Usually it came easily to her, but this time...

She had another go. Woolly sheep. Cute chubby ones. In a green field studded with buttercups and daisies. Lambs, like fluffy clouds with black stick legs, queuing politely, waiting their turn to trampoline from the springy summer turf, over the trimmed hedge. Background done. Sheep done. Now jump. Every time the sheep moved, they changed shape, and so did the hedge they were leaping over. *Bugger off. I want to go to sleeeep.* No chance of that. Not with Dilys, Tamsin, Chas and Guy, Will and Nesta all lining up to pole vault an ever-growing mountain of Pearl's furniture.

'Breakfast in five minutes,' called Gail, tapping on Will's door.

'Make it ten,' Will answered. He'd only been home an hour, creeping in at six. He sat on the bed in his brand-new Radney the Robot boxers and put his head in his hands. Why, oh why had he done it? Gone and got involved with the mad woman again. They'd both been unhappy at waking up next to each other, but Will had politely managed to continue play-acting and stretched to give Lexi a good morning kiss. She'd screamed as if he'd gone at her with a bloodied hatchet, and they'd leapt off opposite sides of the bed.

'Keep away from me,' she'd yelled. 'Ugh, it's revolting.'

Will had dropped his chin and his eyes. Revolting. A bit pink and shrivelled maybe, but revolting was a slight exaggeration.

'Not that,' said Lexi, crossing her arms over her breasts. 'Your chin, your hair, your breath. Everything.'

It was enough to give a man a complex.

She tugged at the sheets, ripping the top one off the bed. Will had expected her to wrap herself in it, but no. 'Filthy,' she screamed. 'They're filthy, and the whole room smells.'

Hadn't Shakespeare put it in a more genteel fashion? The rancid odour of the double bed or some such.

Lexi took a step towards him. 'Out. Out.'

Once would have been enough. He ran for the shower room. This time, he was happy to scrub away. He was the contaminated one.

She was in the hall waiting for him. 'It'll take me all day to clean this place,' she said. He could see her shaking.

'Let me organise help. I know this little cleaning agency. Very efficient.' Sympathy overcame the fear and dislike. This compulsive cleaning problem needed treating.

'Efficient?' She looked like a little schoolgirl who'd been promised help with her homework.

'Very.'

'Do you think they'd come today?'

'I'll ask as soon as they open and let you know. Now, why don't you go back to bed and rest?'

'Not that bed,' whimpered Lexi. But she walked slowly up the stairs.

Will shook himself. If he didn't make a move soon, he'd be going to the office in his underpants. The smell of coffee and toast wafted up from the kitchen as he made his way downstairs.

Gail was making notes in her diary and eating breakfast at the same time.

'Busy today?' he asked.

'Got shopping to do for Miss Jenkins, more ironing, have to walk Perry and offices to clean at five-thirty.'

'Could you fit in a new client this morning?' asked Will, pouring coffee. 'I saw her yesterday, and she was asking about help with the housework. She's very particular. House-proud.'

'Nesta would do it for me. I'll phone her after breakfast.'

'Nesta?'

Over cereal and toast, Gail gave Will a potted version of Saturday's adventures.

'Today's got to be an improvement.' He put on his jacket and picked up the car keys. As he got to the door, Gail called him.

'Will, have you forgotten anything?'

'Oh yes. The client. It's Mrs Camberlege. Alexandra.' He jotted her address and telephone number on the pad. 'I'll let her know to expect you.'

'Morning, Gorgeous. Wish you were here because I'm writing this in bed. Your adoring Bradley.'

Bradley. Another postcard featuring sea, sun and sand. Gail wiped the corners of her eyes with a tissue. His message made her smile and then want to cry.

She turned her attention to the cheap brown envelope, the only other post. It didn't have a window, so it wasn't a bill. And it wasn't franked. There was a proper stamp on it. And it wasn't sealed.

She opened out the single sheet of paper. It was from the surgery. Would she make an appointment to see Dr Holliday concerning her recent blood tests?

Yes, she would. When she had time. There was so much to organise, so much to do and so little time and energy. 'Prioritise,' she told herself, and put the kettle on.

Mrs Gail Lockwood, Woman of the Year three times in succession, sat on the squashy cushions. Hair, make-up, nails and clothes all immaculate.

Richard Madeley leaned towards her. 'I'm sure we're all dying to know, Gail, how you run a home, care for a lodger, your daughter, young grandson and aged mother and, at the same time, manage such a hugely successful business. Do tell us.'

There was a hush as every woman in the studio audience held her breath.

'It's all down to two things.' The Woman of the Year looked ten years younger than she had any right to. She paused for effect, leaned back and crossed her slim legs.

'And they are?' Judy Finnigan moistened her lips with the tip of her tongue.

Gail Lockwood held up one elegantly manicured finger. The diamonds adorning it flashed at the camera. 'I prioritise,' she said, and lifting a second finger, 'and delegate.'

There was spontaneous applause from the enraptured crowd.

Prioritise and delegate. Yeah, that's exactly what she'd do. She opened her diary, placed a pen and notepad next to it and sipped her mug of tea while she stared at the ceiling, waiting for inspiration. None came. 'Come on, Gail. Get your bleeding act together.' She reached for the phone.

'Laxi-Lexi. Course I'll do it.' Nesta sounded delighted. 'You can trust me. I'll give her and her whole place a good going over. We'll know all her slimming secrets by the end of the day. I'll be with her in half an hour.'

Next, the doctor.

Gail recognised Cat-Woman's voice. 'There's a cancellation at ten this morning. You could take that or wait for Thursday fortnight.'

Thursday bloody fortnight. No, I can't wait that long. *Mother could be dead and buried by then and me in a padded cell, waiting to be taken to court and charged with matricide. With a blanket over my head and the paparazzi flashing cameras.*

'I'll take it.' Leave a note for Dilys, let her sleep. See the doctor. Drop some work off for Tam, visit Mother, call at the garage...

It only took five minutes to get her day planned.

The phone rang.

'Gail? Chas here. I was wondering if Girls Will could look after the business for me this afternoon. I have to go out. By Girls Will, I mean you personally.'

Gail agreed. One phone call was all it took. Now her day had to be replanned. But she'd drop anything for Chas. Literally anything.

'And how are we today?' Doc Holliday's pen was poised over the prescription pad.

'Suicidal. Matricidal and any other bloody 'cidals going. And you wanted to see me.' Gail flipped her letter onto his desk.

'Hurrrumph.' He was not amused, and Gail wasn't really interested. She yawned.

'Your levels are very low,' he said, 'as I suspected.'

Well done, Sherlock Holmes. 'So, what are you going to do about it?'

'I think we might try stronger HRT tablets.'

'You already have.'

'Oh,' said the doctor. 'And are they working?'

Gail gave his question a moment's thought. 'Maybe it's not my hormones. Maybe it's my life,' she said.

Doc Holliday showed no reaction. His head was already over his prescription pad. Gail stood up and crept out so as not to disturb him.

'Gwanny!' The blade of a toy helicopter snagged her tights as Jack attached himself to Gail's legs.

'Come in,' said Tamsin, pushing the door wide.

Gail dragged her left leg and Jack towards the living room. 'F-f-flipping heck, Tam.' She stood in awe and took in her surroundings. The room had been painted and papered, the suite recovered, the carpet replaced, the coffee table rediscovered. 'It's fantastic.'

'Sit down, Mum. I'll make us some coffee.'

''Snice 'n' tidy,' said Jack.

'It certainly is,' said Gail, sitting without having to clear a space.

'Zez helped Mummy. Look.' He pointed at the cushions. 'Zez made 'em and this.' The covers. 'And this.' The curtains.

'Oh.' A terrible thought hit Gail like a punch to the stomach. Zez, sorry, Jez made curtains... sewed. No, he couldn't be. He wasn't, was he? Please, God, don't let him be gay.

Jack clambered onto Gail's lap and knelt to whisper wetly in her ear. 'Zez sleeps in Mummy's big bed. It's a secwet.'

Gail squeezed him close. For once, God had answered. 'Thank you, thank you,' she said, and Jack laughed, thinking it was for him.

'Want some work?' Gail asked as they drank their coffee.

'Yes, please.'

Gail put her briefcase on the table. 'The business stationery's in there but my mobile number's not on it. Anything you can do on your computer?'

'Yeah. No probs.'

'And, if I let you have my car this afternoon, could you do Miss Jenkins's shopping? I've got the money and list here and the address to deliver it to.'

'Yeah. Sure.'

'Right. I'll see you at two. I'm off to walk Perry now.' And after that, she'd pay a visit to Guy's garage and see what she could sniff out.

'*You're in the wrong business. Forget cleaning.*' Gail's *agony aunt had decided to accompany her on the drive into town.* 'A *detective agency is what you should be running. You've one agent out casing Lexi's joint and now you, masquerading as DI Lockwood, are off to interrogate a suspect.*'

Gail ignored her. As she reached the main road, her mobile began ringing. She stopped to answer it.

'Hiya, Gail. Just to let you know I'm off home now.'

'No, Dilys. Wait there. Put the kettle on. I'll be back before it boils.'

Holding up two lines of traffic as she performed a five-point turn on a main road gave her a feeling of power. Her agony aunt disappeared. Probably scared.

'Balls,' Gail shouted at a fellow motorist as he mouthed an obscenity at her. She flicked a V at another one. *Go on, stop the car and get out. I'm dying to smack someone.*

Dilys had drawn sad eyebrows to match her mouth. Turned down at the corners.

Sorrow, so-o-o-row... Gail couldn't get the song out of her head as they stood together, ironing.

'Give me some work to do,' Dil had pleaded, 'otherwise I'll go mad.' Her face was lined from jetlag and sagging from distress, and Gail had done as she'd asked, knowing it was the best thing for her. Keep her mind and body occupied so she didn't dwell on her problems. What she could do with was a man. Couldn't we all? Someone to wine and dine her, no strings attached.

'You could do with a... an interest.' Gail changed her mind at the last second.

'An interest? Such as?' Dilys dumped another pair of jeans onto the new ironing board.

'A hobby. I don't know.'

'I'll take up crocheting, make my own shawl so I can sit by the fire.'

A ship floated across Gail's ironing board. It was a cheery little vessel painted in bright red and shiny blue. Not so long ago, a lone yachtsman. Today, Captain Gail and her crew. It was scary, considering she didn't know if she could pay her own bills, let alone Tamsin's and Nesta Neate's. At this rate, she'd soon have more staff than customers. And now she was about to add Dilys.

'Be my business partner. We could work really well together. By this time next year...'

'...we could be millionaires,' they finished together, and for the first time since arriving home, Dilys smiled. A watery one, yes. But still a smile.

'Partners?'

'Partners,' said Dilys, lifting her iron and clanking it against Gail's to seal the deal.

22

Wednesday, 8 March

Gail was eating a cheese sandwich and applying foundation when she remembered the offices to be cleaned. 'Five-thirty,' she gasped, spitting crumbs.

'No, it's half past one,' said Dilys, who'd refused cheese because it began with C. It was also Cheddar and she wasn't hungry.

'I've got to get to Chas's now. And at five-thirty, I'm booked to be in two places at once. Shutting up shop for Chas Henderson, Gentlemen's Outfitter, and Grey and Grimm's solicitors' offices.'

'I can do the solicitors,' said Dilys.

'Yes, but what about the cleaning equipment? And you look knackered already.'

'We can ask Tamsin or Nesta to give me a hand.'

It had to be Tamsin. There'd been no word from Nesta to say she'd finished at Lexi's. 'I could pick up Tam, then drop you off at Hill House to give Nesta a hand, then, if you call at Chas's shop later and...' Gail put a hand to her head. 'Oh shit. This is getting complicated.'

'That's why you've got a partner,' Dilys told her. 'You finish getting the slap on and get to Swooney Clooney's boutique, and I'll sort the rest.'

It was the old team. Except for Bradley. His face appeared in Gail's magnifying mirror as she thought of him. She scrubbed at it with a tissue. Bradley was the past. Chas was the future. The immediate future anyway. She decided to wear her red suit. After all, it was an upmarket shop.

'Hi-ho,' said Dilys as they left the house.

'Hi-ho,' said Gail. '*It's off to work we go.*' It was almost like old times.

Charles Henderson had closed for the lunch break. He ate the last of the tuna salad straight from the Tupperware and then began on his hands. First, massage in the cream. The ultra-expensive stuff containing organically grown Aloe vera, Royal jelly as used by Cleopatra, almond oil, beeswax, jojoba and evening primrose. It was also fortified with vitamins and guaranteed to eliminate free radicals, whatever they were.

Once the cream was absorbed, he turned his attention to his nails, checking each cuticle. Only when he was completely satisfied that his hands were sheer perfection did he open the brand-new bottle of nail polish. Clear, of course. He wasn't Boy George.

It was the first thing Gail noticed when she walked in. Bloody hell. Dilys was right. Sodding nail varnish. Mind you, he had the most beautiful hands.

'Darling, you look wonderful,' Chas enthused. 'Now, you will be all right, won't you? You shouldn't be busy. You know how to work the till—it's your old one. If I'm not back by closing time, lock up and put the keys through the letterbox.' He took hold of both her hands and pecked the air either side of her face. 'Bye, sweetie. Don't go measuring any inside legs, will you?'

He almost minced out.

Gail plonked herself on the stool behind the counter. What was all that about? He must have sniffed the nail polish fumes and had a change of personality. Talk about a luvvie.

Surely he isn't...?

'Gail, you've got to stop thinking like this.' Her agony aunt leaned against the till. 'First Jez and now Chas. Still, there's no point in chasing after him if he prefers men.'

'Chasing? I'm not bloody chasing him.'

Her agony aunt went to sulk in the kitchen.

It was a long afternoon. A couple of office types came in to browse. 'Can I help you, sir?' 'Just looking.' That sort of thing.

Gail was visibly twitching. There was so much she could have been doing. She could have set up her ironing board in the kitchen for starters. How about writing out some invoices? Yes, she could do that. As she lifted her briefcase, a customer walked in.

'Good aft...' No, this couldn't be happening. God couldn't have such a wicked sense of humour. Guy. Gail fiddled with the clasp on her briefcase, playing for time.

Guy's eyes roamed the shelves, ceiling, floor. Anywhere to avoid contact with Gail's.

Gail recovered first. 'Mr Henderson's not here. He's been called out on urgent business and asked me to step in. Actually, he called my company, Girls Will. I expect Mother has told you about it.' She had to draw breath. Anyway, she'd told him about it and so had Bradley.

'I didn't come to see Mr Henderson. I came to buy a suit,' said Guy. He was more composed than she was.

Gail drew several breaths. Cool, calm, relaxed and in control. 'Can I help?' she asked.

'I thought dark blue,' he said. 'Not navy. Something a little lighter.'

That shouldn't be difficult. Chas's organisational methods included colour coordinating everything. Gail led the way to the blue section. It was all very professional. She played the sales assistant, he the customer. As if they'd never met before.

Guy tried on two suits and settled for the first. 'And a shirt and tie to go with it.'

'Any particular colour?'

'White shirt.'

That was easy. Gail carried it across to the counter. Her hands were shaking, her temper bubbling just beneath her ready-to-burst-into-beetroot skin. She had to know what Guy was up to with her mother but could hardly come straight out with it. Not unless she was Dilys. Or DI Lockwood.

I am arresting you for the heinous crime of conning an old lady out of her belongings. Anything you do say may be given in evidence...

'My mother,' she began. It was a start.

Guy turned his attention from the tie rack to the sales assistant. 'Your mother is a wonderful woman,' he said, with no sign of a smirk. 'Exciting, entertaining, amusing.'

You what? I've known her all my life and never noticed.

'I never know what to expect.'

Neither do I, so that's one we agree on.

'She never ceases to amaze me.'

That's two.

'One day she's a Twenties flapper, the next a Sixties mod or a Fifties Hollywood star.'

Can't argue with that.

'A truly wonderful woman, truly...' His voice faded away like the end of a soundtrack to an old black and white movie, one starring Guy Reeves as Cary Grant and Pearl Proctor as Audrey Hepburn.

Gail's knees threatened to jack-knife. 'Got to sit down,' she mumbled, but he wasn't looking or listening.

'My God,' she exhaled, with her bum safely on a stool. 'I think he loves her.'

The tie was proving more of a challenge, which was fortunate. Guy, examining the entire collection twice, gave Gail a chance to recover. By the time he'd opted for the royal blue, pure silk tie and handkerchief set, adorned with fat, naked and sexless cherubs, Gail was able to act the unruffled assistant.

At the till, she added up the gentleman's purchases. Eight hundred plus. Firkinell. It was Dilys's expression but the only one suitable. Guy hadn't asked for any prices and she hadn't looked. A hot flush attacked from all directions. Gail kept her head bowed.

'What's the damage?' asked Guy.

She struggled to tell him. 'It's all excellent quality, and you get what you pay for and...' Just get on with it. 'Eight hundred and fifty-five pounds and ninety-nine pence.' There. She'd said it and nearly fainted in the process.

Guy unzipped a cheap wallet and pulled out a wad of notes. Gail blinked and zoomed in on the wad. She knew the old trick of wrapping real money around pieces of paper, but Guy hadn't played the old trick. He counted seventeen fifty-pound notes onto the counter and added the extra six pounds.

Gail was too shocked for speech. Good job too, she told herself afterwards, otherwise she'd have been at his throat, wanting to know where he'd got his money from. Were the proceeds from Pearl's antiques paying for him to dress like a popstar? Was his bank account filled with money filched from flocks of silly old ladies? But no, it was Chas's shop and she was being paid to mind it. Girls Will could do without tabloid headlines.

Company Director garrottes customer with pure silk tie.

She managed to remain professional until the door clicked behind Pearl's mechanic and then, 'Funck you,' she screamed at the top of her voice. 'I'm going to find out what you're up to if it's the last thing I do. You... you... ageing bloody gigolo.'

Ageism reigned.

'Over there. Be with you in a sec,' shouted the young woman.

'I'm not deaf,' said Chas, doing as he was told. Not so much as a cup of tea or 'hello, sweetie'. Not like the old days.

Chas had fond memories of them. When he was treated with respect at a photoshoot, when he'd been the young man with taut muscles, posing in the nylon Y-fronts or mini briefs—in packs of two—featuring saucy slogans. He'd been one of the favourites for formal menswear, in dinner jacket and bow tie, staring at the camera with chin in hand and furrowed brow. And they'd loved him in casuals. The sea in the background, him in Levi's and T-shirt, holding a coil of rope and staring thoughtfully out at the horizon. And his hands. Once upon a time, they'd adored his hands, and he'd modelled rings and wristwatches worth millions of pounds for all the major catalogue companies. He still kept them in tip-top condition, and they looked as good as they had at twenty, but no one was interested. He was too old.

He watched a young upstart. Talk about scruffy. The youngster, all chin-stubble and a dragged-through-a-hedge-backwards hairstyle, perched on the edge of a double bed to model striped pyjamas more suitable for a man triple his age. Chas shook his head. He wouldn't be seen dead in night-wear like that, yet he was considered too old to be photographed in it.

Holding his hands in front of his face, he checked them once again. Immaculate.

'Ready?' called the photographer.

Chas stood and hitched up the extra-large bath towel wrapped around his nether regions.

'All you have to do is open the door and remember to smile as you step inside, and could you place your hand on your back, maybe, and perhaps the tiniest limp? Good. Good.'

A professional to the last, Chas limped, clutched the base of his spine and even remembered to smile as he demonstrated the walk-in bath.

Dilys, Nesta and Gail stood at the cracked wash-basins. It had been Dilys's idea to go to the Monday night meeting of Flabfighters.

'We could go home and put our feet up,' Gail had suggested.

'No, I'd sooner be doing something,' said Dilys, so Gail hadn't argued.

'That Lexi's a right nutter,' Nesta diagnosed as she washed her hands.

'Tell us everything you know,' demanded Dilys.

Nesta didn't need encouragement. 'The place was bleedin' spotless, but she got me cleaning everything. And she helped. She couldn't wait to get her rubber gloves on and get stuck in. You could do heart trans-plants on her kitchen table or floor or even in her loo, for that matter. There isn't a germ daft enough to go near the place. The woman is mad.'

'Obsessive-compulsive disorder,' murmured Dilys.

'What's that when it's at home?'

'It's what our old boss said Lexi has, but we didn't know what she was compulsive about. We do now. Cleaning.'

Cynthia's voice penetrated the toilet walls. 'Line up for the weigh-in. Line up for the weigh-in.'

'Are you sure you're up for this?' Gail asked Dilys. 'You must be knackered.'

'I'm sure I want to keep busy and there's no way I'm tired,' said Dilys, rubbing the tail end off her left eyebrow and covering the smudge with her fringe.

'Hang on to that for a minute, will you?' Nesta took off her coat, folded it and passed it to Dilys. Then she removed her long pink cardigan, rolled it up and stuffed it into her tartan shopping bag. She unpinned a large gold-coloured brooch in the shape of a spider and dropped it on the top, unclipped her earrings, removed her engagement ring and peered down at herself, checking to see if there was any extra ballast she could dispose of. 'Ooo, nearly forgot.' She fished in the pocket of her skirt and produced the inevitable bag of sweets. 'Pineapple rock, anybody?'

Dilys and Gail declined.

'Suit yourselves.' Nesta popped two large chunks into her mouth and added the remainder to her shopping bag. 'I'm going for Slimmer of the Week tonight. It's been salad for dinner and tea the last seven days.'

Gail covered her smile with her hand and kept her eyes averted from Dilys.

'Besides, I'm bound to weigh less because I cheated last time.'

'Cheated?' Dilys and Gail cried together.

'Yes. I stuck the brass weights off the kitchen scales in my drawers.' Nesta stood in line, crunching her pineapple rock, while Cynthia stood, in charge of the scales, looking like a stick of rock. She was wearing pink tights, a tiny pink leather skirt and a pink fluffy off-the-shoulder sweater. *The right colour for my agony aunt*, thought Gail, *but definitely not the right outfit*. It was an effort for Cynthia not to wrinkle her nose in disgust as Big Nesta ambled forwards to step on the scales.

'What are you eating?' she asked, examining Nesta from swollen feet to bulging cheeks.

Nesta bit down on the rock. 'Celery.'

Cynth looked at the scales and did a quick double take. 'You've lost weight,' she squeaked. She gave the scales a thump. 'Six pounds. How have you managed that?'

'Salad,' crunched Nesta. 'It's all that's passed my lips.'

'That and lies,' whispered Dilys.

'W-w-well done,' stammered Cynth, and turned to Dilys, who was already standing on the scales.

'Six pounds. How have you managed that?'

For a moment, Dilys thought she'd got stuck with Cynth in some sort of time warp. *Six pounds. How have you managed that? Six pounds. How have you managed that?* On and on for ever. A split in the space-time continuum. They'd used the plot more than once in *Star Trek* and it had been in *Groundhog Day*.

Gail prodded her. 'That's brilliant.'

Dilys came back from the future or the past or wherever it was where Cynthia was asking for eternity how she'd lost six pounds.

'How? Do tell us?' Cynth urged.

'It was easy,' answered Dilys. 'It's being bloody miserable that did it.'

Cynthia simpered and moved on to Gail.

'A pound less than last time,' she said. She didn't ask how Gail had managed it, but Gail told her anyway.

'Hard work's my secret,' she said.

The three ladies from Girls Will took their seats and awaited Cynth's proclamation. Who would reign supreme this week?

Cynth stood tall, straight and upright, sticking to her stick-of-rock look. She clapped her hands together, which was completely unnecessary, as the audience were, as always, agog to hear the news. 'This week, we have a draw for Slimmer of The Week,' said Cynth. 'Will Nesta Neate and Dilys Lloyd please come up on the stage.'

Nesta surreptitiously slipped the two chunks of pineapple rock she'd been about to pop into her mouth back into the bag. She stood, shoving her chair back into the knees of the woman sitting behind her, and shambled out into the aisle. Dilys followed.

'Now, Nesta here,' said Cynth, painting on a smile, 'has already told me that her results are from sticking to the Flabfighters' Diet, and I expect Dilys is the same. Aren't you, dear?'

Dilys opened her mouth and, like a goldfish, closed it when she spotted the you'll-be-sorry-if-you-open-your-big-mouth message that was spread across Cynth's face.

'Two more successes for Flabfighters.' Cynthia's voice rang out. She led the clapping.

Dilys stared unseeingly at the other club members. This was supposed to be her moment. She had wanted this for so long and what a let-down it turned out to be. *What's the big deal? What's it all about? Losing a few pounds. Losing a daughter. Losing a job. Slimmer of The Week? Loser of The Year, more like.*

She lurched sideways and crashed to the floor. Immediately, Cynth and Nesta were leaning over her.

'Get your boobs out of her face. You're suffocating her. Give her some air.' The stick of rock was in charge. 'We need to raise her legs and loosen her clothing.'

Someone handed a folded coat to Cynthia, who placed it under Dilys's feet. Gail was already undoing the buttons at the neck of Dilys's blouse.

'It's jetlag,' she explained. 'She only got home from Australia the day before yesterday and she's worked all day today. I'll take her home.'

Dilys wondered why the clapping had stopped and the acoustics in the church hall had changed. The mumblings from her fellow Flabfighters echoed, as if they were all in some huge subterranean cavern. Still puzzled, she allowed Nesta and Gail to help her sit up. Five minutes later, they took her out to Gail's car. With their hands beneath her elbows, her feet barely touched the floor.

They laid her on the back seat. Nesta pressed a king-size Mars bar in her hands. 'Sugar. That's what's lacking. Get that down you.'

Dilys clutched the Mars and did nothing. All she wanted was to sleep. Nesta, kneeling on the passenger seat, took the chocolate off her, tore off the wrapping and force-fed her patient. Before Dilys had finished the last mouthful, they were back at Gail's.

Ten minutes later, Dilys was in bed with Nesta sat one side of her and Gail the other.

Nesta dunked a biscuit into her tea. 'She'll sleep the clock round,' she predicted.

Twice, thought Dilys as she closed her eyes.

23

Thursday, 9 March

Without breathing, Bradley carefully placed his paperback and glasses on the table and, dropping to his hands and knees, crawled quietly behind the sofa. There was a second knock at the door. He risked a quick peek. Yes, it was definitely Brenda's silhouette he could see through the glass panel.

This was bloody stupid. Hiding from a woman. But what a woman. Brenda was a man-eater and she'd set her sights on him. Talk about scary. Give him a Jehovah's Witness at his door any day.

'Braaaddy. Braddy Waddy, darling.'

Oh Christ. Braddy was bad enough. But Braddy Waddy. Hell's bells. And Bloody Braddy's knees were beginning to hurt, taking all his weight on the stone tiles. He rolled onto his side and stifled a giggle at the silliness of it. A grown man hiding like a little kid.

'Oh, come on, Braddy. Open up. I know you're in there.'

Of course she did. She knew his every move. He couldn't take a leak without her knowing about it. Ever since he'd arrived, he hadn't been able to go anywhere without Brenda being behind him or at his side or hanging on to his arm. He'd heard via the gang's grapevine that they were considered 'an item'. Over his dead body.

Bradley laid his head on the floor and wished it would open up and swallow him. It was either that or leap off the balcony. This wasn't what retirement was supposed to be like.

'Braddy, sweetie.' Her voice was soft. 'Brenda doesn't mind if you're having a shower. Let me in, love. I could scrub your back for you.'

Braddy collapsed onto his back, kicked his legs in the air and shoved a fist into his mouth. Scrub his back? Not bloody likely.

'I'm going to wait here if it takes forever,' sang Brenda, leaning against the door. 'Don't be shy. Come out and let me rub you dry.'

That did it. Third floor or not, he was going over the top. Rolling back onto his hands and knees, he crawled across the floor and slid open the window leading to the balcony. Now for the great escape.

Another tap at the door. 'Braddy Waddy. Icka Brenda's waiting.'

You'll have a bleeding long wait, thought Bradley. *Now, if I climb over the railings and hang on, at arm's length, I should be able to reach the balcony beneath.* He'd seen it done a hundred times and by a hundred different actors, so it couldn't be too difficult.

Jimmy'll take pity on me and either hide me in his flat or let me out of it so I can hole up somewhere until Brenny Wenny's cooled off.

He clambered over the wrought iron railing and stood, his back to the view, his toes wedged between the iron bars. So far, so good. Next, into a crouching position, hold the rails, lower himself and it would be, 'Hello, Jimmy.'

But the next words he said weren't, 'Hello, Jimmy', but 'Hello, Nurse' when he opened his eyes in hospital.

'You are nasty accident,' said the nurse.

That's what my mother used to say, was what his normal reply would have been, but Bradley discovered that his voice was the croak of a frog with tonsillitis, and to add to that, his face didn't want to move. His mouth would only open as wide as the slot on a cash machine.

'Have nasty accident,' corrected the nurse, shaking her head.

He wasn't going to argue with that. He'd certainly had one. It felt as if Brenda had been scrubbing his back with a bus and drying him off with a brick wall.

'You want us call someone. Jimmy, p'raps?'

'Jimmy?' How did she know about Jimmy?

'You are asking for Jimmy. I call him for you?' She put her hand to her ear as if she were holding a telephone.

'No, not Jimmy,' said Bradley. 'Don't call him. Call Gail.' He wanted her to know he was suffering, and she might worry about what had happened to him when the flow of daily postcards came to an end. He didn't want her to think it was because he'd stopped caring. He relaxed back onto the pillows and closed his eyes so that he could picture Gail getting on a plane on the first stage of her mercy dash to his bedside. A man had to have dreams.

Dilys groaned, yawned, rubbed her eyes and lay, staring at the strange clock on the wrong side of the bed. It told her she'd been sleeping for fourteen hours. She was at Gail's. Yes, it was all coming back to her. Australia. Girls Will. Flabfighters. The blood, sweat and tear-stained tapestry of her miserable life.

May as well go back to sleep. There's nothing to get up for. Nothing to look forward to. I wonder if you can put yourself into a voluntary coma? That's not fair on Gail though. Lying here in her spare bedroom, waiting to conk out.

She sat up, kicked back the duvet and struggled out of bed to stagger to the bathroom.

'Dilys?' It was Gail calling up the stairs. 'Cup of tea?'

Dilys, trying to make out who or what was staring back at her from the bathroom mirror, made a noise, which could have been a yes or a no, and lurched back to the bedroom.

Five minutes later, Gail appeared carrying a tray. 'Tea and toast.'

And marmalade and a bunch of flowers all on a tray with a lacy cloth over it. All to make her feel better. To let her know that someone cared.

'Eat up,' said Gail. She was using her bright and cheery voice.

'I've come to a decision,' said Dilys, rubbing off the remains of her fuzzy eyebrows. The rest were probably on the pillowslip. 'I'm never ever watching *Neighbours* again. Nothing Australian. I'm not even going to drink their wine.'

Gail didn't like to say that Dilys's dilemma was nothing to do with Australians. It was her daughter, born and bred in Chenwick, who'd caused the trouble. So, using her bright and cheery voice again, she said, 'Cheer up. You're home now. You're a company director as well as Slimmer of The Week. Eat your breakfast, and here's the paper if you fancy a read. I'll leave you in peace.'

Dilys munched her way through the toast, inch deep in marmalade. Her appetite was coming back. Then she turned her attention to the Echo. It was all the usual stuff. The same people in trouble, the same arguments about the retail park, a couple of wedding photographs that she skipped quickly, and finally the hatches, matches and dispatches column. One of Anne's schoolfriends was announcing the safe arrival of Roman, brother to Kylie, Charlotte and Elton. Quite an eclectic taste in music there.

Deaths. Dilys scanned the names, then did a quick calculation of the average age. Somewhere in the eighties this week. That meant she had another thirty years to go. What was she going to do on her own for thirty bloody years?

She flicked over a couple of pages and then stopped.

The advertisement took up about an eighth of the page. She read it twice. The first time in amazement, the second in delight. Plans began to form in her head. What had Gail said about taking up an interest? This could be it.

'Gail,' she yelled. 'Come and see this.'

Gail arrived breathless and worried. 'What's up?'

Dilys shoved the paper at her. 'Look. *Zany Scrapes*. They're holding their first ever convention here in Chenwick of all places. Unbelievable.'

'Come and meet the actors. Dress as your favourite character. Sit on the casting couch,' read Gail. 'Saturday the seventeenth of March.'

'Unbelievable,' repeated Gail, gasping for breath. *Zany Scrapes on Planet Zog* had managed to do something she couldn't—put a smile on Dilys's face.

Gail was prioritising. Before phoning her mother and asking a few probing questions, she'd answer all the messages that had been left for Girls Will. Business was looking good. The diary was filling. At this rate, she'd be down the job centre, startling Master Potter by asking him to find some hard workers for Girls Will. As she put down the phone, it rang. She grabbed it quickly before it had chance to wake Dilys, who'd gone back to sleep.

'Meesees Lockwood?' An unknown voice and a strange accent.

'Yes,' said Gail.

'I have some bad news for you.'

Bugger. What now?

'Meester Bradley Jones wishes to speak with you.'

Was that it? The bad news? Bradley wanting to speak to her?

'Gail, I've had a bit of an accident.' Bradley's voice sounded far away, which it was, and about as weak as the tea he drank. 'I fell off my balcony.'

'Fell off... are you all right? How the hell did you manage that?'

'I was escaping the enemy. Pity I was on the third floor.'

'Third floor?' Gail cringed at the thought. 'Bloody hell, Bradley. I hope you were drunk enough that it didn't hurt.'

'No. Stone-cold sober, and it does hurt. Cuts and bruises all over and concussion, and I'm here all alone with no one to look after me. I keep having this recurring dream about you sitting by my bedside, holding my hand and mopping my fevered brow, and I wanted to know if there was the remotest possibility of it coming true.'

He wanted her to fly out there? He had to be joking. Gail took a deep breath. 'You're joking, aren't you?'

'No, Gail, I miss you, and I hate it here in Spain. The hospital won't let me out for about a week and then only if I have someone to look after me, and I want to come home.'

He certainly sounded miserable. Gail's heart did a quick bounce at the thought of him in hospital in a foreign country. 'Oh, Bradley. I'm sorry. I can't come.'

'Oh, Gail.'

Was that a sob? 'But if you can get on a plane, I could meet you and you could stay here with me until you're fit and decide what you want to do with the rest of your life.'

'You'd do that for me?'

'There's not a lot I wouldn't do for you, Bradley.' As she said the words, she realised how much he meant to her. He was such a good friend, always there when she needed him. Now he wanted help and there was no way she would let him down.

'I'll call you again as soon as I've got things worked out.' There was a moment's silence. 'Gail?'

'Yes?'

'You're sure about this?'

'Of course.' She put down the phone. *I just hope Dilys has vacated the spare bed before you get here,* she thought, *and having a man in it will give Mother something else to talk about.*

Mother. Yes, she'd call Pearl next, but before she had a chance, the phone rang again.

'Chas here. What are you doing tonight? Fancy dinner?'

Dinner? George Clooney in a white suit leading her to a corner table in the window of a flash restaurant overlooking a myriad of tiny lights twinkling over an exotic harbour. He pulled out a chair for her, poured champagne into her glass and took charge of the menu. He gazed deeply into her eyes. She knew that in the subdued light from the perfumed candle her wrinkles were hardly visible.

'Tonight?' She turned the page of her diary, playing for time. 'Yes, tonight looks fine.'

'I'll pick you up at eight.'

Eight. It's two-thirty now. That gives me five and a half hours to get ready. The ironing will have to wait, and Nesta can tackle Grey and Grimm's. Now, what'll I wear?

She sat dreaming for two minutes until the phone rang again. Was it ever going to shut up?

'Hiya, Mum.' Tamsin's voice was brighter and cheerier than her own had been when speaking to Dilys. A sure sign that she wanted something. Probably babysitting.

'Can you babysit tonight?'

Gail cut her short. 'No, sorry. I've got a hot date.'

'A what? Did you say date?'

Gail confirmed there was nothing wrong with her daughter's hearing.

'With a man?' Shock, horror.

'No, a monkey.'

'Mother.' Not bright and cheery. This time, it was a wail. 'You're too old for dates. Oh, God, it's horrible. A woman of your age.'

Gail interrupted. 'What age? I'll have you know that with the wonders of modern medicine, I could still have a baby if I wanted and then it would be me asking you to babysit.' She'd momentarily forgotten the hysterectomy.

'You should be past all that s-s-' Tamsin could hardly bear to say the word in relation to her parent but finally spat it out. 'Sex stuff. Ugh. I don't want to think about it. Too much information already.'

'Sorry about the babysitting,' said Gail, and because she was bristling about the ageist comments, she was compelled to add, 'I would have but getting laid is higher on my list of priorities right now.' She went to put the phone down gently, but Tamsin beat her to it, only Tam didn't do it gently. Gail shook her head and rubbed at her ear to get rid of the echoing.

Daughter down. Mother to go. She dialled Pearl's number. There was no answer, and as Pearl didn't consider an answerphone one of life's necessities, she couldn't leave a message. 'It'll keep,' said Gail as she went upstairs to see if Dilys was still breathing.

Oh, the flesh was weak. And so was the mind in Will's case. He'd made up his mind to tell Lexi it was all over between them. Whatever 'it' was. Only sex. Nothing else. No conversation. No companionship. No shared interests, if you didn't count the sex. She could find herself another stud. And then the phone rang.

'You know what I fancy tonight, Mr Bassett?' Lexi purred down the line.

He started to shake, visibly. Enough that Gina noticed and mouthed, 'You all right?'

Will nodded and mimed holding a cup and sipping. Gina took the hint and went to put the kettle on. It was almost time to go home, and they usually had coffee before leaving.

Once he was alone, he sat straighter at his desk, drew a deep breath and came out with it. 'I'm sorry, Lexi. Tonight's out of the question and'—he breathed out—'so's any other night. It's time we cooled it.'

'Seven o'clock,' said Lexi, and the line went dead.

He rearranged himself through the lining of his trouser pocket and told himself she'd have a long wait. OK, telling her over the phone was the coward's way out but he'd done it. Not that she'd taken any notice. Not her. Lexi was a control freak. Think how she controlled herself.

Gina returned with the coffee and drank hers while she finished off the filing. Will sat at his desk, sipping slowly, telling himself that a night at home with Gail would fit the bill. Rest and relaxation and *Zany Scrapes on Planet Zog*. He could watch the recording again and study it at leisure. When he'd taken the advertisement about the convention, he'd decided immediately that there was no way he was going to miss it, especially when the organisers promised to put him a free ticket in the post. If he was going, he'd want an outfit, and, as yet, he hadn't even decided which character to go as. There were only six to choose from. Five, actually. He could hardly turn himself into Betty Bowk, the professor's beautiful daughter. But he could be the mad professor or the evil Emperor Zig. Their costumes should be simple enough to duplicate. For a second, he contemplated becoming Kurt King, superhero, but no, everyone would want to be Kurt. So, what did that leave? Either Blublobbery, the friendly alien who looked like a mutant jellyfish, or Radney the Robot. Becoming either would take thought and ingenuity. Will guessed there'd be fewer aliens and robots because they'd be more of a challenge. He wasn't sure about the net and rag draped alien. He'd no sewing skills. So, Radney it was. He might draw up a few plans when he got home.

'No arguments,' said Dilys. 'I've made up my mind. I'm going home, and no, I don't want a lift. I'll get a taxi.'

They sat over a cup of coffee while they waited for the taxi to arrive. Gail was bubbling over with her news. She told Dilys about Bradley's accident first.

'And you're going to nurse him? On top of everything else? Mother, daughter, grandson, lodger, job.' Dilys checked them off on her fingers.

'Yes, and guess what? Chas has asked me to go out for dinner with him tonight.'

Dilys didn't look impressed. She wrinkled her nose. 'You don't really fancy him, do you?'

'A George Clooney double. Who wouldn't?'

'Me. He might look like him but he's only Chas Henderson, and he wears nail varnish. He's probably gay.'

'No, there has to be a good reason for the nail polish.'

'Oh, yeah, and what would that be?'

'Perhaps it's that stuff you paint on to stop biting your nails.' Gail knew she was clutching at straws. Chas's nails hadn't been bitten in his life. They were almost too perfect.

'Take care, Gail. He's all right but, like I said, he fancies himself.'

A horn honked outside. Dilys stood up, kissed Gail, picked up her suitcase and bumped into Will as she rushed out of the door.

'Oops, sorry, Will.'

'Sorry, Dil.'

Will and Dil. *It sounds like the title of a second-rate sitcom*, thought Gail as she poured coffee into Will's mug.

'Coffee?'

Will nodded and sat where Dilys had been two minutes earlier. The seat was still warm. 'How's Dilys coping?' he asked.

'She's posted a letter to her daughter, and now she'll sit back and wait for a reply. Until Hell freezes over if necessary.' Gail wondered if she was wasting her breath, as Will seemed far more interested in the wall.

It was actually the contraption on the kitchen wall, the one that held rolls of kitchen paper and cling film, which kept attracting Will's attention. At the bottom of it dangled a big roll of Bacofoil. He'd be needing loads of that.

24

'Does this look all right?'

'I'd prefer pink,' said her agony aunt.

'No surprises there,' Gail told her as she did a twirl in front of the full-length mirror.

Her agony aunt gave a snort and disappeared.

Gail was wearing her black dress and had added a gold shawl. Gold bracelets, earrings and sandals completed the effect she was hoping for. Sophisticated and sexy. She'd washed her hair and dried it, head hanging upside down to get added bounce, and shunned the jar of Funky Gunk. Tonight, she'd go for smooth just in case Chas wanted to run his fingers through it. Yes, smooth, sophisticated and sexy.

Chas complimented her as soon as she opened the door to him, making the five hours of preparation all worthwhile. Face pack, hair-free legs and armpits. A stray whisker plucked from the chin with the aid of new tweezers, her specs and the magnifying mirror. Body lotion slapped all over. Toe and fingernails painted gold. By the time every wrinkle and bulge had been overhauled, she'd felt almost too knackered to go out. Gail reminded herself that, if she was lucky enough to get her kit off, her body was just about as good as she could get it at short notice.

Chas, in a charcoal suit with black T-shirt beneath, was film star material. She wanted to ask if anyone had ever requested his autograph. 'Could you sign this for me, Mr Clooney, sir?' The autograph book changed into a lace thong. Gail blinked back to reality.

'Ready?'

'Yes.' She pulled her shawl around her shoulders and prayed that she didn't break out in goosebumps or catch pneumonia. It was chilly outside and she was off out, half naked, as Pearl would have put it, and not a thermal vest or a woolly scarf in sight.

He took her to Mad Hatter's, a classy restaurant a couple of miles out of town. Chas held the door open for her, and she stepped into the dimly lit interior. The building was low ceilinged with ancient beams. Real ones. Walls had been knocked down to convert the whole place into one long room with recesses leading from it.

They were led to one of four tables in a deep alcove. Glass-encased candles flickered on the windowsill, and there were more on the table, creating a pool of light on the crimson cloth. *A fire hazard if ever there was one*, thought Gail, slipping the shawl from her shoulders and letting it drop over the back of her chair. She had a vivid picture of herself, arm aloft, clinking champagne glasses with Chas and the fringe of the shawl catching fire. Now, that would be a hot date.

They had begun their starters, melon fans with raspberry coulis, when the evening turned into a nightmare. A woman walked past the entrance to their alcove. Gail spluttered on a chunk of melon and dabbed at the raspberry running down her chin.

No, it can't be. I must be hallucinating. Shouldn't have had two glasses of wine on an empty stomach. Hell. That's all I need. Mother.

The woman was disappearing through the door to the ladies loo. It was Pearl all right. Who else had radioactive hair? And Wednesday legs, as Bradley had so often described them. Wednesday gonna break? What other woman of seventy-three, but passing herself off as sixty-three, would dress as a sixteen-year-old? Forgetting the fire risk, Gail pulled her shawl back around her shoulders and suppressed a shiver. Definitely Pearl. Platform-soled snakeskin sandals to match the snakeskin blouse, which was tucked into a black skirt with a split up to mid-thigh.

Chas, fortunately, was unaware of her predicament. He was talking about somebody called Avril and he seemed to expect Gail to know who he was on about. Gail bowed her head as Pearl reappeared, a fresh Cupid's bow in Post Office red adorning her lips. From beneath her lashes, Gail watched her mother teeter over the thick red carpet in the ridiculous shoes and that dreadful skirt. The most you could say for it was that it enabled her to give her varicose veins a good airing.

Chas carried on his monologue. Pearl passed by. Gail lifted her head and resumed eating. She watched Chas's lips move but didn't listen to the words.

If Bradley were here now, we'd both be hanging on to each other, laughing. I'll have to tell him all about this when he comes home. But what the hell's Pearl doing here anyway? And who's she with?

DI Lockwood made her excuses to her partner and slipped from the table. Pretending she didn't know the location of the washroom, she took a right turn and, keeping close to the wall, made her way to the opening of the next alcove. She waited, feigning interest in the painting hung on the wall, an old-fashioned country scene of a barn, chickens and a smock-clad farmer leaning on a five-barred gate. Taking a compact from her bag, she flicked it open and, with her back to the alcove, peered into the mirror. An old trick but a good one. With a bit of head twisting and mirror slanting, she finally zeroed in on the couple in the corner. The gangster from the park. Between finger and thumb, he held a black grape from the cheese platter. His moll sidled closer to him. They were sitting at the same side of the table as each other, on a pew-style seat. The moll giggled, leaning into his side, opening her lips so that he could pop the grape into the mouth that smiled as widely as the slot on a Victorian pillar box.

DI Lockwood, mission accomplished, went back to her seat and her wild salmon parcel with herbs and honey wrapped in filo pastry. If the suspects were on the cheese course already, they should soon be vacating the premises and she could relax. Then, with a sudden bump, she gave up the police force and became a concerned daughter again. Could Guy really love Pearl, or was he using her for what he could get? In this case, money. But what had Nesta said about Guy's first wife? She'd been an eccentric dresser, all that theatrical Regency style. So, did Guy really have eyes for Pearl? Was he going for the same type all over again? He'd struck gold if he was. No one else dressed as eccentrically as her mother.

'A natural blonde,' Chas droned on. 'Turned heads wherever she went...'

His bloody wife. Was that his only topic of conversation? Gail considered trying to steer the chitchat in another direction but changed her mind as the grape-eating incident did an unasked-for replay above the candle flames.

Her mother was besotted with the man. Her lips, like a vampire's after a binge, had pouted seductively at Guy. If a woman of her age could be described as seductive. Ugh. And double ugh. Her mouth dropped open, her eyes glazed over in sudden realisation, and her fork clattered to her plate.

Chas didn't notice. 'I remember our first annivers ary...'

Gail clamped a hand over her open mouth to prevent a groan from escaping. *Oh my God. I think Mum's too old to be going out with men and Tamsin thinks I'm too old to be going out with men.* She glanced at Chas, who was still wittering on about the attractions of Avril.

Why do we need men anyway? Roger was nothing but trouble and heartache, and Dad hardly said a word and moped about from the day he retired until the day he died, which wasn't long afterwards.

The steamed pudding arrived. Rich dark chocolate with a melting milk chocolate centre, served with double cream and a strawberry and mint leaf on the side.

Chas had stopped talking. 'I'm so sorry,' he was saying. 'I loved Avril, you know.' He put his hand over Gail's and squeezed it. 'Kick me next time I mention her name. They should lock me up. I must be mad talking about another woman when I'm out dining with such a gorgeous one.'

Gail managed a half smile, half grimace. His hand was warm. His touch welcome. That was what she missed. Human contact. To touch, hold hands, feel the warmth of another body next to hers and know she wasn't alone in the world.

With her right hand, she spooned up a million calories. Her left hand, beneath Chas's, turned so that their palms touched. She returned his squeeze.

Enjoy it while you can, Gail. And good luck, Mother. She raised her glass and made a silent wish. *Let's hope neither of us get hurt.*

So much for a night in. 'You're a weak man, William Bassett,' Will Bassett told himself. 'Just because Gail's gone out with that bloke who looks like a shop dummy doesn't mean you have to go out too. Be honest with yourself. Are you really going to finish with Lexi, face to face, or are you off on one of your fantasies again?'

Deep down, he knew that being free of Lexi would give him an immense sense of relief. Safety even. There again, a regular leg-over, not many men would say no to that.

Ten minutes later, he was pulling on the handbrake of the car. He switched off the headlights and sat. So far so good. He'd managed to park the car, not land the spacecraft. In future, his space fantasies would be saved for *Zany Scrapes*. Later, he might attend a few other conventions. *Star Trek. Doctor Who.*

'Your mission is to rid yourself of this alien female,' muttered Will, immediately lapsing into character.

'Aye, Captain.'

'Make it so.'

Now, how was he going to tell Lexi he didn't want to be her sex slave? The perfect solution would be if she dumped him, but how was he going to manipulate her into that situation? He opened the car door and, as the interior light was on, glanced at his watch. An hour and a half late. Lexi would be in a bad mood. That could only be to his advantage.

The door was unlocked. He walked into the hall. She was wearing nothing but earrings and rubber gloves and was on her hands and knees, her back to him, scrubbing the gleaming floor. As she scrubbed, her hips swayed and her bottom wobbled. He was instantly at attention. *Just one more time*, his swollen brain begged inside his jeans. *Once more can't hurt.*

He gave a cough. 'Sorry I'm late.' He was about to make up an excuse but decided against it.

Lexi swivelled around until she was sitting on the tiles, facing him. The front of her hair was damp and a trickle of sweat glistened between her breasts.

'You've got clothes on,' she said accusingly.

Apart from the first time they'd met, which was business, he'd never got further than the doormat before having to strip.

They both looked at his jeans, his rainbow striped shirt.

'Out, Out,' screamed Lexi, pointing at the door.

Will turned and heard her gasp as she caught sight of his ponytail, which was held by a fluorescent green scrunchie with a plastic model of a sumo wrestler stitched to it. He couldn't believe his luck. She was throwing him out. He'd never come back. He reached the door when she screamed again.

'Stop.'

The command was so loud, so shrill, so forcefully emitted that he obeyed without thinking.

'Strip.' Lexi pointed to the carved wooden chest where he was expected to deposit his polluted clothing.

It was back to Plan A. He stripped and, wearing only the sumo scrunchie, obediently followed his mistress up the stairs.

He removed his scrunchie and stepped into the shower. *It's not a containment field, neither is it a decontamination unit*, he reminded himself. *It's a bloody shower, and that's all it is.* He made it a quick one and stood waiting for Lexi to allow him into the white chamber. Holodeck. Bedroom.

Plan A began as soon as he was seated in the towel-draped chair and Lexi was in charge of the hairdryer. He waited patiently until his long tresses were almost dry before beginning Stage One. Nonchalantly, he lifted his right hand to scratch the side of his head. No reaction. On to Stage Two. He wiggled his little finger in his earhole. There was an intake of breath from behind him. He tensed. Cause of death—bashed by a BaByliss. Haemorrhage caused by a hairdryer. Nothing happened, so it was on to the third and final stage.

In cold blood, in the brilliant light from the hundred and fifty watt bulb, and with no rehearsal, Will removed his finger from his ear, held it in front of his face to see exactly what he'd dragged out from the depths of that orifice and, using his thumbnail, dug beneath the little fingernail and flicked the contents into the air.

The hairdryer caught him a blow on the left side of his head. He shot from the chair and turned to face his attacker. *Now*, he thought. *Now you tell me to get out and never darken your door again*, but he hadn't counted on Lexi's sexual appetite. She'd been expecting her orgasm almost two hours ago and had decided that better late than never should apply to their evening.

'Back into the shower with you,' she yelled, pointing the dryer like a Smith & Wesson .38 revolver.

Will obeyed from force of habit. He picked up the soap. Why hadn't she chucked him out? Why had his plan failed? What could he do that was worse? More disgusting?

The new idea hit him harder than the hairdryer had. Leaving the shower running, he let himself out onto the landing, ran down the stairs and opened the wooden chest where he'd deposited his clothes. Fumbling for his jeans, he reached into the pocket... Plan B had to work. Every woman hated bbf.

It took courage to boldly go back to her. He wet his hair before returning and sat motionless while she dried it. Lexi put down the dryer, walked around the chair to face him and held out her hands. He took them in his and stood up. Unusually for him, his penis didn't. They both stared down at it. Lexi in horror. Will in admiration. How had he managed that? He must be cured. So, while her eyes still concentrated on the lower half of his torso, he did it.

This time, he used his index finger, poking it into his navel, wiggling it and coming out with...

Here's one I made earlier, he wanted to shout. *Scraped from the lining of my pocket.*

...a little ball of belly button fluff.

Mrs Alexandra Camberlege finally said the words he longed to hear. 'Fuck off out of my life.' Of course she was hitting him at the same time, her balled fists beating at his head and shoulders, but it was worth it. Will ran for the exit, grabbing in the open chest for his clothes. He'd learned his lesson. No more exploring strange new worlds for him.

25

'In last week's exciting episode, our intrepid hero, Kurt King, nominated best pilot in the Universe for six star-years running, was locked inside a time machine, stolen from Professor Bowk by the evil Emperor Zig. Through the window of his time machine prison, Kurt could see his beloved Betty Bowk, bound and gagged.'

The screen, which had been in black and white, exploded into colour. Dilys gave a squeal of delight. To celebrate the programme's success, the producers had decided that from episode twenty-five onwards, the monochrome would have to go. Perversely, this defeated what they had originally set out to do, which was create a spoof of the old forties and fifties science fiction adventures.

Kurt King had dark brown hair with blond streaks. His eyes were violet, probably those fancy-coloured contact lenses, decided Dilys. No one could have eyes that colour.

'By the time I have finished sending you back in time,' leered the evil Emperor Zig, 'you will be a leetle boy once more. Ha, ha, ha.' His depraved laughter echoed around the set as he twiddled the red, amber and green painted disposable paper plates that passed as knobs and were carelessly glued on the side of the large open-fronted crate in which Kurt sat.

Dilys knew that the crate, sorry, time machine, wasn't really open. An invisible force field was holding the hero captive.

Kurt King began to shake, as if he were sitting on top of a badly balanced washing machine performing its fast spin cycle. The picture blurred, then cleared to show the face of a teenager with dark brown hair and blond streaks. He also wore violet contact lenses. The screen blurred again. The camera took a close up of Betty Bowk in a long pink nightie. Her gag was missing. Her mouth opened to let out a squeaky scream.

Shakily, the camera moved back to the time machine, where a small boy of about five sat wearing a badly fitting dark brown wig with blond streaks. His eyes, wide in fear and amazement, were brown.

'One more twist and you will be a baby,' threatened the emperor. 'Two more and you will cease to exist.'

And return to Betty Bowk with gag back in position and dainty wrists secured by huge loops of rope. She squirmed in her chair, rolled her eyes and made a valiant attempt at slipping her hands free.

'Bloody hell,' shouted Dilys. 'Talk about a wimp. You can get out of there. Our Nesta could get her thigh through that.'

Professor Bowk's head popped out from behind a polystyrene rock.

'Stop, or I shoot!' Professor Bowk stepped from his hiding place, holding a foil-covered Fairy liquid bottle in his hand.

'That's right. Fill him full of bubbles,' shouted Dilys.

Behind the professor stood Radney the Robot, all peeling silver foil and peeping bits of brown cardboard. Behind Radney, Blublobbery shuffled in. The friendly alien was, true to its name, blue.

Dilys catapulted from her armchair to press Pause so she could take in Blublobbery. If she could duplicate the costume, she might pluck up enough courage to go to the *Zany Scrapes* convention. No one would ever recognise her underneath that lot.

She pressed Play.

Blublobbery, on invisible feet, shuffled across to Radney. From beneath its rags, a hand and arm materialised, clad in a long blue ruffled evening glove. Blue fingers tugged at the robot's cardboard leg until Radney shambled over to the time machine. Slowly, Radney turned the time dials back. The little lad disappeared to be replaced by the teenager, who in turn disappeared to be replaced by Kurt King. A star sparkled on his teeth as he smiled. Leaping from the time machine...

'Why didn't you do that before, you pillock?' shouted Dilys.

...he crossed the floorboards in two giant strides and tugged at the ropes securing his beloved. Betty fell into his open arms. Their lips brushed.

No one noticed evil Emperor Zig drag the time machine away.

'Will the evil emperor escape?' asked a deep voice. 'Will he use his depraved invention again? Can our hero, Kurt King, stop him? Tune in same time next week and all will be revealed.'

Dilys stopped the tape and rewound it to where Blublobbery made its entrance. Blublobbery was the shortest of all the characters. Well, she was no Amazon. She pressed Pause again and knelt on the rug in front of the screen. The friendly alien was an unknown human beneath an umbrella-like framework strewn with enough rags and old net curtains to ensure the actor's anonymity.

Dilys had enough old clothes and net curtains lying about. There was even a golf brolly somewhere. 'I can do that,' said Dilys. 'I can be Blublobbery. All I'll have to buy is some dye.'

She switched off the television and went to make a cup of chocolate. 'Yes, you begin with C,' she said to the tin of Cadbury's, 'but for tonight, you can be BD. Bedtime drink. OK?'

As she whisked the powder into the boiling milk, she thought of her best friend. 'And who's making your bedtime drink, Gail?'

'Would you like a brandy with your coffee?'

'Would I?'

'This could mean you have your nightcap here in Mad Hatter's and then there's no excuse to ask if he'd like to come in for a nightcap?' Her agony aunt had a habit of turning up when she wasn't needed. 'Or,' she continued, 'you could say yes, and have cocoa later.'

'Brandy always sounds so sophisticated,' replied Gail, 'and that's what I'm trying to be.'

'Yes,' she said. It meant she could stop thinking. Her thoughts were too confused. Addled by alcohol, with a touch of lust thrown in. And her agony aunt had been no help.

The first part of the evening, all Chas had talked about was his wife, Avril, then he'd apologised and asked Gail about herself, but when she'd started telling him, he'd sat staring into space, leaving her with the impression that he either wasn't listening or was bored out of his skull. She was tempted to test her turning-a-deaf-one theory by throwing in a few gory details about the mother with the dog-pee-on-snow hair colour, or how about a graphic description of that row of stinking cat saucers?

They had moved to a huge squashy sofa in the new conservatory. Pearl and Guy had left an hour previously, too wrapped up in each other and around each other to notice Gail, Chas or anyone else in the restaurant.

Gail, drifting in her alcohol-induced stupor, was aware of Chas's hand resting on her knee. She was

also aware that she was the envy of many of the other
women in the place. She sipped her brandy and tried
to smile. Yuck. She'd sooner have had a nice glass of
paraffin. Quick, get the chocolate mint to take the
taste away.

Once the mint was unwrapped and in her mouth,
she picked up her coffee cup and leaned back into
the cushions, concentrating on not spilling anything.
She felt bloated. A four-course meal, wine, coffee,
mint, brandy. No wonder.

She stifled a yawn closely followed by a burp.

'You're beautiful,' he murmured.

She knew it was a lie. Passable in a good light,
yes. Beautiful, no. If Bradley had told her she was
beautiful, she'd have asked him what he was after and
probably thumped him at the same time. So, what
was Chas after? He'd wined and dined her and was
now whispering sweet nothings. Did he really want
to get her into his bed? Did she really want to get into
it?

'*Sweet nothings, ooooo sweet nothings.*' The tune
danced through her head, but she couldn't remember any more of the words.

Chas removed the hand resting on her knee and
picked up his brandy goblet.

Gail, sick of chanting the same couple of words,
gave up on the sweet nothings and changed her tune
to, '*Do you think I'm sexy?*'

While he paid the bill, she went to the ladies. In
the oval mirror above the washbasin, her face was
sagging. Dark rings were forming under her eyes. As
dark as the fillings in her back teeth, which were on
full display in the mirror as she yawned widely. With
a fingertip, she patted the beneath-the-eye begin-
ning-to-crepe skin.

She smoothed in a little extra foundation, which
promised instant lift and wide eyes. *I reckon Cin-*

derella was in her fifties and that's why she had to get home before midnight, so she didn't turn into a crumpled, exhausted old bag and frighten off Prince Charming.

Chas was waiting outside the door. 'Your place or mine?' he asked, lifting his eyebrow and giving that dangerous smile, the one that belonged to the real George Clooney.

Gail shivered and pulled her shawl tighter around her shoulders. Would she be having second thoughts if she were with the real one? Huh. As if she'd ever be in that situation. Mr Clooney was a fantasy and therefore OK to dream about. On the other hand, this Clooney lookalike was real flesh and blood and male urges and instincts and had been without his wife for six weeks or more, even longer if Avril had been denying him his conjugal rights because the chiropodist was keeping her happy.

She came to a decision. 'Home, and don't spare the horses. My home. It's been a lovely evening but I am getting tired. I've been so busy lately.'

When the taxi stopped outside her house, Gail gave Chas a peck on the cheek. 'Thank you for a lovely evening,' she said. She'd been rehearsing it all the way home.

Five minutes later, she was sitting in front of her dressing table mirror, slapping cleanser on her face. It was an effort but she had too many make-up-stained pillowslips already. As she smoothed in the age-reducing moisturiser, knowing it was too late to bother and she could have bought the jar that wasn't age-reducing for a couple of quid cheaper, she thought about the blonde bimbos who hung on to footballers' arms. What did they call them? Trophy wives. That was it, but with her and Chas, it was the other way around. She certainly wasn't gorgeous enough to be the trophy, but he was.

Pearl's voice suddenly filled the bedroom. 'Beauty's only skin-deep.'

'Yes, Mother,' said Gail, shaking her head to rid herself of the spectre of the split-skirted vampire. Some of those old sayings were perfectly true. Chas was a head-turner all right but...

'I *did* have a good time. I *did* enjoy myself.' She rubbed in the hand lotion as if she were trying to remove a layer of skin.

Come off it. Who are you trying to kid?

Gail wormed her way into the middle of the double bed and, rolling onto her side, wondered what it would have been like to lie there and gaze into the eyes of Mr Clooney.

'Shit. He isn't George.'

'*No, but you could have closed your eyes and pretended,*' said her agony aunt, clad in pink spotted pyjamas. '*Then you could have crossed off "get laid" from your to-do list.*'

No. It had been a pleasant enough evening, apart from the Pearl episode, but it hadn't exactly been a laugh a minute.

'*Describe your date in three words,*' challenged her agony aunt.

Gail's response was immediate. 'Humourless. Sexless. Magicless.'

Dilys lay in bed, dreaming of the *Zany Scrapes* convention. Should she go? What sort of people went to these things? Sad bastards, probably.

'Is that what I am?' she said, sitting up in bed and staring into the darkness. 'Dilys Lloyd. Failed wife. Failed mother. I even failed my driving test twice. Dilys Lloyd. Complete failure.'

She groped around until she found the switch for the bedside light. That cup of chocolate had been very wet. What she could do with was something to soak it up. A couple of minutes later, she was back in bed accompanied by a whole family-sized chocolate Swiss roll.

'Dilys Lloyd,' she began again. A shower of cake crumbs hit the duvet. 'Messy eater.' She wondered why she was talking aloud when there was no one to hear her. 'Shouldn't talk with your mouth full,' she told herself. Aloud. There was a couple of inches of cake left. She forced it all in and sat chewing. Oooh, it was good. Chocolate sponge cake rolled around a creamy chocolate filling and covered in real chocolate. With a moistened finger, she picked up the stray crumbs, switched off the light and snuggled under the duvet. Overdosing on chocolate always lifted her spirits. 'Goodnight, Dilys Lloyd. Company director, Slimmer of the Week and about to be the best bloody Blublobbery seen outside the television studios.'

Chas hung up his suit, dropped his shirt into the laundry basket and sighed. Damn Avril and her chiropodist. They were welcome to each other. It was back to being single for him. A different woman every night and a row of fresh notches on the headboard of the king-size bed. He stared at his reflection in the mirror and lifted an eyebrow. It had taken him months of practice to perfect that. Good-looking or what? Of course he was. So, why was he getting into bed alone? OK, perhaps he was out of practice. It had been a while since he'd bedded anyone other than Avril. A couple of years. But his charm had always worked on the ladies before, so why not now? Why was Gail Lockwood so different?

He looked into the mirror. 'Who could resist you?' he asked his reflection.

Guy rolled over and admired the view. Pearl's pink hairnet, handstitched with sequins, sparkled in the light from the streetlamp outside the window, vying with the golden glow of her hair.

Pearl rolled onto her back and gave a loud snore.

Guy, propping himself on one elbow, watched her sleeping and smiled.

'I suppose I'll have to sleep with you,' she'd told him. 'No choice now you've sold my bed.'

Bradley gave a low moan. He had another six nights lying on the breeze-blocks that the hospital was passing off as a mattress. Breeze-blocks covered in shiny plastic that made him sweat and creaked and groaned every time he moved. And he had to survive five whole days of Brenda playing nursie, spoon-feeding him with cornflakes and threatening to kiss him better.

On the white expanse of the ceiling, he pictured his plane sinking through thick grey clouds and landing in fine drizzle. Perhaps there'd be a rainbow. Wonderful British weather. And there was Gail... He drifted into sleep, imagining her wrapped in his arms, making love on the airport tarmac. It was marginally softer than the hospital bed.

26

Monday, 13 March

The bosses and employees of Girls Will were holding their Monday morning meeting in Tamsin's tidy flat. Jez was certainly performing miracles. The coffee table was empty. Gail placed the paperwork on it, crossed her fingers and announced, 'Girls Will is going well, better than I ever hoped.'

'We've got enough work for this week and next,' said Dilys.

'And we're getting several phone calls a day,' said Gail. 'I'm hoping we can get enough work to keep the four of us busy.'

'You will, Mum. I know you will.' Tamsin had never looked happier.

'If you can contact the people on this list. They're all prospective customers. Here's my diary so you can make appointments. And can you type out these invoices?'

Tamsin nodded. 'Fine. It'll all be done before Gran gets here at lunchtime.'

'Will Guy be with her?' asked Gail. She wanted a few words with him. About missing furniture.

'Dunno,' said Tam, getting up in answer to a wail from Jack's bedroom. 'See you later,' she called over her shoulder.

Dilys was happy for Nesta to drop her off in town. Her task was to get Mrs Carrington's shopping. No supermarket stuff. It was all from the posh places. The little deli and the organic shop, which meant Dil could seek out some sky-blue Dylon at the same time.

Nesta had an appointment with her doctor. Blood pressure. 'See you up at Hill House,' she wheezed as she squeezed behind the wheel of her Mini.

Gail took a deep breath. It was up to her, then. She was the only one left, the only one to tackle Alexandra Camberlege's pristine palace.

'Oh, hello,' gushed Lexi. 'If it isn't William Bassett's non-wife. In the flesh. Tell me again, what is it you are to him?'

'Landlady,' snapped Gail. 'And I'm also in charge of Girls Will.' *Leave Dilys out of this.* 'It's my company, so you've got the boss today.'

'Goodie.' Lexi rubbed her hands together. 'You can start with the bedrooms. Wait there while I run up and check they're ready for you.'

Gail stood in the hall, admiring the wooden chests standing on either side of the door, not knowing that the one on the right was where her lodger's underpants lodged while he was up the stairs giving Mrs Camberlege her weight-reducing treatments.

'Ready,' called Lexi.

Gail picked up her basket of cleaning equipment.

'Five bedrooms, three ensuite, and the family bathroom.' Lexi waved a hand to denote the upper storey of her kingdom. 'That should keep you busy.' She made a dramatic Hollywood-style descent of the curved staircase and disappeared.

Gail opened the first door, stared at the immaculate interior of a long-unused but well-dusted bedroom and sighed. This was the Lexi Game. Nesta had told her all about it. A sort of Hunt the Thimble crossed with Hide and Seek. Apparently, Lexi left something in each room. Maybe it was a book on the bed or a curtain hanging skew-whiff. It could be a lone fingerprint on the mirror or a hairbrush adorning the dressing tabletop at not quite a ninety-degree angle.

'There's never any cleaning to be done,' Nesta had assured Gail. 'She does all that before we get there. All we have to do is spot the deliberate mistake. Then she thinks we've done a real good job.'

So, *where and what is it today?* Gail hunted around. Not a thing out of place, unless... yes, it had to be. The valance around the bed was slightly, ever so slightly, rumpled. Gail smoothed it and stepped back. Perfection or what?

She moved to the next room. Easy. A hair on the silk eiderdown. Then she discovered half an inch of sludge in the crystal shell that held the soap. Bathroom done.

The next few were more difficult. A fingernail-sized scrap of paper beneath the bed. A thread of cotton hanging from a curtain. One of the hangers in the wardrobe facing in the opposite direction to the others. Now, who did that remind her of? Chas.

It was the first time that morning she'd thought of him. *That should tell me something,* she thought, turning the hanger around. But as his face appeared on the inside of the wardrobe door, her knees went weak. God, he was gorgeous, and she must have been a bloody idiot to spurn his advances. Spurn his advances? Sounded like something from a historical novel. She put Chas in white armour on a white horse. No. It didn't work. He was useless as a knight. Much better to leave him as he was. A Clooney lookalike. At that, he was perfection.

Lexi's room was the final challenge. Gail glanced at her watch. Playing this bloody stupid game was as time-consuming as doing the actual cleaning. Then she reminded herself that Lexi thought she was doing the actual cleaning and, because she was doing a thorough job, she was putting right the dreadfully untidy wrongs that littered the beautiful house.

Right. Lexi's bedroom. This could be a toughie.

Gail opened the door. The mistake leapt at her, hitting her like a slap in the face. Her hands shook as she crossed the room towards it. With no glasses on, she had to be sure.

Lexi's bed was unmade. The covers thrown back, the bottom sheet creased. A dent on each pillow. More than a dent on the one. Gail advanced slowly. She picked up the object from the pillow and turned it in her fingers.

The scrunchie was fluorescent green and had a white sumo wrestler stitched to it.

'Hiya, I'm back.' Nesta bustled into the room. 'Bloomin' 'eck, Gail. What's up?'

'Nothing,' said Gail, stuffing the scrunchie into the pocket of her jeans. And then, because she could see Nesta didn't believe her, she felt obliged to add, 'Just fed up with Lexi's silly games. There's nothing at all to clean.'

'That's 'cause she's already done it all.' Nesta nodded and her chins wobbled. 'Here. Have a chunk of peppermint rock.'

Gail crunched on the rock. So, Will and Lexi were definitely having a relationship. She'd guessed as much. But why would Lexi leave the scrunchie for her to find? Unless... no, she couldn't possibly be. Lexi with her figure, money, house and car couldn't possibly be jealous. Gail nearly choked on her rock.

'You all right to finish up here?' she asked Nesta. 'I'm off to the airport.' Bradley was being released early due to good behaviour.

Nesta nodded. Her chins wobbled again.

Bradley ran his fingers through his lopped off hair. The Kevin Keegan curls had gone. The short style suited him and showed off the bruises around his eyes, which the curls might well have covered, or at least shadowed. Now, they were on full display. He was all out for the sympathy vote. As he reached the doors, he thanked the attendant who had pushed his wheelchair.

'I'll walk from here,' he said. 'I want to impress the girlfriend.'

And he did. Only, Gail wasn't exactly his girlfriend. And his walk was more of a pronounced limp. When he saw her waving to him, he added thumps to his lumps and bumps. His heart had grown some lower limbs that were stamping up and down in his chest.

'Bradley!' Her voice was all concern. She stood on tiptoe to plant the tiniest of gentle kisses on his cheek.

'You smell wonderful,' he said. 'Of polish.'

'That'll be Mr Sheen,' answered Gail.

'Should I be jealous?'

Gail laughed and stood back to take a good look at her old boss. The white suit and the golden tan were pure BJ, but the long curls had vanished. 'You'd look younger and fitter if it weren't for the limp and the bruises,' she said.

'And I'd look happier if you loved me.'

'I do love you.' Gail thumped his arm, and he groaned. 'Come on, let's get you home. I hope you can manage the stairs. I'm not carrying you up to bed.'

'How did you know that was one of my favourite fantasies?'

Gail laughed again. Bradley was back, and it felt wonderful.

Will was waiting on the step as the Clio drew up outside the house. Gail wanted a few words with him. Her hand slid into her pocket and squeezed the scrunchie. Will and Lexi. If they were an item, it would explain a lot. Like Lexi searching her out and asking about her husband.

'Good grief, Bradley. You look as if you've fallen off a third-floor balcony,' Will quipped.

'Funny you should say that.' Bradley grimaced.

Will helped him out of the car.

'Come on. Let's get you into bed,' said Gail. 'You look exhausted.'

Bradley winked. 'Talk about a fast worker.'

'Sorry to tell you this, Gail, but your mother's waiting inside.' As Will spoke, Gail saw the net curtains twitch. Yes, that would be Mother. 'And she's got her boyfriend with her.'

It was Gail's turn to groan. She wanted a word with Guy too. Prioritise, she told herself. Get Bradley settled first, then tackle the furniture thief and leave Will until last. Or leave Will out of it altogether. Were his affairs any of her business?

They were barely through the door when Pearl leapt into action, her radioactive hair frizzed out by the energy vibrating from her.

'What's *he* doing here?' she screamed, pointing a witchy finger at Bradley.

'Moving in.' Bradley gave his widest grin.

'*Mother*,' wailed Gail in exasperation.

Bradley flopped into the nearest armchair. 'You carry on. I'll just sit here quietly. I've been missing this particular soap.'

'Bradley's had an accident. He's going to stay here,' said Gail.

Pearl managed to leer and interrupt at the same time. 'Until he gets better, I suppose. And how long is that going to take, eh?' She prodded Bradley's leg with her foot. A foot shod in a white pointed-toed, stiletto-heeled shoe. A foot at the end of a leg clad in black tights. 'He's the sort who'll turn into a permanent invalid.'

Gail looked around for help. There was none. Will had done a disappearing act. Bradley sat with an inane grin on his face. And Guy, well, he was less than useless, hiding behind a newspaper, pretending nothing was happening.

And while Gail searched for help, Pearl continued. 'Fill the place up with men, why don't you? First, William Bassett, then that Chas bloke. Yes, I've heard about him. And now Bradley Jones.'

It took a split second for Pearl to suck in a breath. Gail took advantage of it and, trying to change the subject, said, 'I've been meaning to ask you, Mum, what's happened to all your furniture?'

'We sold it at an auction,' said Pearl. 'And, while we were there, we bought you a present. Another man for your collection.'

For a moment, Gail thought Pearl was about to hand Guy over, but the gnarled hand, with the huge solitaire diamond engagement ring—the what?—went right past his head and dipped behind the sofa to drag out a life-size cardboard cut-out of George Clooney.

Gail's knees went weak as they always did at the sight of her hero. The shock of the ring and the present left her speechless. A condition her mother had never been in.

'Of course,' Pearl carried on regardless, 'one man's enough for me.'

This was Guy's cue. He dropped the newspaper, stood up and placed a hand protectively on Pearl's shoulder. 'We've come to tell you we're getting married,' he said.

Weak-kneed and speechless, Gail sank, missing Bradley's lap by inches and landing on the arm of his chair. She gave a yelp as he pinched her bum.

'Congratulate your mum,' he said, 'and say thank you for the nice present.'

27

'Shock. Horror. Shock. Horror,' chanted Gail. It was the only way she could explain what she was feeling. Lying in the scalding bath of Time Out bubbles, she considered submerging herself until she stopped breathing. It was impossible to get her head around her mother remarrying. At her age. And so soon.

I've been blind. And stupid. I thought Mum and her Jag were ready for the scrapheap. But the car wasn't in for repairs, and Mum's about to start a new life.

The scrapheap loomed in Gail's imagination, but this time, jutting from the top of it was a springboard, and the whole family were queuing up on it. Gail leapt first and landed on her feet, and in her red suit. Tam followed her, somersaulting through the air and coming to rest on Jez's lap in the made-over living room. Finally, Pearl flew from the springboard, zooming downwards until she dropped directly into a huge meringue of a wedding dress.

Aaah, Guy's new suit. Another mystery solved. A bath was the best place for thinking. He'd bought it for his wedding, and she'd thought he'd paid for it from the proceeds of her mother's furniture, when in fact the happy couple had been selling stuff off so that their worldly goods would fit into one house. Guy's house, which her mother had already moved into, taking Arnie and the cat-gang with her. Mother, living in sin with Guy.

Bradley lay back on the pillows, the ones Gail had plumped up for him, and sipped the tea and nibbled the toast Gail had made for him. He let out a sigh of pure pleasure. His first night back in Britain, where he belonged. And better than that, he was living under the same roof as Gail. When Gail came to bed, there'd only be a wall separating them. Oh, for a sledgehammer.

For fifteen years, he'd considered Gail his best friend, and it hadn't been until all his plans of an early retirement in the sunshine had been made that it had hit him. People often fall in love with their best friends. He had, and it was hard to believe. All those years working together and not realising how much she meant to him.

He sent out a prayer of thanks to Jimmy, who had arranged his escape. Poor bloody Jimmy. 'I don't know why I'm doing this,' he'd said as he drove Bradley to the airport. 'I've had a respite from darling Brenda since you arrived.'

'You're a real mate,' Bradley had told him.

'If I had any sense, I'd turn around right now and deliver you into her clutches. She's itching to nurse you back to health. No doubt, she'd dress in a nurse's uniform too. You'd only have to ask.'

Bradley shuddered and pulled the duvet closer to his chin at the thought of it.

The rap on his door shattered the image of Brenda in black stockings and blue cotton minidress with white pinny and matching cap. Not that Bradley had seen a nurse dressed like that this century. He was reinventing images from old *Carry On* films.

'Come in.' He crossed his fingers, hoping it wouldn't be Will making a late-night visit.

It was Gail in a fluffy red dressing gown, the material far too thick and not the slightest bit see-through. She sat on the bed and took his empty mug from him.

'You OK?' They both said it together.

Bradley gave a minimalist nod. His head was aching.

'Dunno,' said Gail.

'Want to talk about it?' Bradley held out his hand.

'It's Mother. Getting married. Do I really want to murder her, or is it my hormones playing up? I don't know what to think.'

'Be glad,' said Bradley, without hesitation. Gail was holding his hand. 'She won't be needing you so much. She'll have her husband. And be very glad she didn't ask you to be Matron of Honour.'

For the first time since Pearl had dropped her bombshell, Gail smiled. 'Thanks, Bradley. I've missed you.' She stood up and bent to kiss him, aiming at his forehead. He jerked his head up quickly, but not quickly enough. The kiss landed on his nose. 'Goodnight,' she said.

'You're not going, are you? You're not going to leave me here, all alone and sick? I've got a terrible headache. What if I slip into a coma during the night?'

'I'll leave a note for my great-great-granddaughter to kiss you in a hundred years' time and wake you up.' Gail laughed, dodged his grasping hand and was out of the door before he could say 'paracetamol'.

'Tomorrow's fairly quiet,' said Tamsin. The Girls Will diary sat on her lap, her finger tracing the few jobs listed for Tuesday. Jack sat on Gail's lap. Nesta's lap held a giant paper bag filled with Pick'n'Mix. And Dilys sat, trying to hide her hands in her lap, tucking them into the folds of her skirt. In a hurry to complete her Blublobbery outfit, she'd dyed her net curtains before buying any new rubber gloves to replace the split pair she'd thrown out. The results had been amazing. Sky-blue nets with matching fingers, palms, nails... everything as far as her wrists.

'It'll be even quieter once I've told Lexi,' said Gail, trying not to stare at Dilys's hands, which were an azure blue. Hands that were discreetly unwrapping a nut praline.

'Tell 'er what?' demanded Nesta, peeling the paper from a hazelnut whirl.

'Tell 'er what, Gwanny?' Jack was going to have a gift for impersonation once he'd managed to get his tongue around his Rrrrs.

Gail took a deep breath. 'Tell her we're not going to work for her any longer.' She popped a Turkish delight into her mouth.

'You must be mad,' piped up Dilys.

'I'll second that,' added Nesta. 'Talk about money for old rope.'

'Old wope, old wope,' chanted Jack, chewing one of Nesta's caramels.

'We can't do it,' said Gail. 'The woman's sick. She should get help.'

'And is that what you're going to tell her? Sooner you than me,' said Nesta, combining a strawberry creme with an orange one.

Arnie circled three times before plucking at the purple silk with his magnificent claws.

'Naughty boy. Shoo.' Pearl clapped her hands loudly but not loudly enough to bother the ginger tom, though he did stop treading on the material long enough to stare up at her. 'That's my wedding dress,' she told him. 'Now, get off it, or I won't bring you any smoked salmon back from my reception.'

Arnie leapt from the chair over which the dress had been draped. Pearl didn't mind the cat hairs and didn't bother to brush them off, but she didn't want to be ironing the long silken folds of the floor-length ballgown she'd discovered in the Sue Ryder shop. It fitted perfectly and was a real bargain at ten pounds. Of course, it wasn't the right time of year to be posing outside the registry office in a strapless gown but that had been easily solved. In one of the boxes she hadn't unpacked since her move to Guy's was the most wonderful green chenille tablecloth with a long gold fringe around its edges. Folded in half, it would make a perfect cape and keep her shoulders nice and warm. The fringe would match her shoes and her hair.

Pity about Guy putting his foot down about brides-maids. Gail and Tamsin would have looked a treat, the two of them in green dresses with purple cloaks, and Jack could have been a pageboy. Never mind Gail would have probably been awkward and refused to wear whatever was chosen for her anyway. Guy was right. Small ceremony followed by big party for all their friends. And to prove how magnanimous she could be, she'd posted invitations to everyone, including Dreadful Dilys and William Sponging Bas-sett. They should be receiving them, first class, that morning. She decided to hand-deliver the final one to that idiot, Bradley Jones. It would mean he'd re-ceive his at the same time as everyone else and allow her to check up on what he was doing. *I'll add a PS,* she thought. *Tell him not to wear that white suit. If I'm not wearing white, I don't see why anyone else should.*

Lexi stood, panting, in the middle of the immacu-late sitting room. She'd finished cleaning it from top to bottom and wondered where she should place the inch length of white cotton in the white room. On the carpet or a cushion or under the white vase of white lilies? It was the only way she could be sure that the staff of Girls Will were doing their job properly. If the cotton was still there when they'd gone, she'd have no hesitation in sacking them and getting another agency to do the work for her.

Checking her watch, she realised that there was only half an hour left to polish and hoover upstairs before her cleaning ladies arrived. She ran from the room and was about to dash up to the bedrooms when the door knocked. Smoothing down her hair, she went to answer it.

'It's you. You're early,' she cried in dismay.

'Yes, we should talk.' Gail pushed her way in. 'I'm sorry, Lexi, but we can't do the cleaning for you. There's nothing for us to do, is there? You've already done it all before we get here, and I really feel we can't take your money. It's unethical.' Gail was pleased with the word. Unethical. Yes, that was good.

'B-b-but...' began Lexi, 'b-b-but...' She burst into tears.

Gail was frozen to the spot. Bloody hell. She'd expected tantrums, not tears. How was she going to deal with this?

'I can't do it all on my own.' Lexi, the slim, beautiful and rich siren who had lured Will Bassett into her bed and let Gail know about it in her own inimitable way, began to sob.

Gail pulled a tissue from her pocket and passed it to the transformed Mrs Camberlege. The snivelling, pitiful and crumpled sick woman who couldn't stop cleaning.

Lexi wiped her eyes and nose and then began a fresh bout of crying. Gail held out her arms and, like a child, Lexi fell into them.

'Get some help,' she said. 'See a doctor. Tell them all about it. I'll come with you if you want.'

'Would you?' Lexi sniffed.

'I'll phone now. Right now.' *Before you have chance to change your mind.*

'It's Dr Holliday.' Sniffing suited Lexi. Made her seem more human.

Cat-Woman, the evil receptionist, answered the phone. 'Nothing for at least a fortnight,' she trilled, sounding ecstatic about the long wait.

'It's for Mrs Alexandra Camberlege,' said Gail.

'Bring her straight in.'

Money talks, thought Gail as, with her arm still around her charge, she led her out of the door and towards the dusty, old and battered Clio.

'Hiya, Boss,' cried Dilys, cheerfully, peeping around the bedroom door. 'You respectable?'

'Yep,' said Bradley, folding his newspaper and removing his specs.

'Then I won't bother coming in,' quipped Dilys, but she was sitting on the bed before she'd finished speaking. 'How are you?'

Bradley groaned.

'Oops. Silly question. You look black and blue.'

'Not as blue as you. What have you been up to?' Bradley stared at Dil's hands.

'Dyeing some curtains,' said Dilys. 'Without gloves on. Fancy a cuppa?' she asked, changing the subject. 'Gail asked me to call in and check on you, but I'd have come anyway.'

Over a pot of tea, with added hot water for BJ so it was weak and willing, they exchanged news. Bradley gave a condensed version of life in the sun and being chased by Brenda, the femme fatale. Dilys gave a colourful version of her daughter's wedding and the birth of Girls Will followed by a technicoloured account of the blossoming relationship between Gail and Chas Henderson, poncy owner of the gentlemen's outfitters and possessor of painted nails.

'But he is bloody good to feast your eyes on,' she finished, not noticing BJ's face turn white, albeit with black and blue splodges.

'Getting on well, are they?' asked Bradley.

'Must be. He took her to that posh place, Mad Hatter's. Costs a bleeding fortune there.'

Bradley gave a huge sigh.

'You getting tired? I'd better go and leave you in peace. Oooh, nearly forgot.' She tossed a paper bag onto the bed. 'It's Arnica from the health shop. I got you tablets and cream. S'posed to be good for bruising. Want a quick rub down? Anything I can get you before I leave?'

Yeah, that sledgehammer, thought Bradley. *First, I'll knock down the wall that separates me from my love and then I'll knock out that bastard who's chasing my woman.*

'Stick the plug in the bath for me,' he said. 'My head hurts when I bend over.'

'Aaah.' It was a cross between a groan of pain and a sigh of relief as, five minutes later, Bradley lowered himself into the hot water. Gail had given him some bubbly stuff that purported to ease aching muscles and relax the mind. It wasn't working. He settled back on the inflatable head cushion and tried not to think of Gail with another man. His unsuccessful attempts were disturbed by the bathroom door crashing open.

'Pearl!' Bradley diverted a floating cushion of bubbles so that it sat over his private parts.

'I wondered where you'd got to,' said Pearl. 'Thought you were supposed to be too sick to get out of bed. I've brought you this.' She approached the bath.

Bradley slipped further into the bubbles and held out his hand to take the envelope she was offering him.

Pearl snatched it away. 'You'll get it all wet,' she snapped, 'and they cost a lot of money. It's an invitation to my wedding. Don't RSVP. I'll expect to see you there.' It was a royal command.

'I won't disappoint you,' said Bradley.

He thought he heard Pearl mutter, 'Pity', as she dropped the invitation onto the bathmat and flew out of the door.

Cat-Woman was all smiles. 'Hello, Mrs Camberlege. Doctor won't keep you waiting more than a few minutes.'

And, to Gail's disgust, he didn't.

Once Lexi was in with the doctor, Gail sifted through the old magazines on the table. The Chenwick Echo's magazine dated January. She remembered it well. Madame Gladys and her amazing horoscopes. This was the issue Bradley had read out to her because she hadn't had her specs and, from what she remembered, Madame Gladys had been spot on. Awkward family, money in the bank and...

Gail did a double take. Virgo. Yes, she was reading the forecast for Virgos. She checked the date on the front cover. Yes, it was the same one Bradley had read to her, but the horoscope was nothing like it.

'Family,' it said. 'A close family member could change their ways. Money. Invest wisely. Keep frivolous purchases to a minimum.' *Frivolous purchases? Don't make me laugh.* 'Love. A bleak time for Virgos. Long-term relationships should be nurtured.'

Gail checked the other star signs. Perhaps Bradley had read the wrong one by mistake. No. And then the light bulb above her head switched on. Idiot. He'd made it all up, and what had he said about love?

'Don't let the man of your dreams slip through your fingers.'

'The man of your dreams.' The agony aunt was back again. 'It's not Will. It's not the doctor.' She had a smudge of Passionate Pink lipstick on her front teeth. 'It's certainly not Guy. It's not even Chas. Now, tell me, who does that leave?'

'Not *Bradley. Definitely not Bradley. No. Bradley's lovely and caring and fun but no way is he the man of my dreams.*'

The pink lady gave a condescending pink smile. '*Methinks the lady doth protest...*'

'Bugger off,' hissed Gail.

The agony aunt disappeared just as Lexi re-emerged, after sobbing her heart out under the watchful eyes and attentive ears of Doc Holliday. She was clutching a prescription for Prozac and a sealed letter she was to present to an eminent psychiatrist who, the doctor had assured her, would soon have her sorted out.

Cat-Woman purred goodbye.

'You *can* beat this,' said Gail as they crossed the car park.

'Mmm,' mumbled Lexi, then for the first time, she noticed the chariot that had carried her to the surgery. 'Is that yours?' Her nose wrinkled in disgust.

''Fraid so,' said Gail.

'I won't take up any more of your time. There's a taxi rank around the corner.'

'Fine.' *Beating your illness is going to be a long job. God help your eminent shrink. He'll be seeing one himself before he's through with you.*

Gail was still seething at the way she'd been dismissed without a thank you as she placed Will's evening meal on the table.

'Chicken casserole, and you can try this for afters.' From the greatest height she could manage, Gail dropped the fluorescent green scrunchie onto Will's plate. The sumo wrestler glowed a poisonous white against a piece of chicken breast.

Will had the decency to choke on a chopped carrot and Gail had the pleasure of thumping him in the middle of his back. Hard.

'*Ouch.* How did you find that?'

'You mean where did I find it.'

Will coughed and pulled at his ponytail—a sure sign of guilt. 'I left it at Lexi's.' His voice was barely more than a squeak. 'I've been having a thing with her.'

Thing? A thing that involved me being the wife? No, don't scream, Gail. Keep your mouth shut. He's about to spill all and you want to hear it. Shove his dinner back in the oven to keep warm.

'It's such a relief to tell someone,' said Will. 'She's weird, you know, Gail. Seriously weird. It was like being in a vortex, getting sucked in and...'

Dropping the sumo onto Will's dinner had produced the same effect as a dam bursting. Everything poured out. Thankfully, he didn't get too explicit when it came to the sex scenes. If ever two people should never have met, it was this pair. A science fiction fanatic and a woman with compulsive behaviour disorder. And somehow, from the gospel according to her lodger, he'd managed to fit his obsession around Lexi's.

He didn't draw breath until the final scene had been related.

Gail, elbow on the table and her hand covering her mouth to disguise the smile brought on by the revelation of the belly button fluff, waited a full thirty seconds before making any comment. 'You say you are never going to see her again.'

'Never,' vowed Will, shaking his head.

'Sure?'

'Positive.' He reached across the table and took her hand. 'I'm lucky to have got out of the mess in one piece. The whole experience has made me grow up.'

'Not before time,' Gail couldn't resist adding.

Will squeezed her hand. 'Thanks, Gail. You're a real pal. It's been great to offload it. Can I have my dinner now?'

*Blublobbery, on invisible feet, shuffled across to Rad-
ney. From beneath its rags, a hand and arm materialised, clad in a long blue ruffled evening glove. A
close-up showed the blue fingers tugging at the robot's
cardboard leg.*

Dilys had watched that snatch of video a thousand
times. The outfit propped against her sofa looked
exactly like a deflated Blublobbery. Dil had painstak-
ingly stitched strips of her dyed blue net curtains and
assorted pieces of material to the stripped spines of
a golfing umbrella. All dyed blue. Once the umbrella
was opened and she was beneath it, she was a dead
ringer for the *Zany Scrapes* alien life form. The ma-
terials, all with frayed hems and of varying lengths,
either touched or dragged along the ground, making
her invisible. Originally, she'd hoped to find gloves
in case she wanted to put out a hand to greet any
of the actors or draw a cup of tea under her cover,
but after combing every charity shop, junk shop and
dress shop in Chenwick, she hadn't been able to find
a pair of long ruffled evening gloves in blue or any
other colour. She'd even considered asking Pearl if
she had any. Then, once she'd dyed all her material,
there was no need for gloves. Her hands and arms,
almost up to the elbows, were blue. Now, checking
them, it looked as if the colour was fading.

Thinking about Pearl reminded her of the surprise
invitation she'd received in that morning's post. It
had requested an RSVP. Dilys turned her attention
from her outfit and, using blue fingers, stamped
Pearl's number that was at the bottom of the invitation into her phone. She needed to know if the
invitation was for real. Anne and Roger had made a
fool out of her, and she was damned sure Pearl and
Guy weren't going to do the same. And, at the same
time, she could ask Pearl if she had any blue gloves.

'Of course we want you to come. We want every-one to join us and share in our happiness,' crooned Pearl.

Dilys spluttered. Was the mad old bat being forced to read words from a card that Guy had written for her?

'Well, if you're sure, I'd love to come,' Dilys an-swered politely. *I want to see the bridal gown, and it'll kill me if I have to wait for the photos to be developed. Pearl's bound to come up with a showstopper.*

'Now, if you don't mind, I'd like to get back to sleep,' said Pearl, doing a loud, theatrical yawn.

'There's something else I'd like to ask you,' she said quickly. 'I was wondering if you have any blue gl–'

Too late. Pearl had ended the call.

'Sleep? It's a bit early, isn't it?' Dilys shouted down the phone, knowing it was a pointless thing to do. As she replaced the receiver, the clock struck nine and the table teetered a step away from her. The phone hopped in agitation. On the wall, a picture of Chenwick town centre in 1926 tilted to one side.

'Firkinell.' It felt like an earthquake. Dilys waited a moment to see if there was going to be anoth-er tremor. No. Everything was back to normal. She looked out of the window to check if anything had fallen. Maybe a small tree or a bit of house. The only casualty she could see was a couple of slates fallen from the roof to the pavement. Back in the hall, she straightened the picture and moved the table to its original position. Then, holding up her hands, she mimed strangling Pearl.

She could manage without the gloves. She turned her hands over and glared harder at the backs. Would the dye survive until the convention?

'I'd sooner re-dye you than ask Pearl for a favour,' Dilys decided, clapping together the hands that wouldn't have been out of place on a frozen corpse.

Pearl slammed her mobile down on the bedside table and turned her attention from Dilys to Guy. It was like being a teenager again. Pearl could go so far and no further. 'It's not because I don't love you,' she explained. 'It's just that it's been such a long time.'

'I can wait. We've got all the time in the world,' Guy answered.

It wasn't strictly true. Spring chickens they were not, hence the early night. It was time to take the plunge. Pearl knew not to be the one above. That way, her face would sag, her wrinkles become exaggerated. If Guy saw her like that, he'd think he was in the sack with an ugly pug. She couldn't risk it. Not even with the curtains closed and the lights off. Giving a moan, she urged Guy on top. And then it happened.

The earth moved.

Bradley limped around the bed, did a U-turn when he reached the wall and retraced his steps. Ten three-quarter laps and his sore muscles were aching more than ever. Stopping in front of the bay window, he bent double. 'Eeeargh.' Sodding agony but it had to be done. Tuesday already and he had to be fit enough for the Wedding of the Year by Saturday.

'*Button up your overcoat*,' he sang, pulling the belt of his purple silk quilted dressing gown tighter, '*let your balls hang free.*' He'd never been sure of that second line or the next one. He straightened, puffed and tried to reach his toes again. '*da da care for yourself.*'

'*You belong to me.*' Gail, coming through the door with a tray in her hands, finished it off for him.

'I wish I did,' said Bradley, taking the tray from her. 'Hey, I can't eat all this.' He sniffed appreciatively at the two plates of chicken casserole.

'I thought I'd eat with you, seeing as you're confined to your room.'

Bradley set the tray down on the little table in front of the window. 'Not for long,' he said. 'I've got to get fit, pronto. Got a big date coming up.' He took Pearl's invitation from his pocket and waved it in front of Gail. 'You shall go to the ball, and I'll be your Prince Charming. You can save the last waltz for me.'

'Bloody hell,' swore Gail, dropping into a chair. 'What's come over Mother? Everyone's got an invitation.'

'Everyone?' asked Bradley, seeing Gail being whirled around the dance floor by Charles Henderson.

'Everyone who's anyone,' affirmed Gail. 'Now, eat up before it gets cold.'

Bradley sat on the opposite side of the little table. It was like being married. Eating dinner together. He stretched out his foot and rubbed Gail's ankle. It was hard and cold, not in the least what he'd expected.

'And stop doing that,' said Gail, who had her legs tucked well under her chair. 'You're making the table wobble.'

'Right away, ma'am.' *You idiot, Bradley Jones. Can't you tell flesh from wood? Surely you knew Gail would be soft and warm.*

The table wobbled again and took on a life of its own, shifting itself a few paces from them.

'*Bradley.*'

'It wasn't me. I think Chenwick's getting an earthquake.'

'An earthquake?'

'Well, more of a tremor. Nothing to worry about.' He pulled the table back towards them. 'It's all over now,' he said, stabbing a potato with his fork. 'You know something, Gail? I'm as vulnerable as this spud. At your mercy.' He burst into song. '*If you want my body... I couldn't fight you off if I tried.*'

And God, Gail, how I wish you would.

28

Wednesday, 15 March

It was Wednesday, half-day closing in Chenwick, and Chas was beginning to wonder if he'd ever be able to get into his shop so that he could open for half a day. He put his shoulder to the front door again and pushed. Surely the postman couldn't have delivered enough junk mail to block the entire entrance?

The door gave a fraction. Chas rubbed his sore shoulder and tried again. He was getting there, albeit an inch at a time. He breathed in and, squeezing through the gap, flicked on the light switch. Nothing. Nothing except thick choking dust.

'My God, the damned ceiling's fallen in.' The earthquake. An excited newsreader on local radio had been discussing it with the good residents of Chenwick as Chas was having breakfast.

Brushing dust from the sleeve of his jacket, he felt in his pocket for his mobile. Get the cleaners in and phone the insurance company. Could he claim, or was it an act of God?

'Gail?' his voice wailed. 'This is an emergency. There's been a major catastrophe. How soon can you get here?'

'We always said we had a lumpy ceiling in here. Good job we didn't get the earthquake while we were actually in the shop.' Dilys was kneeling in the rubble, picking up the manageable-sized pieces of plaster and dropping them into binbags.

Nesta heaved the full bags out of the front door and onto the pavement.

'What do you want doing with the clothing?' Gail asked. Most of it could be brushed off or sent to the dry cleaners. The shirts in their packets would be good as new after a wipe with a wet cloth.

'Throw it out. All of it. It's ruined,' moaned Chas. He was standing helplessly in the far corner, nearest the kitchen door.

'You could have a sale,' suggested Dilys, moving from her knees to her bottom. Gail had warned them all to wear their oldest clothing, so she wasn't fussed about her holey jeans getting covered in plaster dust.

'No, no. Hopefully the insurance will cover,' said Chas, waving his hand ineffectually. Dilys was too far away to see if his nails were painted.

'I could murder a cuppa,' she said, raising non-existent eyebrows.

Chas was too deep in shock to take the hint. Nesta dropped the bag she was carrying and climbed over the mess to put the kettle on.

'We could all do with a break,' said Gail. 'Let's retire to the kitchen, away from the dust.'

Dilys didn't need telling twice. 'My throat's as dry as a...' One glance at Chas, all dove grey suit and pink accessories, made her change her mind. 'As a polystyrene rock from Planet Zog,' she concluded politely.

Chas followed them into the kitchen but declined to join them at the scrubbed pine table that had replaced BJ's Formica-topped job. The matching chairs had plump gingham cushions to match the curtains at the tiny window.

'Bit of a change since we were last here,' observed Dilys.

'Yeah.' Gail picked at a pulled thread on her old grey sweater and sneezed as she brushed at the knees of her faded red never-jogged-in jogging bottoms.

Nesta produced a homemade cake from the depths of her shopping bag. It was already cut into eight equal slices. After a quick fight with the cling film, she put two slices onto each of four plates and passed them around.

'It's all right. It doesn't begin with C. It's VS,' said Dilys to Gail. 'Victoria Sponge. You can eat it.'

Chas refused his offering and left the room. Gail's eyes followed him.

'Sorry. What did you say?' She bit into her first slice.

'Nothing,' said Dilys, catching escaping crumbs in her blue palm.

Gail ate her cake and wondered if she should go after Chas. He'd hardly spoken all morning, just watched them working and not lifted a finger to help. They'd not exchanged more than a few words since the night at Mad Hatter's, and Gail surprised herself by admitting she didn't really care.

'Bradley would have mucked in along with us,' Dilys was telling Nesta. 'This one's too frightened of chipping his nail varnish.'

Gail knew her friend was right. Perhaps not about the nail varnish, but Bradley wouldn't have stood and watched them. He'd have lugged out the crumbling plaster and been there with the mop and bucket, to say nothing of the kettle. And he'd have got them to sponge off the merchandise before getting it back on sale.

'I'll go and see if he's OK,' she said. 'The cake was lovely, Nesta. Thanks.'

'Do you want another piece?'

Gail shook her head. Dilys reached for the plate, took what looked like the larger slice from it and passed the final piece to Nesta.

Chas, hands clasped, head uplifted and eyes on the gaping hole in his ceiling, appeared to be praying. *This is an omen*, he told himself. *This place was never meant to be. My world is falling apart.*

Gail came to a halt in the kitchen doorway, not wanting to disturb whatever was going on, but Chas was disturbed anyway as the front door was pushed open. A blonde head popped around it.

'Oh, Charles, darling.' The woman in the pale lemon suit with matching bag and stilettos tiptoed into the sales area. 'I've made a terrible mistake. That chiropodist...' She fished in her bag for a tissue to dab at her dry eyes. 'Please, darling, won't you come home?'

Chas shook his head. All that dust must have affected him. He thought he could see, and hear, Avril. He blinked hard. The vision of loveliness was still there. The words spoken were real. The weight that had been sitting on his shoulders all morning lifted. He held out his arms and, as Avril ran towards him, he knew his prayers had been answered. *There is a God. He's telling me this place wasn't meant to be. My place is beside Avril, and now she's come back to me, looking like an angel.*

Gail, witness to the scene, turned to make her way unnoticed into the kitchen, but that was not meant to be either. Chas heard her. Saw her. He took in the baggy-at-the-knees jogging bottoms, the hair almost grey from dust, the smudged face. Whatever had he seen in the drab Mrs Lockwood? His Avril would never allow herself to look like that. His Avril wouldn't crawl around on her hands and knees, grubbing in the dirt.

Gail, through the crack in the closing door, watched Chas's Barbie doll fall into his arms.

There was a new young waitress in the Central Cafe.

'The other one probably got sacked for offering pots of monkey pee to the clientele,' said Gail. She was sitting with Dilys and Nesta in the corner, waiting for three all-day breakfasts. Plaster clearing was good for the appetite.

'Mrs Avril Henderson, the original bimbo,' said Dilys. 'I suppose that means we've lost a customer. He didn't last long, did he?'

Gail didn't answer. No, he hadn't lasted long. Not in his shop. Not in her life. Still, she had the cardboard cut-out Pearl had bought for her, and it was as good as Chas Bleeding Henderson any day. Just as much personality for starters.

'Penny for 'em,' said Nesta. The food had arrived, and Gail hadn't noticed.

'I was wondering if one of you would walk Perry this afternoon,' Gail lied.

Nesta waved a hand. 'I will.'

'You've a heart of gold,' said Gail.

'In the body of a blue-arsed fly,' finished Dilys.

Guilt. That was the feeling creeping over Gail. Definitely guilt. Here she was lying on the bed in the middle of the afternoon when there were a thousand and one things she could be doing. Should be doing.

'Poor Nesta was wandering over the park dog walking. Dilys Lloyd, a partner in the business, was scouring Woolworth's for cheap cleaning fluids and a big bag of dusters while, the accused, Your Honour, lay in bed dreaming. That is correct. Dreaming.'

The jury, as one, gave a sharp intake of shocked breath.

'Lazy cow,' muttered their spokesperson who was dressed from head to toe in pink.

Gail stretched, about to leap off the bed to begin task number one, but decided to await the verdict.

May as well relax with that bit of sickly sunshine trickling through the window and shining right onto her. This was bliss. The bath had made her feel so sleepy. Task number one should be to clear the plaster dust out of the bath and plughole. Forget that. Half an hour wouldn't hurt. Bradley was having a snooze in the next-door bedroom, so he was OK. The shopping could wait, and when she was on the way home from the supermarket, she'd call in at Guy's to see if Mother needed any help and then pop into Tamsin's to make sure she was all right.

'Guilty. Guilty. Guilty,' mumbled the twelve good men and true.

The judge straightened his wig and his glasses and prepared to announce the sentence.

Gail never got to hear it. A shadow suddenly blocked out the sunshine. For a split second, she thought it was the executioner come to cart her off to the gallows, but once jolted out of her half sleep, she could see a man-sized shape blocking out the sun. The window cleaner was scrubbing away with his chamois. She yawned and rolled off the bed. He'd be wanting a cup of tea. She always made one for him.

'Did you know that there's a robot in your back bedroom?' Johnny Sparkle—it couldn't possibly be his real name—slurped at his tea with three sugars.

The expression on Gail's face told him all he needed to know.

'You oughta go up and take a gander,' he said.

'I can't. It's the lodger's room, and he keeps it locked.'

'No bleedin' wonder. Tell you what, love, you can nip up me ladder if you like. You oughta know what's going on in your own house, and I'm telling you there's summat strange up there. I wouldn't want me wife sharing her home with some sort of nutter.'

What was that about—nutter? He wouldn't want his wife sharing with one? Gail only knew nutters. They dogged her every step. She had one for a mother, she worked with a couple, she had two nesting under her own roof. So, was she a nutter too? Birds of a feather and all that.

'If you want to take a look, I'll hold the ladder steady for you.'

'I don't like heights,' Gail confessed.

'It'd be worth it,' encouraged Johnny.

No, it wouldn't, thought Gail. Hadn't she got enough to cope with without any weirdness in Will's bedroom? What he got up to was his own affair.

'You sure?'

'Positive.'

As Johnny Sparkle secured the ladders to the roof rack on his van, she thanked her lucky stars that George Clooney was under her bed and not leaning against the wardrobe. A robot in one room, Swooney Clooney in another. What would Mr Sparkle have made of that?

Dropping a teabag into her mug, she wondered who Bradley would choose. Bo Derek emerging from the waves? No. He was more of a Xena man. Xena, warrior princess. Yes, Bradley would be into leather miniskirts.

Handley and Lanyon's supervisor, ladies' department, hid discreetly behind a rail of tweed skirts to watch the man. 'Suspicious,' she whispered to the young assistant. 'You did right to call my attention to him.' They didn't get many men limping through the underwear and dress section. Probably one of those tran... What was the word?

From her surveillance point, she saw him take a mango-coloured woollen dress—low neckline, long sleeves—and hold it up against himself. She'd read about his sort in the Sunday papers. He seemed pleased with the dress and, folding it over his arm, made his way to the hats. The man tried them all and chose the one that didn't fit. Far too small for him. Balancing the hat on top of the dress, he ventured into the lingerie section.

'Enough is enough,' hissed the supervisor and marched towards the trans...whatsit.

'Can I help you?' she boomed.

'I'd like some underwear, please.'

'What size?'

'Twelve and 36B.' He'd had a job lot of brassieres in the shop once and had got used to sizing up the ladies.

You never are a twelve, the supervisor wanted to scream but didn't. Of course, the 36B was entirely up to him and how much stuffing he used. The most sensible course of action was to humour this transylvanian—got it—and get him off the premises as quickly as possible. 'A smooth line would be the most suitable,' she said. 'It won't show through that fine material.'

29

Saturday, 17 March

The convention was due to last all day. The wedding was an afternoon do, beginning at two-thirty.

Will was well-organised. He packed his Radney suit into a large box. There was no way he could wear it on the way to the convention. There was probably a law against driving whilst clad in cardboard boxes. His long plait was twirled around and clipped in a bun at the back of his head so that it wouldn't peek out of his costume and ruin the effect.

Every little detail had been taken care of. Box full of robot. Suitcase full of wedding gear. He'd use the community centre loos rather like Superman did the phone box. From Will in jeans, to Will as Radney, and finally Will as respectable wedding guest.

His watch told him it was already five past ten. Good. He didn't want to be the first to arrive. He picked up box, case and car keys and, whistling, ran down the stairs.

The convention was due to last all day. The wedding was an afternoon do, beginning at two-thirty. Trust Pearl to choose the same day as the convention.

There was no way Dilys was going on the bus dressed as Blublobbery. Instead, she decided to splash out on a taxi and then decided she couldn't do Blublobbery in a taxi either. Gingerly, she closed the umbrella covered in the torn strips of dyed curtains. Then she opened it again, even more gingerly. It worked. Splitting a couple of dustbin liners, she used them to wrap up her precious costume. She'd get a taxi home afterwards, ask the driver to wait while she did a quick change and then he could take her to the registry office. The floaty violet dress she'd worn to Anne and Roger's wedding was hanging on the door, ready for her.

A horn tooted outside. 'Five past ten. Right on time,' said Dilys. She didn't want to be the first to arrive. As she picked up the skin of the empty Zog alien, her heart gave a nervous flutter. She wasn't sure which was going to be the biggest ordeal—the convention or the wedding.

With a clumsy gait, which came easily when wearing cardboard trousers, William Bassett, alias Radney the Robot, lumbered towards the door of the main hall and flashed his ticket to the man in the black suit. Through the slit in the box, which formed the robot's head, Will saw the man grin at him. Friendly lot, these Earthlings.

Turning his head, a feat in itself, Will took in the transformed community centre. The walls were draped in black cloth decorated with stick-on silver stars. In one corner, Kurt King's spaceship had come to land, sitting precariously on its rusty metal legs. Large polystyrene rocks loomed in unexpected places and also helped to cordon off an area in front of the stage that was laid out with neat rows of seats. Bollocks. That could prove a problem. Sitting down was not a normal position for a robot.

Will clunked his way over to the bar only to be confronted by problem number two. How the hell was he going to take a drink? It might be early but he was in dire need of one.

'Pint, please, love. And one of those bendy straws.' Problem solved. With a bit of fiddling about, he even managed to insert a gloved hand between boxes and reach the wallet in his jeans' pocket.

With his back against the bar, Will surveyed his fellow Zoggers. A large banner spanning the room announced that as their official name. It read 'Welcome, Zoggers.' As far as he could tell, he was the only robot on the premises. His fellow Zoggers had all turned up as the beautiful people, mostly Betty Bowks and Kurt Kings. A few of the older ones sported wild hair and thick spectacles—Mad Professor Bowks—or were tripping about as Evil Emperor Zigs in long robes and jewelled crowns.

'Would you like a drink, Betty?' It was Will's attempt at socialising. The girl with the long dark hair and incredibly long and luxuriant false eyelashes didn't bother replying but continued her wiggle across to a muscular Kurt King whose every ripple was visible beneath skin-tight silver Lycra.

Will twisted his head, trying to take another suck at his beer and only succeeding in poking himself in the eye with the bendy straw. '*Ouch.*'

'You could make a hole for your mouth,' suggested someone from behind.

'Pardon?'

A three-point turn brought him into eye contact with the speaker. Would have brought him into eye contact if the speaker had any eyes.

'Blublobbery,' cried Will, delighted to see someone as stupidly dressed as himself.

Blublobbery held up a biro in a blue fist. 'Shall I?' it said.

Will bent his hinged knees so that the friendly alien could reach. There was a sudden plop as the biro pierced his 48 x 200g processed peas box, otherwise called Radney's head, and made contact with Will's chin.

'There,' said Blublobbery, directing the end of the straw through the mouth hole.

'That deserves a drink,' said Will. 'What'll it be?'

'Pardon?'

Will raised his voice and repeated the question.

'Gin and tonic, please,' said the alien.

The voice was muffled behind the layers of blue material, but Will, scrabbling around for his wallet, realised it was a she.

Blublobbery produced an arm from between the fronds of her disguise. It was blue to the wrist, pink above. Blue fingers closed around the stem of the glass before drawing it inside the assorted bedraggled fronds. A couple of seconds later, the glass reappeared empty. 'Thanks, I needed that.'

'Do you come to these things often?' Will shook the cube on his shoulders. He hadn't meant it to sound like that. Like a chat-up line.

Blublobbery wobbled, presumably shaking her head beneath the structure supporting all that material. 'My round,' she said.

She was enjoying herself. At a bare five feet in her flatties, the fronds of the brolly dragged the floor, completely concealing her identity. Radney towered above her. Was his head inside the top box or further down? She risked a crick in the neck to peer up through the narrow-as-a-letterbox section of net-only that she'd incorporated as her spy hole. The robot could be anyone under that get-up. It was sort of exciting, talking to a total stranger. She could tell him anything, and he'd never know if she was telling the truth or not. On the other hand, he could do the same. Oh well, who gave a toss?

Together, they wandered around, taking in the exhibits, the cheap props from the series, still photographs of the characters, tattered copies of original scripts. When it came to the talks, they stood, side by side, the only Radney and the sole Blublobbery there, while everyone else sat.

'The secret of *Zany Scrapes on Planet Zog*'s success lies firmly in the homemade, dare I say badly made'—there was a rumble of laughter from the appreciative audience—'props and scenery. These give Zog something unique in these days of hi-tech special effects.'

A cheer erupted.

The devisor of the series was followed by the scriptwriters and the actors.

'I'm parched,' hissed Blublobbery. 'Fancy another drink?'

Together, they shuffled back to the bar.

'What a prat,' Blublobbery hissed. Her blue hand appeared and pointed at the muscle-bound version of Kurt King. 'He's got a silver star stuck on one of his front teeth. And he's really enjoying himself.'

'How can you tell?' asked Radney.

'He's had a permanent stiffy since he arrived,' Blublobbery announced.

Will was enjoying himself without a permanent stiffy. His companion had a beautiful voice. He thought he'd heard it before, and recently. That receptionist from the doctors', maybe? What did Gail call her? Cat-Woman. That was it. She could be Cat-Woman. She could be anyone. Old or young. A beauty or ugly as sin. It didn't matter. She was fun to talk to, fun to be with. At last, he'd found her. A woman he could talk to, not lust after.

The talks were still going on. The schedule was over-running. Blublobbery was having a good time until she caught sight of the clock above the bar.

'Oh, no. It's almost two o'clock,' she cried. 'My taxi will be waiting.' And, with a rustle of dyed blue net curtains, she was gone.

'Hang on,' Will called after her. 'Am I ever going to see you again?' He ran to the door as fast as his cardboard layer would allow. Too late. Her taxi was already halfway down the road. It was a modern version of *Cinderella* but ten hours too early and no slipper.

Dilys, her Blublobbery umbrella folded, sat in jeans and T-shirt in the back of the taxi. 'Bugger,' she swore. 'He was a nice bloke. Why didn't I ask him his name?'

30

Turquoise was Tamsin's colour choice. She knew it suited her fair skin and blonde hair. The dress was longer than she would normally wear, but Jez said if the neckline was low, then the skirt shouldn't be too short, and she had to agree with him. The big hat reminded her of a picture from *Alice in Wonderland*. The Duchess. She gave it a tug so that it tilted slightly.

'You look pwetty,' said Jack.

'So do you. Handsome, I mean,' said Tamsin before turning around to check. When she did, she screamed. *'Jack. Oh, Jack.'*

Her son grinned up at her, a half-melted Freddo bar in his fist and chocolate smeared from ear to ear. The hated expression she'd heard Dilys use sprang to mind. It was as if he'd been sucking a cow's behind.

'In the bathroom, quick,' she yelled, 'and don't touch anything.'

'I was hungwy,' sobbed Jack as she scrubbed his face with a soapy flannel.

'I'm hungry too, but Granny Pearl's going to give us a lovely dinner after she gets married.' The ceremony was at two-thirty, half an hour for photos, and with any luck, they'd be sitting down to eat by four. 'Let's have a quick sandwich,' she said.

By the time Jez arrived, Jack was clean and tidy and sitting on the armchair, too afraid to move.

'You look sensational,' said Jez, eyeing up Tamsin. 'Both of you.' He picked up Jack. 'So, what do you think of us?'

Tamsin smiled at the two men in her life. They both wore black trousers, white shirts with matching waistcoats and bow ties covered with tiny Daffy Ducks. The only difference was that Jez didn't have a chocolate smudge on his collar.

Not a Windsor knot. Bradley undid his tie. The knot bore more than a passing resemblance to a Terry's Chocolate Orange, or had that come into his head because the tie was orange? Yep, a smaller knot for today. Orange tie, olive green suit, yellow and green bruises. That Arnica stuff had done the trick. Speeded up the whole process. Bradley could walk without limping and sit down and stand up without groaning.

The red suit would have to do. It was smart, it was new and it was all she had. Thursday and Friday had been hectic. As Will had predicted, Girls Will was really taking off. Great but there'd been no time to scour the shops for a new outfit.

'Can I come in?' It was Bradley tapping at the door. He didn't wait for an answer. 'I got this for you,' he said, but Gail didn't see the bag. She stared at her ex-boss. *How didn't I know he's this gorgeous? Have I been blind for the past fifteen years?*

'Bloody hell, Bradley. It is Bradley, isn't it? Don't you look good.' She couldn't resist putting out a hand to stroke the lapel of the olive suit, and Bradley couldn't resist taking her hand and planting a kiss in her palm.

Gail dragged her hand away. 'That tickles.' Tickle wasn't the word. A tickle would demand a scratch or cause a laugh. Tingle was nearer the mark. 'I didn't tell you before but that new haircut really suits you. You look...' She was stuck for words.

'This is for you,' Bradley repeated to cover her confusion, and his confusion. He held out the Handley and Lanyon bag. 'Aren't you going to open it?' As she made no move to, Bradley tipped out the contents onto the bed. The mango-coloured hat rolled onto the floor. 'I knew you didn't have time to go shopping, so I did it for you.'

Gail opened her mouth, but her voice box remained firmly closed. She picked up the dress. She picked up the cream undies. She picked up the hat. All in silence.

Bradley stood helpless, arms at his sides. 'I've got it all wrong.'

'No.' It was a squeak to herald the arrival of a bucket of tears. Tears that convinced Bradley he'd got it all wrong.

He shook out his three-pointed orange hanky, the one he'd taken half an hour to fold, and passed it to her. 'Sorry,' he said.

'No,' wailed Gail. 'Don't be sorry. No one's ever done anything this nice for me before.' She shoved him away and out of the door.

Bradley sat on the top of the stairs to wait for her. He'd never understand women.

Gail was stunned. Had Bradley chosen all this on his own? She pulled the undies on, then the clothes, then finished off the outfit with the hat. It all fitted perfectly, even the pewter-coloured shoes. She'd never worn that pinky-peach colour before but had to admit it suited her.

Ten minutes later, after repairing the tear-damaged make-up, she was giving Bradley a huge smile and doing a twirl on the landing.

'Absolutely gorgeous,' said Bradley, taking her in from head to foot and lingering on the bits in between.

Arnie sat in his hated cat basket, whiskers twitching. Pearl was next to him in the back of the black Armstrong Siddeley, the gleaming bonnet of which was adorned with gold ribbons.

'What do you think, Puss?' asked Pearl. 'Will I do?'

Arnie's unblinking eyes took in his mistress. Purple silk and green chenille. Gold fringe and sandals. Her hair brighter than ever after she'd convinced Sharon from the salon to put a colour reviver on it.

Arnie mewed. Pearl took it to be in approval. She scratched his head with an emerald fingernail. Unable to choose between the same green as her chenille tablecloth cum cloak or the deep purple of her charity shop frock, she'd compromised and used both bottles of nail varnish. One hand in each.

Very soon, Guy would be putting a ring on her purple hand. He'd spent the night in a room at The Red Lion. Pearl was all for sticking to traditions, and not letting the groom see her before the service was one of them.

The car drew up in front of the registry office. The door opened for her. Pearl climbed graciously out before bending back in again to lift up Arnie, basket and all. The nail polish hadn't been the only point she couldn't decide upon. Bible or bouquet had been another. Eventually, she had twined roses around Arnie's basket, together with his Best in Show rosette. For a woman who had told her intended he had to sleep elsewhere on the eve of their wedding, she wasn't averse to breaking the rules when it suited her.

'I'm probably the first woman in history to carry her favourite cat up the aisle,' she whispered in the ginger moggy's ear, forgetting momentarily that there was no aisle. The front path would have to do.

She turned, hitched the tablecloth further onto her shoulders, heaved the giant tomcat and basket in front of her and walked regally up the asphalt to where a group of her overwhelmed friends, relations and others waited.

She was halfway before Guy managed to close his mouth, which had dropped open on seeing this vision of loveliness, and dash towards her.

'Oooof,' slumped Pearl. 'Give us a hand with this, will you? Arnie must have put on some weight.'

They entered the registrar's office carrying Arnie-in-the-basket between them.

31

Jack was full of ice cream. Chocolate, banana, strawberry and the white one. 'You spoil him,' his mum had told Gwanny Pearl. Now Jack was bored. There was no one to play with. No children anywhere.

The little boy searched the room for something to do. He wanted a playmate. And he found one.

Arnie was delighted to be let out of his basket. He rubbed his fat ginger body around Jack's legs before setting off to explore. Jack dropped to his knees and crawled behind the tomcat, waggling his bottom as Arnie was doing.

'Meow,' wailed Arnie.

'Meow,' wailed Jack.

It was the meowing that gave their game away. Gail poked her head under the table. 'Hello, what are you up to?'

'I'm a cat,' said Jack, 'and I'm following Arnie.'

'Arnie!' Sure enough, the ginger terror with the intact testicles was there too, about to sharpen his claws on Bradley's olive trouser leg. Gail ducked under the table, which came as one hell of a surprise to Bradley, who thought his luck was in and immediately followed suit.

'What are we doing?' he whispered, staring at Gail and Jack.

'We've got to catch Arnie before he wrecks the place.'

'Let him. This whole wedding's run like clockwork. A bit eccentric maybe, but not a single hitch so far. Oh, and, Gail, I'm stuck.' Bradley arched his back. The table wobbled. This time without the aid of an earthquake.

'Jack, it's up to you. Be a big brave boy. Catch Arnie and put him back in his cage... erm, basket.' She didn't have to repeat her request. Still on hands and knees, Jack was close to reaching the land speed crawling record and in hot pursuit of Arnie's upright tail.

Gail winced at the sight of Arnie's exposed nether regions before turning to Bradley. 'Are you really stuck?'

'No. C'm'ere.' He put his hand behind her head and drew her towards him.

Strangely, Gail didn't find herself resisting. Must be the champagne. The kiss lasted half a second. Strangely, Gail didn't find it long enough.

'I'm having a fantastic time,' said Bradley. 'Fancy a dance?'

'Under here?' Silly question.

'It's a bit cramped, don't you think?' Bradley held her hand, and together they struggled out from their hiding place.

'Gwanny Pearl.' Jack's sticky hands tugged at the gold fringe. The green chenille slipped to the floor, trapping Arnie beneath it.

'Hello, Jack, darling,' cooed Pearl.

Jack jumped up and down in agitation. 'Arnie can't bweave.'

'Can't what, my precious?'

Jack pointed to the hump under the green cloth. 'It's Arnie.'

'Good boy.' Pearl patted Jack's head. 'He's in time to see us cutting the cake.' She turned to Guy. 'We can cut it now, can't we, darling?'

'Yes. Everyone's finished eating.'

Pearl freed the trapped cat and lifted him onto the table. Before anyone could say 'knife', he was rubbing his hairy hips around the bottom layer of the three-tiered, purple-iced wedding cake.

'Knife,' said Pearl. The master of ceremonies passed her a huge silver weapon, simultaneously banging his gavel on the table, loud enough to quieten the guests and startle Arnie, who leapt into his mistress's arms. The cake knife narrowly missed the cat's hanging sandbags.

Everyone was given a slice of cake and Arnie was put back into his basket.

Jack picked the icing and marzipan from his por-tion and pushed the rich black cake through the wire of Arnie's basket. Putting his empty plate carefully on the floor, he began removing his shoelace.

'She hasn't got a boookay,' he told Arnie, 'so, I'm mekking one.' He plucked the drooping flowers growing from Arnie's prison.

'What are you doing?'

Why did grown-ups always ask that? Jack smiled sweetly up at Dilys. 'Gwanny's s'posed to thwow these.' Jez, not knowing that his girlfriend's gran was about to break with tradition and replace flowers with an Arnie-in-the-basket, had explained all about the throwing of the bouquet to the little boy. Jack had been looking forward to it all day. He held out the flowers and shoelace. Dilys obligingly tied the lace around his makeshift offering and watched him dash off to present it to Pearl.

She wouldn't mind having a bash at catching that. She chewed on a blue finger as she realised what her last thought had been. Catch the bouquet? Get married again? No, no, no. Husbands were definitely not on her menu. A little flirting was OK and she wouldn't say no to a bit of how's your father as long as there were no strings attached. And friendship. Friendship was good. A man who would share her interests, someone she could have a laugh with, like Radney the Robot. She pushed her way through the dancing guests. Fred of Fred's Fries caught her arm.

'Allo, love.' He lifted her hand and did a double take. 'Blimey, you're cold. Come and 'ave a dance. I'll soon warm you up.'

She was rescued by Sharon. 'Give over, Fred, or I'll tell your missis about you. Eh, Dil, what's going on?' Her head bobbed to where Dilys had been aiming. 'Gail and your old boss.'

'Gail and my old boss?' repeated Dilys. 'Nothing. Just good friends. Always have been, always will be.'

'Nah. There's more to it than that. Go and 'ave a gander.'

Curious, Dilys went to have a gander. Her partner and her ex-boss were certainly sitting very close. Close but not touching. Dilys parked herself on the opposite side of the table to get a good view.

'I'm glad you came,' said Gail.

'Your mother's invited the whole of bloody Chenwick, but it was still a shock when she asked me,' said Dilys. 'You look nice.' She'd been so busy trying to assess the situation that it had taken a while to notice Gail's dress. 'Where'd'ya find that?'

Gail blushed. 'Bradley bought it for me.'

Firkinell. Shaz was right. A bloke didn't buy a girl a dress for nothing. They must be an item. Who'd have thought it? Dilys raised a perfectly drawn eyebrow in what she hoped was a questioning expression. BJ didn't react.

Gail flapped a hand in front of her face. 'Is it warm in here or is it me?'

Warm? Dilys wanted to shout. *It's simmering.* They were like a couple of pots coming up to the boil. How long would it take before the lids started rattling? Bradley Jones and Gail, well, they'd always got on like a house on fire. Dilys gave a little giggle. Simmering, boiling, on fire. All hot stuff.

She was about to excuse herself—there was no way she was going to play gooseberry—when there was a commotion from the top table. Pearl was about to throw her bouquet.

'Come on,' urged Dilys.

Bradley was on his feet first.

Pearl proudly showed her wilting flowers to her guests and explained how her *grandson*—Gail wasn't the only one who noticed she'd missed 'great' off—had made it for her and was impatient to see it thrown.

'So, without further ado...' Pearl turned her back on her guests, lifted a pale skinny arm and tossed the flowers over her head.

Bradley was a full foot off the floor, arm out-stretched. He didn't want to catch the thing but if he could bat it in Gail's direction. He tapped it sideways.

Lousy shot, thought Dilys as it bypassed Gail and arced over her own head, directly into Tamsin's waiting hands.

The expectant hush was filled with Jack's voice. 'Mummy's got to marry Zez now, hasn't she?' The laughter covered Tamsin's embarrassment.

Will, standing at the rear, began pushing his way through the melee. He was sure he'd seen a blue hand go up. Could Blublobbery possibly be at Pearl and Guy's wedding? 'Excuse me. Excuse me.'

'Mr Bassett. How are you?' Doc Holliday had never asked him that before.

'Fine, thanks. I've lost someone.'

'I'm terribly sorry to hear that, but time heals, you know, and they've no doubt gone to a better place.' The doctor was waffling.

'My condolences,' said a new voice. Was it the voice he was searching for? Cat-Woman. She purred at him and placed a consoling hand on his arm. A normal flesh-coloured hand tipped with false nails shaped into sharp points.

'Excuse me,' he said again and pushed his way to the bar. Cat-Woman was not his Cinderella.

'Pint, please.'

The barmaid picked up a glass.

'Lemonade.'

The barman screwed the top off a bottle and poured the fizzy liquid into a tumbler.

Out of the corner of his eye, Will saw money being exchanged and the lemonade being passed from the barman's hairy fist into a smaller one. Hairless and blue.

'Blublobbery,' he yelled.

For once in her life, Dilys was stuck for words. Even swear words. Will held her blue hand and led her towards an empty table. 'Let's talk,' he said, and for once, he meant it. No ulterior motive. He'd found a friend, someone he could chat to and be comfortable with. It was so refreshing after Lexi. With Dilys, there would be no sex and therefore no complications.

Gail closed her eyes and sank onto Bradley's shoulder. She felt drunk but that wasn't possible. Two glasses of champagne with dinner and soft drinks ever since that encounter under the table. The music was slow and romantic. Bradley's arms were around her, holding her close, and the sensation she was experiencing was stirring up old memories. The last time she'd felt like this was... When? Not with Roger. Not with Chas. Not with the couple of short and unconsummated relationships in between the two.

'Be honest,' said the uninvited guest at the wedding, the pink agony aunt. 'You've never felt like this before. Fifteen years with Bradley as a boss and not so much as an erotic dream about him, then he leaves for pastures new and turns into...'

Gail breathed in Bradley's aftershave. Pull yourself together. You're dancing with your best friend. It's the atmosphere in here. All lovey-dovey, and you want to be part of it.

'Best friends can make good lovers,' said the agony aunt as she waltzed away.

Pearl and Guy entwined, also waltzed past, followed by Tamsin and Jez. And there wasn't space to slide a piece of paper between that pair. Behind them loomed Doc Holliday and Cat-Woman and there wasn't space to slide a printed prescription between them.

'Bloody hell,' gasped Gail. 'I never guessed the two of them were at it. Must tell Dilys.' But Dilys was engrossed, elbows on the table, blue hands either side of her face, talking to Will. Besides, Gail didn't want to let go of Bradley. The kitchen staff of The Red Lion must have added a secret ingredient to the food. Had they replaced the monosodium glutamate with aphrodisiacs?

Funny things, weddings. People attending them tended to act out of character. And they always made you think back to your own big day.

Gail saw herself as a nineteen-year-old, madly in love with the man standing next to her. All the girls had fancied Roger with his Elvis quiff and his smouldering eyes, and she'd considered herself lucky to get him. How wrong could she have been?

'You're miles away,' said Bradley.

'I was thinking about Roger,' Gail admitted. 'Our wedding all those years ago. Dilys reckons Roger still has a look of Elvis about him. An aged Elvis, all beer belly and dyed hair.'

'Think about me instead,' he whispered in her ear.

Gail thought. Madly in love hadn't worked. Once the lust had worn off, there'd been nothing left. She'd never be able to say that about Bradley because they'd always be friends, always be able to laugh and talk together, and so far, lust hadn't come into it. Not on her side, anyway. But was that the truth? Wasn't there a little tingle, a warm glow, a tiny shiver?

'I could do with some fresh air,' she said.

The staff were setting up the evening buffet.

'We don't have to stay here,' said Bradley. 'Why don't I take you out for a meal?'

'I'd really like that.' The truth was out. 'But what shall I tell Mother?'

Bradley shrugged. 'You'll think of something.' With his hand on her waist, he guided Gail towards Pearl.

Gail stalled, playing for time. 'Dilys and Will are having a good time.'

'They certainly are,' confirmed Bradley.

'Tam, Jack and Jez look happy.'

'They certainly do.'

They'd reached Pearl and Guy, and Gail had run out of time. After dithering over what excuse to give for their premature departure, she stated the fact bluntly. 'We're leaving now.'

'Have a lovely time, the two of you.' Pearl's purple silk rustled as she reached out to kiss them both.

'That ring on her finger's had a magical effect,' said Bradley.

'Let's hope it lasts,' said Gail as, hand in hand, they ran down the steps of The Red Lion.

32

'Do you fancy Mad Hatter's?' asked Bradley as they sat in the taxi.

'How about a pizza and we take it home?' said Gail. It was infinitely preferable to the posh restaurant.

They sat, knees touching, on the sofa that still hadn't been paid for, and shared a Hawaiian Special. They laughed about old times, wondered if Pearl would kill Guy on her wedding night and hoped Tamsin would finally settle down.

Bradley made mugs of drinking chocolate, and they sipped them in silence.

Gail carried the empty mugs into the kitchen and turned on the tap. If she washed them now, she could put off the inevitable for a little longer. But what was the inevitable? A kiss goodnight or...

'We can do that in the morning.' Bradley crept up behind her.

Gail dried her hands. They were shaking.

'Your place or mine?' he asked.

This couldn't be happening. She was in bed with her ex-boss.

'Be gentle with me.' Had she really said that? She'd heard it in an old black and white movie once, just as the bedroom door closed. The next scene was the breakfast table. Films weren't like that anymore. Scenes of acrobatic couples causing headboards to bang against the wall from their energetic lovemaking flashed through her mind, making her more nervous. Was that the way everybody did it now?

'I'm not sure I remember how to do this,' she panted, sure a heart attack was imminent. 'I'm a born-again virgin.' Now she was rambling as she always did when nervous.

'Oh good,' Bradley murmured into her cleavage.

Gail's breathing was definitely laboured. Perhaps she should take a snort of Ventolin? Too late. His tongue flicked over her left nipple. She stopped breathing.

He moved to cup her face in his hands. 'God, you're beautiful,' he said without his glasses on.

I am? When did he last get his eyes tested?

Then he kissed her, making her forget her stretch marks and the hysterectomy scar. She forgot about being a grandmother and a cleaning lady. And was completely oblivious to George Clooney beneath the bed.

'You really should pay for that suite.' The agony aunt made an unwanted appearance. Gail's eyes widened, and she almost went to cover herself up. 'You've managed everything else on your to-do list.'

The to-do list appeared one job at a time on the wall, the agony aunt smiling proudly beside it.

Get a job. Check.

Sort out family relationships. Check.

Do roots and nails. Double Check.

'You've even discovered the man of your dreams,' she whispered, 'and you're about to get—'

'Thanks for your help, I think,' said Gail. 'Now, sod off.'

Acknowledgements

Thanks go to all at Cahill Davis Publishing for their help and patience. I am grateful to my dear friend, Betty Moulder, who gave me the initial idea for this novel, and many thanks go to Teresa Ashby who ordered me to send it out into the world.

About the Author

Lynne Hackles has been writing for many years. Her short stories have appeared in women's magazines in the UK and abroad. She has regular features in Writing Magazine and has had a children's novel for pre-teens and four non-fiction books published. She has also ghosted a book. Lynne is a creative writing tutor for a correspondence course and has led workshops and given many talks.

Until the first lockdown she was of no fixed abode as she and her husband had been travelling for three years all over the UK in their motorhome. After all the campsites closed they lived on a friend's drive for seventeen weeks before moving into a house and selling Bill, their beloved motorhome.

Lynne is known for her sense of humour and has been told she should be doing stand-up comedy. She says she knows there is a difference between comedy and humour and she can't stand up for long due to a life-time back problem.

Back in 2007 she appeared on Deal or No Deal and was described by Noel Edmonds as having warmth, colour, energy and positivity. He also thought she was a little crazy as she gambled between 10p and £75,000. She won the big money.

Find out more about Lynne on her website www.lynnehackles.com